A Passage to Self in Virginia Woolf's Works and Life

Masami Usui

GENDAITOSHO

All rights reserved. No part of this publication may be reproduced or transmitted in any from or by any means, electronic or mechanical, including photocopying, recording, or by any information storage or retrieval system, without prior permission in writing from the copyright holder.

MASAMI USUI
A Passage to Self in Virginia Woolf's Works and Life

Copyright © 2017 by Masami Usui
ISBN 978-4-434-23935-9

First published in October, 2017 by GENDAITOSHO
2-21-4, Higashionuma, Minami-ku Sagamihara-shi,
Kanagawa, 252-0333, Japan

Contents

Acknowledgments ... vii
Preface ... ix

Chapter:1
Woolf's Search for Space in *Between the Acts* ... 1
   I. Introduction ... 1
   II. Pointz Hall as an Ideological and Cultural Shelter ... 5
   III. Pointz Hall as Lost Paradise ... 16
   IV. Conclusion ... 22

Chapter:2
A Paradox of 'A House of History's Own':
in Virginia Woolf's *Orlando* and *A Room of One's Own* ... 27
   I. Introduction ... 27
   II. A Paradox in a Relationship between Literature
      and Architecture ... 29
   III. A House of Men's Own in Orlando ... 34
   IV. A University of Men's Own in *A Room of One's Own* ... 41
   V. Conclusion ... 45

Chapter:3
Animal-Assisted Therapy
in Virginia Woolf's *Flush, A Biography* ... 49
   I. Introduction ... 49
   II. The Dual Therapy: Barrett Browning's Flush
      and Woolf's Pinker ... 50

    III. The Encounter between Barrett Browning's Agony
         and Flush's Sympathy ··56
    IV. The Resolution between Barrett Browning's
         Liberated Self and Flush's Domesticated Self ···············63
    V. Conclusion ···71

Chapter:4
In Quest for Herstory: Virginia Woolf's Novels and Sir Joshua Reynolds's Portraits ···············77
    I. Introduction ··77
    II. The Signifier of Portraits ···79
    III. The Predicted Future in Children's Portraits
         in *Mrs. Dalloway* ···82
    IV. The Concluded Fate in Lady / Gentleman Portraits
         in *Between the Acts* ··87
    V. Conclusion ···95

Chapter:5
Against "Once a Lady Athlete, Always a Lady Athlete" in Virginia Woolf's *Three Guineas* ···············99
    I. Introduction ··99
    II. Diagram of Men and Athleticism ·······································101
    III. Diagram of Women and Athleticism ·································107
    IV. Contest of Diagrams of Sex / Gender and Athleticism ········113
    V. Conclusion ···121

Chapter:6
Julia Margaret Cameron as a Feminist Precursor for Virginia Woolf ···············125
    I. Introduction ··125
    II. Women as Prisoners of Victorianism ·································126
    III. Women as Outsiders against Victorianism ······················133
    IV. Women as Artists ···137

    V. Conclusion ··· 143

Chapter:7
Miyeko Kamiya's Encounter with Virginia Woolf:
A Japanese Woman Psychiatrist's Waves of Her Own ······ 147

    I. Introduction ··· 147
    II. Kamiya's Recreating Woolf's Voice as a Victim
       of Sexual Abuse ··· 150
    III. Kamiya's Encoding Woolf's Lesbian Tendencies,
        Mental Breakdown, and Creativity ······························ 156
    IV. Kamiya's Reviving Woolf as a Bombardment Victim ············ 163
    V. Conclusion ··· 167

Chapter:8
The Trauma Caused by Mothers' Deaths
in Virginia Woolf and Kyoko Mori ································ 173

    I. Introduction ··· 173
    II. The Image of Woman: Breaking the Beauty Myth ················ 176
    III. The Paradox between the Private and the Public ················ 183
    IV. The Pursuit of Women's Language and Art as Forms
        of Self-Expression ··· 189
    V. Conclusion ··· 192

About the Author ··· 195

Acknowledgments

I would like to thank Professor Emeritus Yoko Sugiyama for her long-standing affection and encouragement since my graduate student days in Japan. Thanks are also especially due to Professor Emeritus William Johnsen of Michigan State University and Professor Emeritus Linda Wagner-Martin of the University of North Carolina at Chapel Hill who supervised my doctoral dissertation on Virginia Woolf which was the beginning of my Woolf studies. I am also very glad to thank Dr. Makiko Minow-Pinkney for her support and encouragement. I am grateful to Hiroshima University and Doshisha University which enabled me to continue my research on Woolf for years.

Preface

This book is a product of my research and writing on Virginia Woolf conducted during the wake of the millennium, specifically between 2000 and 2007. During that time, my research was divided into two types; Woolf studies and Asian American literature and studies. Though I was deeply involved in many types of research on Asian American literature, I never abandoned my Woolf studies which originated from my Ph.D. dissertation and became a regular participant in the International Virginia Woolf Conference and the Modern Language Association Convention held annually in various parts of the world.

I began my studies on Woolf at Kobe College in Nishinomiya, Japan, and deepened my studies during my graduate days at Michigan State University in East Lansing. After I received my first M.A. in English from Kobe College in 1985 and stayed at the doctoral program of Kansei Gakuin University for one year, I decided to study in the United States and arrived at Michigan State University in the fall of 1986. I finished my M.A. program in 1987, was admitted to the doctoral program in the same year, and in 1989 completed my Ph.D. dissertation entitled *Search for Space: Transformation from House as Ideology to Home and Room as Mythology in Virginia Woolf's Novels* (UMI Micro-film #9012076). During that period, I was fortunate to be involved into newly emerging feminist literary criticism and Woolf studies which largely influenced me and guided me during the completion of my dissertation. Though ten years had already passed since

Elaine Showalter's landmark book, *A Literature of Their Own: British Women Novelists from Brontë to Lessing*(1977), that period was blessed with a number of other seminal books: Showalter's *The Female Malady* (1985), Toril Mori's *Sexual / Texual Politics* (1985), Makiko Minow-Pinkney's *Virginia Woolf and the Problem of the Subject* (1987), and Jane Marcus's *Virginia Woolf and the Language of Patriarchy* (1987). At Michigan State, Professor Linda Wagner-Martin led me to an advanced level of literary criticism and women's studies.

Overall, my Woolf studies form the core of my literary critical approach which also incorporates feminism and New Historicism; this became the primary approach in my other studies as well, especially Asian American literature. As for my post-graduate Woolf studies, a paper that was part of my dissertation was accepted for presentation at the 1989 Modern Language Association Convention in Washington, D.C. Mark Hussey, who chaired the session at the MLA, edited the book and the revised version of my paper was included in *Virginia Woolf and War: Fiction, Reality, and Myth* in 1991. The period between the late 1980's and the beginning of the 1990's witnessed a remarkable increase in Woolf studies in the United States. Hussey was one of the leaders in the younger generation in Woolf studies and started the Annual Conference on Virginia Woolf, currently called the International Virginia Woolf Conference. As a regular attendee of this conference on Virginia Woolf, I presented my research a total of seven times at the conference between 1992 and 2004. In 2000, I was back at the MLA Convention in Washington D.C., to present my paper on Woolf. Some of the revised presentation papers were published in the proceedings: *Virginia Woolf: Themes and Variations* (1993), *Re-Reading, Re-Writing, Re-Teaching Virginia Woolf* (1995), and *Across the Generations* (2003). Shorter articles were published in

Virginia Woolf Miscellany (1991 and 1999), and in *Virginia Woolf Bulletin* (The Virginia Woolf Society of Great Britain) in 2000. Between 1995 and 1999, I was appointed as international associate editor of *Woolf Studies Annual*, another by-product of the Annual Conference on Virginia Woolf. The decade after my dissertation in my early academic career was filled with the growth of my Woolf studies.

    I am grateful for research grants that I received that allowed me to continue my studies on Woolf. The Fukuhara Research Award, which I received in 1994 for "In Search for Space and Self: Virginia Woolf's Novels and British Portraits," enabled me to do research on Woolf and British portraits, especially those by Sir Joshua Reynolds. The 1995 Grant-in-Aid for Scientific Research (A) by Japan Society for the Promotion of Science generously provided funding for "Against Ideology: Virginia Woolf Studies in Japan during the World War II." The 2001 Doshisha University Research Grant for "The Prologue of Encoding the Gender Texts by Virginia Woolf from a Twenty-first Century Perspective," and the 2006-2009 Grant-in-Aid for Scientific Research Fundamental Research (C) for "Women Artists and Transnationalism" were also invaluable for my work. With an extended perspective and themes, including Woolf studies, I am currently working on "A Passage to the Borderless Intellectual Property: In Search for Coexisting Discourse of Global Culture and Literature." That is generously funded by the 2014-2018 Grant-in-Aid for Scientific Research Fundamental Research (C).

    All the papers included in this book were previously published in Doshisha University's journals, both *Doshisha Studies in English* (The Literary Association of Doshisha University) and *Doshisha Literature* (English Literary Society of Doshisha University). I deeply appreciate the editors of those journals and also my colleagues at the English Department of Doshisha University as well as my former colleagues at the Faculty of Integrated Arts and Sciences of Hiroshima University. Since these papers were originally published at the beginning of 2000, I decided to maintain the 16th edition MLA citation style. In order to publish them in book form, I have revised the papers with updated references.

Chapter 1

Woolf's Search for Space in *Between the Acts*

I. Introduction

In Between the Acts, Virginia Woolf explores the significance of space which was embedded between the two world wars. As it was Woolf's last work before her suicide, *Between the Acts* is considered Woolf's suicide note where she was struggling with her last search for space and self in the middle of her anxiety about death, which was induced from both her manic-depressive illness and the approaching crisis of World War II.[1] Having been an advocate against World War I, Woolf again attempts to express her own pacifist beliefs within a paradoxical frame consisting both of the Geman Blitz, and a pageant that is held in an open theatre of the British country house, Pointz Hall, which is located in a "remove village in the very heart of England" (13).

Though Woolf started writing *Between the Acts* in April 1938, she stopped writing it in May 1940. It was completed in February 1941, and published by Leonard Woolf in July, four mouths after Woolf's suicide. Considering the fact that World War II broke out in September 1939, and as suggested by many critics, the title, *Between the Acts*, embraces the conflicting space between the two world wars. Most of them compare the relationship between the last stage of Woolf's psychological strife in her creative activities and the outbreak of the world war. Since the end of the 1980's, however, the ideological and political concepts began to be examined more closely and profoundly in interpreting the text of *Between the Acts*. Alex Zwerdling and Gillian Beer show some excellent examples.

But, why did Woolf use June 1939 as the time of *Between the Acts*? It is three months before the outbreak of the war on September 1 when the German army entered Poland on Adolf Hitler's orders with Great Britain's last warning on September 3 that the German army should withdraw from Poland. The coming danger and extreme strain in this historical turning point is described in a feedback process from her own experience of the Blitz from 1940 to 1941. In an essay written in 1940, Woolf expresses the intense sense of anxiety owing to the German air raids before she and Leonard evacuated to Lewis.

> The Germans were over this house last night and the night before that. Here they are again. It is a queer experience, lying in the dark and listening to the zoom of a hornet which may at any moment sting you to death. It is a sound that interrupts cool and consecutive thinking about peace. Yet it is a sound — far more than prayers and anthems — that should compel one to think about peace. Unless we can think peace into existence we — not this one body in this one bed but millions of bodies yet to be born — will lie in the same darkness and hear the same death rattle overhead. Let us think what we can do to create the only efficient air-raid shelter while the guns on the hill go pop pop pop and the searchlights finger the clouds and now and then, sometimes close at hand, sometimes far away, a bomb drops.

(Woolf, "Thoughts on Peace in an Air Raid" 243)

It was in the fall of 1940, that Woolf underwent real air raids near her home in London. Her house at Mecklenburgh Square was destroyed by a bomb; a few weeks later, she witnessed the terrible ruins of her former residence at Tavistock Square. While going through her life as a victim of the German air raids, Woolf was striving to write what would be her final novel.

By June 1938, Winston Churchill had already launched the British policy and strategy in case of German air raids in London. In the same year, in case of gas raids by the Germans, approximately 38,000,000 gas masks were delivered to Londoners (Gardiner 10). Churchill himself established the Cabinet War Rooms, in the basement of the Government Offices which faces St. James' Park. Between September 7, 1940 and the end of July 1941, around 50,000 high explosive bombs were dropped on London (Ellis 3) Until September 1940, approximately 177,000 Londoners had to escape into underground shelters of the tubes every night.[2] In addition, early plans for evacuating the school children, mothers and babies, and disabled people from London had been established in 1938 at the time of the Munich Crisis, and was carried out on September 1, 1939.[3] The pageant in the novel is performed "against a backdrop of military training for World War II as RAF planes fly overhead" as Hana Wirth-Nesher points out (188). As an emergency strategy in case of the air raids, the underground escape movement and the mass evacuation to the country contrasts strikingly with the pageant in the open theatre found in the novel. Moreover, the paradox is emphasized as if Woolf were criticizing the citizens' misjudgement of "phoney war," which expresses, especially, the Londoners' disappointment when "the widely predicted air raids failed to materialise" during the fall of 1939 through the spring of

1940, as Robert Jackson refers to (3). Woolf intended to establish this intertwined conflicting space, which predicts the coming crisis and chaos, that would destroy not only the physical buildings and towns, but also the human spiritual, psychological, and absolute meanings of life.

Another conflicting space is emphasized when Woolf shows the contrast between the performers of the pageant, consisting of the village people and its audience of the Olivers, their friends from London, the local gentry, and its newcomers. The irony exists in the fact that the villagers' ancestors had settled there before the Norman Conquest in 1066 and whose names were listed in Domesday Book of 1086 (134). Miss La Trobe, an outsider to Great Britain and satirist of its history, produces the pageant where the amateur actors and actresses, as offsprings of England, play the creators of English history. Miss La Trobe's pageant shows a greater paradox, for the villagers' ancestors had been in existence in England even before the privileged people's ancestors established their own society. By spreading this paradox in the open theatre in June 1939, at the same time in the approaching crisis, Miss La Trobe aims to attack the British Empire and all its ideologies. Wirth-Nesher remarks that Miss La Trobe is in "a double exile" because she is "an artist in time of war, questioning the ethics and efficacy of art on the homefront, removed from men in battle" and she is also "a single woman dedicated to art and exiled from procreation of the species, emphasized as woman's role even more acutely during wartime" (196-97). In order to accomplish a multilayered conflicting space, Pointz Hall and its pageant embody the ideologies of the British society and history as a cultural shelter. The hall eventually portrays a lost paradise in the turning point of the British history and its people when they are crucially confronted with World War II.

II. Pointz Hall as an Ideological and Cultural Shelter

Pointz Hall alludes to the accumulated and multilayered ideological features of English history as it is illustrated in the country house owned by the Olivers for one hundred and twenty years, the site where a medieval barn was originally founded. The "Noble Barn" that had been built originally founded. The "Noble Barn" that had been built over seven hundred years ago and reminded some people of a Greek temple, others of the middle ages, most people of an age before their own, scarcely anybody of the present moment" (61) is "as old as the church, and built of the same stone, but it had no steeple" (18). This twelfth-century building is one of the earliest surviving fortified manor houses with a simple yet solid structure consisting of a hall and an open roof. James Chambers states that since stone was very expensive, except for the cathedrals and castles, a limited number of knights and wealthy merchants could use it for their houses (19). Thus, Noble Barn parallels England as a powerfully-controlled stable state since feudalism was established by William the Conqueror in 1066. At the beginning of the pageant, two unknown girls represent "England"; a rosebud-like tiny girl is old England and a carpenter's daughter with roses in the hair is medieval England. The female icons which enshrine the birth of the British Isles and the foundation of England ironically contrast a male-power, the consequence of which is reflected in the establishment of Noble Barn and the following feudal age.

As the pageant is primarily "set in the reigns of three queens of England: Elizabeth, Anne, and Victoria" (137), the English country houses face the changes during these reigns. The Elizabethan manor house, whose "scar" is observed along with those made by the "Britons," "the Romans," and "the plough" (5) from an aeroplane, can be counted as a great house since Queen Elizabeth I encouraged the lords and knights to build and enlarge their houses for her royal visits (Chambers 57-58). The garden of Pointz Hall was originally founded five hundred years ago; a private chapel changed into "a larder" after the Reformation during the reigns of Henry VIII and possibly Elizabeth I. In a tableau of the reign of Elizabeth I, in a play-within-a-play, with Mrs. Manresa as "Pointz Hall's queenly visitor" (Reginal Abbott 81), there is a mock royal visit, a risk that was enormously high for the country house owners. When the Queen in the pageant recites, "Mistress of pinnacles, spires and palaces," she sweeps her arm towards Pointz Hall (52). The domination of Elizabeth I is, as Beer suggests, situated within a paradox of Woolfs representation of history, which is "stationary, inhabited by replaceable figures whose individuality is less than their community with other lives lived already" (8).

Pointz Hall itself is characteristic of the ideological and idiosyncratic implications of the establishment of the British Empire. The Olivers, who have no connection with the old aristocratic families of this area, represent the upper middle class, which have been working for the British Empire as her subjects and establishing themselves in its society.

> Points Hall was seen in the light of an early summer morning to be a middle-sized house. It did not rank among the houses that are mentioned in guide books. It was too homely. But this whitish house with the grey roof, and the wing thrown out at right angles, lying unfortunately low on the meadow with a fringe of trees on the bank above it so that smoke curled up the nests of the rooks, was desirable house to live in. (7)

In contrast to the great houses whose history traced back to the Elizabethan period, Pointz Hall is considered as one of "villas" which had begun as a country domestic dwelling of a modest size in the eighteenth century and grew in the nineteenth century. Pointz

Hall possesses all the characteristics of the villa in its origin, its development, and such facilities as the library, "the heart of the house" (12) once influenced by the Enlightenment, and overseen by the portraits painted by Sir Joshua Reynolds (1723-92), and its setting in nature. Queen Anne represents Reason in the pageant. The style of Queen Anne thus depicts the Age of Reason in its tastes which were preferred by the newly-established upper-middle class owners.

In its features, the original Pointz Hall resemble those of the British type of Palladian villas. As James S. Ackerman summarizes, Palladianism, whose origin is traced back to an Italian architect, Andrea Palladio of the sixteenth century, was virtually "adapted to country houses of the same size as their Baroque predecessors and contemporaries and to smaller suburban and rural villas of dimensions comparable to Palladio's original model" (155-56). In this process of adaption, Inigo Jone's Queen's House in Greenwich (whose original design was in 1616) is noted to have influenced and inspired the following architects of villas (Ackeman 150). The whitish and greyish features and the simple structure of the Queen's House is reminiscent of those of Pointz Hall.[4] Known as one of the most elegant Queen Anne architectural examples, Andrew Ginger describes Anthony House as having all the characteristics of the villa in its silver-grey, smooth, "simple, well proportioned and refined" mansion (62).[5] Pointz Hall depicts the rising gentlemen's idealized house which originates from the humble residence of the British monarchy, whose original model was designed by the first well-known British architect, Ingio Jones, and later known as a 'Queen Anne architecture.'

The use and development of the villa delineates the dimensional aspects of social, economical, and political changes and stability of the British Empire. According to Chambers, the "English domestic architecture of the eighteenth century was essentially the architecture of educated aristocrats and gentlemen" (125) and "the fashion for Palladian architecture spread easily among classically educated gentlemen" (130). Simpler and smaller in scale and size, "villas" began to be built for the newly-established professionals such as merchants, doctors, lawyers, and soldiers (Chambers 148). The modest size of the house embodies the rising social class and profession of its dwellers and their family background. Bartholomew (Bart) Oliver who is retired from the Indian Civil Service represents the British Empire's colonialism and political force; and his son, Giles Oliver who works as a stock broker in London, is also associated with the British Empire's urban capitalism. This emerging group of rising professionals, engaged in both political and commercial activities in London, the metropolitan capital, shifted their sights to the tradition of the British country estate on a smaller scale. They depended on financial resources in agriculture, and were confronted with the danger of its succession in the twentieth century.

In its improvement as well as its origin and development, Pointz Hall depicts accumulated aberrations and incongruities that have been added with each generation and era. Pointz Hall, first of all, demonstrates the amateur gentleman architect's zeal, travail, and failure in creating the idealized house and garden of the eighteenth century. Because of its simplicity in structure and design, that of villas, amateur gentlemen architects were motivated to redesign both the buildings and landscapes. As Alexander Pope expresses its trend in "Epistle to Richard Boyle, Lord Burlington" (1731), the "'Rule of Taste' became as immutable as the Laws of Nature" (Chambers 130). The "Rule of Taste" means the admiration and imitation of the ancient Roman architecture and its tastes; "Laws of Nature" is based on the idea that nature is "romanticised and idealised as a symbol of harmony and order." The houses were usually built "on high ground with 'commanding prospect'" and the natural-looking gardens were sought and planned "as a landscape painting" (Chambers 125).

> It was a pity that the man who had built Pointz Hall had pitched the house in a hollow, when beyond the flower garden and the vegetables there was this stretch of high ground. Nature had provided a site for a house; man had built his house in a hollow. Nature had provided a stretch turf half a mile in length and level, till it suddenly dipped to the lily pool. The terrace was broad enough to take the entire shadow of one of the great trees laid flat. (9)

The conflict between Nature and man in Pointz Hall is also one between Nature and the amateur gentleman architect, regarding the "Laws of Nature." The reason for building the house in a hollow and facing it north is "to escape from the nature" (8) as Bart explains or "for shelter" as Mrs. Lucy Swithin interprets it (43). Bart's telling of "the famous story of the great eighteenth-century winter when for a whole month the house had been blocked by snow" and "the trees had fallen" (8), accounts for the amateur architect's misjudgement and its ironical consequence of the symbiotic theory of nature and man.

The architectural structure of Pointz Hall with its one wing lacks symmetry, which was preferred in designing villas in the early and mid-eighteenth century, yet was disliked in the late eighteenth century as Mark Girouard mentions in *Life in the English Country House* (96). Pointz Hall demonstrates the procedure of the changed tastes of symmetry.

> For by some lucky chance a wall had been built continuing the house, it might be with the intention of adding another wing, on the raised ground in the sun. But funds were lacking; the plan was abandoned, and the wall remained, nothing but a wall. Later, another generation had planted fruit trees, which in time had spread their arms widely across the red-orange weathered brick. (33)

The process of improvement of Pointz Hall accounts for the failure of building an idealized villa with two symmetrical wings. Wings are generally smaller-sized buildings attached to the house with colonnades or corridors in order to accommodate domestic service area or additional private suites. "Symmetry and correctness of detail were overriding stylistic concerns" (Ginger 21) in designing the villa and, usually, two wings were attached to the house to give it in a symmetrical order. In the pageant, a Restoration comedy entitled "Were there's a Will there's a Way" mocks "Reason," "God's truth," and "a moral" founded in the highly idealized concept and style of the eighteenth-century villa, begins to be reversed, as is seen in the misplaced site and the asymmetrical structure of Pointz Hall.

The asymmetrical structure of the country house allows the greenhouse to the attached to the house in order to expand the space and to enlarge a view by being connected with the garden (Girouard, *Life in the English Country House* 105). As characterized in Pointz Hall, moreover, the garden, designed by Pope's "Laws of Nature" at the beginning of the eighteenth century, was altered and made into an informal and natural garden by using clumps of trees, open lawns, flowers, fruits, and cattle as advocated by Lancelot ('Capability') Brown (1716-83), a well-known landscape gardener who also contributed to establishing Kew Gardens at the end of the eighteenth century (Ginger 21). In Pointz Hall, the Age of Reason is sandwiched between the greenhouse scenes where the young master and mistress of Pointz Hall invite their guests to show them around, using the same phrase, "'Like to see the greenhouse?'" (68&89). During the interval between the Act II and Act III, Isa Oliver invites William Dodge, a young clerk and artist from London, and leaves Giles and Mrs. Manresa to be together. This critical moment is resumed during the interval between the Act III and Act IV, when Giles invites Mrs. Manresa to the greenhouse. The greenhouse is the place where both

Isa and Giles undergo their infidelities. The greenhouse, which affects the irregular structure of the house, but is in harmony with the nature, symbolizes an escape from the strictly regulated manners, morals, and customs of the Age of Reason.

The terrace in Pointz Hall is transformed into the stage of the pageant as Miss La Trobe evaluates its adaptability: "The lawn was as flat as the floor of a theatre. The terrace, rising, made a natural stage. The trees barred the stage like pillars. And the human figure was seen to great advantage against a background of sky" (47). The terrace, which sits between the house and the garden, plays an important role in the view of the park.[6] The limestone and brick, which were employed for the structure of the house by the eighteenth century, are changed into the 1796 product of "much more durable and weather-proof Parker's Roman Cement" (Chambers 156). This cement began to be used for the great Regency terraces not only because of its excellent quality but also because the British government had doubled the brick tax two years earlier in order to finance the British navy against its French counterpart (Chambers 156). The changes found in the terrace, between the eighteenth to nineteenth centuries, originates in the improvement of the architectural technique, structure, and durability of the villa in the British Empire.

The interiors of the house are as important as the outside structure of the house. The portraits are essential because they are the treasures of the house and register the history of the house and of its dwellers. Reynolds's portraits are presented as icons of cultural heritage of the eighteenth century as well as symbols of the human condition of the time. Reynolds's ideas are described in the *Discourses* which are a series of lectures delivered at the Royal Academy. According to Nicholas Penny, Reynolds established the professional status of painters and paintings as "a liberal art" (17). John Walker remarks that Reynolds also instituted "theory" and "a corpus of rules" (174).

Especially for portraits, "there was a greater demand in England than in any other country in Europe" (Penny 17). Boris Ford remarks that the portrait is recognized as a sign which symbolizes the social rank, status, and role beyond the individual (134). In a pair of portraits in the dining room of Pointz Hall, the tension between the female portrait and the male portrait signifies the tension between 'herstory' and history. The man's portrait, "ancestor" of the house, has its name, and even his horse and dog have their names. It is an identifiable individual with a social rank and taste; he is recognized as a country gentleman because of his horse and his "famous hound."[7] On the other hand, the woman's portrait is merely "a picture" without a name and rank, and it was "bought" as a supplemental decoration along side the man's portrait. This "long lady" is portrayed as Diana, goddess of the hunt, as Diane Filby Gillespie concludes by a proof of the arrow (211). In Reynolds's portrait of *the Duchess of Manchester as Diana*, Lady Ann Dawson just before her marriage to Thomas Dawson in July 1754, posed as Diana since Diana was "virgin huntress" (Penny 29).[8] Both an ambiguous identity as an unmarried woman and a mythological allusion as a virgin huntress represents this unrecognizable woman. This pair of portraits not only "establish two poles against which to measure the situations and characters in the book" — one is for generating words and the other for being silent — (Gillespie 212), but also reinforces two conflicting representations of human conditions encoded in the British patriarchal society — a man's recognizable identity and a woman's unrecognizable identity.

Painted by an unknown artist, another portrait of a lady on the top of the principal staircase remains as nameless and unidentifiable as the first woman. Though Lucy insists that the lady is not an ancestress but the family's acquaintance, the ambiguity and anonymity remains in her statements: "Who was she?" and "Who painted her?" (43). Before presenting the pageant which satirizes British history, the portraits are questioned and measured as if they suggest Woolf's definition of women's history. The presence of the nameless lady's portrait implies the complete ignorance or neglect of an ancestress. Though the women's portraits exist outside the frame of history and family history and though they are placed in men's space such as the dining room and the principal staircase, silent communication and agreement exist only between the portraits and Lucy. Both the portrait of the "long lady" in the dining room and the unknown lady's portrait on the top of the principal staircase are silenced selves embedded in the formation of the male-centered ideological and idiosyncratic stream which is tightly attached to the meaning and tastes of Pointz Hall.

Originating in ancient Rome, the villa exists "to provide a counter-balance to urban values and accommodations, and its economic situation is that of a satellite" (Ackerman 9). As a result, the "content of villa ideology is rooted in the contrast of country and city" (Ackerman 12). Pointz Hall, in this respect, connotes the end of this ideology.

> Aunt Lucy, foolish, free; always, since he [Giles] had chosen, after leaving college, to take a job in the city, expressing her amazement, her amusement, at men who spent their lives, buying and selling — ploughs? glass beads was it? or stocks and shares? — to savages who wished mostly oddly — for were they not beautiful naked? — to dress and live like the English? A frivolous, a malignant statement hers was of a problem which, for he had no special gift, no capital, and had been furiously in love with his wife — he nodded to her across the table — had afflicted him for ten years. Given his choice, he would have chosen to farm. But he was not given his choice. So one thing led to another; and the conglomeration of things pressed you flat; held you fast, like a fish in water. So he came for the week-end, and changed. (30-31)

The contrast and connection between country and city is almost broken as urban capitalism overwhelms the agriculture-based country life as it is also broken within Giles. During the last quarter of the nineteenth century, the agricultural economy declined and the profits had been invested in industry (Chambers 219). Like the reign of Elizabeth I, the reign of Queen Victoria, however, was known as the era of "vast 'prodigy houses'" newly built by the great landowners and by "the owners of ships, foundries, mills and factories" (Chambers 219). It was the last era of the historically-established British country house.

The characteristics of Victorian houses are, as the architect Robert Kerr expresses in his ideas, are based on the division of rooms into the masculine and feminine; for instance, the drawing-room is feminine, while the dining-room is masculine (Chambers 221). There is also the division of space into family and servant areas. These intertwined divisions, according to sex and class differences, appear within Pointz Hall. In the drawing-room, Bart is called "Master"; on the other hand, he is called "Bartie" in the kitchen, which is described as the second best room next to the library (22). Both the kitchen and the nursery were inspected primarily by the country house owners in the Victorian Era. The authority in the enforcement of Victorian standard of morals, furthermore, is overwhelming within the home space. In the novel, the "purity and security" of all Queen Victoria's "minions" should be examined and rightly directed, as Budge, an imperial constable in the pageant, insists: *"The ruler of an Empire must keep his eye on the cot; spy too in the kitchen; drawing-room; library; wherever one or two, me and you, come together"* (97).

Moreover, the lily pond, which "for hundreds years, had silted down into the hollow" (28) at Pointz Hall is also proof of the landscape improvement in the nineteenth century. The anecdote of the lily pond, which is mentioned a few times in the novel, is a tragedy of a drowned lady, who committed suicide, as a victim of the woman's subjectivity. When Budge attempts to guard "respectability, and prosperity, and the purity of Victoria's land," he points to Pointz Hall and Victorian scene ends with "'Ome, Sweet 'Ome" said in Cockney (102). The Victorian idealized concept of home which was once engraved in Pointz Hall is questioned between the acts and between Isa and Giles, and it is collapsed between Isa and Rupert Haines as a pair in the three-fold mirror and Mrs. Manresa and Giles as a pair in the greenhouse.

Giles, as the successor of Pointz Hall, is already exempted from the agricultural income and sequestered from farming; instead, his dependence on metropolitan capitalism becomes inevitable. Furthermore, the country encounters an environmental change as the "building of a car factory and of an aerodrome in the neighborhood had attracted a number of unattached floating residents" (47). The contrast and coexistence of country and city diminishes along with the interchanging and intertwining transformation of the urban capital industries and finances at the beginning of the twentieth century.

The uncompleted yet repeatedly redesigned architecture and landscape of Pointz Hall underscores the changes found in the home owners and the succeeding of the families whose social, economical, and cultural conditions have largely influenced the existence, the meaning, and the tastes of the villa. Pointz Hall, at the same time, signifies a series of ideological stances and evidences which are illuminated with the narratives of the pageant that outline the paradoxical history of England. Woolf's presentation of England is thus embedded, illustrated, and encapsulated within the deftly conjoined and intertwined tastes, styles, and significance of Pointz Hall whose origin and improvements ironically correspond with Miss La Trobe's remaking of the English history and recounting the once-internalized voices.

III. Pointz Hall as Lost Paradise

Between the acts — during the intermissions of the pageant — Pointz Hall resonates with quotidian yet ingenious narrative voices in its shift from the ideological and cultural shelter to a Lost Paradise. The air raids are the reality that Giles recognizes.

> Thus only could he show his irritation, his rage with old fogies who sat and looked at views over coffee and cream when the whole of Europe over there — was bristling like . . . He had no command of metaphor. Only the ineffective word "hedgehog" illustrated his vision of Europe, bristling with guns, poised with planes. At any moment guns would rake that land into furrows; planes splinter Bolney Minster into smithereens and blast the Folly. (34)

The "hedgehog" is a military strategy of bombing onto submarines. All of Europe had already been confronted with enormous danger, that of the approach of World War II, and its survival would be determined by the newly developed and largely employed strategy — air raids — which changed the fate of the world ethics since World War I. Above all, technology in general was considered a threat to human existence. The gramophone, for instance, is hidden in the bushes during the pageant. According to Michele Pridmore-Brown, it is used to "deconstruct the role of communications technology in authoritarian politics and in the regulation of bodies" of fascism (411). In her discussion over the interrelation between the island and the aeroplane, Beer analyzes the aeroplane's "menacing" presence in *Between the Acts* where in "the new world of flight and war the old axes are turned, the old geometries of the island giving way" (176). This internalized menace is projected onto the weather forecast, the newspaper, and the letter.

The weather which is discussed before the pageant underlines the ambivalence of the international and national political conditions, for Isa has heard the same discussion for seven summers and connects the seventh one with the rape incident by the guard of Whitehall. Whitehall Palace which had been built primarily for feasts yet destroyed by fire was twice constructed by Inigo Jones in 1619. Between 1939 and 1945, the Whitehall area including Whitehall Gardens and Government Offices was used for war offices, as illustrated by Peter Simkins (68). The elegant Banqueting House of Whitehall Palace hides how the oppressive force led violence when female power is obliged to surrender itself to male power. This rape incident at Whitehall foreshadows the danger of German troops' invasion into England.

As the forecast says, "Variable winds; fair average temperature; rain at times" (16). This unsettled weather is witnessed in the Queen Victoria's reign and realized in the present time, that is, 1939. The greenhouse scene during the interval between the Elizabethan Age and the Age of Reason predicts crisis of the approaching war as William indicates: "'The doom of sudden death hanging over us,' he said. 'There' no retreating and advancing'" and his statement is concluded with Woolf's comments, "The future shadowed their present" (70). The clouds, which are passing across the sky when the pageant shifts its scene from the Age of Reason to the Victorian Age, speak as "bodiless voices" as it "all looks very black" and it is connected with the Germans (91). The sudden shower dropping "like all the people in the world weeping" in present time proves the legitimacy of the "risk she [Miss La Trobe] had run acting in the open air was justified" (107). After the pageant is over, the "old cronies" discuss more openly the approaching war, mentioning that the Brookes "have gone to Italy, in spite of everything" (117); "— things look worse than ever on the continent. And what's the channel, come to think of it, if they mean to invade us? The aeroplanes, I didn't like to say it, made one think" (118). Though Anglo-Italian relationship was about to be built when Prime Minister, Mr. Neville Chamberlain, and Lord Halifax, the Foreign Secretary, visited Rome to meet Signor Mussolini in mid-January 1939, the fall of Barcelona led Chamberlain and Mussolini to opposite directions at the end of January (*The Illustrated London News* Feb. 4, 1939). The German Amy occupied Prague on March 15, and the Italian troops invaded Albania on April 7. The unstable weather that is repeatedly forecast and accompanied with the sense of anxiety, corresponds to the uncertain world-wide political and social conditions which cannot avoid World War II.

Giles' prediction and the weather forecast are both proven when, in the pageant, "The Nineteenth Century," as an era without the army, is over and the "present" begins. After the peak of the British Empire's dominant economic power from the middle of the nineteenth century to the beginning of the twentieth century, moreover, Britain was confronted with the worsened economic position after World War I (Ponting 3). Britain's economic repression in 1930's is a foreshadow of the Empire's entirely destroyed economy after World War II (Woodcock 289-90). There appears real evidence of the coming war when the Reverend G. W. Streatfield asks the audience to donate money in order to repair the "illumination" of the village's old church.

'... So that each of us who has enjoyed this pageant has still an opp...'

The word was cut in two. A zoom severed it. Twelve aeroplanes in perfect formation like a flight of wild duck came overhead. *That* was the music. The audience gaped; the audience gazed. Then zoom became drone. The planes had passed.

'. . . portunity,' Mr. Streatfield continued, 'to make a contribution.' (114-15).

As Kenneth Macksey states, a formation of the squadron shows the already well-organized British Royal Air Force, which had evolved since 1915 when German aircraft first dropped bombs on Britain (62). Carol Mahon remarks that before Britain's declaration of war on Germany, such squadrons as No.19 Squadron and the new Spitfire were flown into Duxford, one of the earliest Royal Air Force stations (5).[9] The terrifying movement and large noise of the squadron which divides the word, "opportunity," into two, represents the destructive force that will never retrieve the divided "opportunity." In an enlarged context, David McWhirter interprets that "personal relations — whether between men and women, social classes, or nations — are increasingly governed by the logic of exclusion, victimization, and violence, even, as Woolf's ominous references to Mussolini suggest, by the ideology of fascism" (794). The forecast substantiates the real menace of the approaching vital and giant force which could destroy the history of England, of Europe, and of human beings in an interrelated context.

The newspapers also play an important role to inform their readers of the previous day's incidents and, at the same time, to create history. Reports from mass-media, which are spread throughout *Between the Acts*, illustrate the destruction of humanity as the result of the striving inhuman armed forces of approaching war. Before the pageant, the rape incident by the soldiers of Whitehall which Isa reads at Pointz Hall and the incident of sixteen people being shot, which Giles reads in a train, are interrelated with each other, even though they happen to be read by different people in different places.[10] At the end of the pageant, "what the *Times* and *Telegraph* both said in their leaders that very morning" (108), that is, the establishment of the League of Nations, is a reminder, after the sudden shower had fallen, which symbolizes "all people's tears, weeping for all people" (107) and alludes to the coming of World War II. The terms, the League of Nations, is cut in the middle as shown in "'Now issued black main fuzzy wig; coffee-coloured ditto in silver turban; they signify presumably the League of . . .'" (108), and the word, "Nations," never appears. The failure of the League of Nations is criticized in the approaching danger of World War II. The pageant is sandwiched between these two mass-media intrusions which imply the progressing history-making news filled with destructive forces and unavoidable conflicts. When the pageant is over and the darkness occupies all the space, the rape incident from the morning newspaper intrudes into silence as the reality and recognition of the destructive forces which enormously influence human conditions. The newspapers, which are crumpled and used to turn out the light by Giles, embody the complete darkness, reminiscent of "Black Saturday," the German raid on the Saturday night of September 7, 1940.

The most intriguing suggestion of the coming war is made in a letter from Scarborough. The silent moment of night when Lucy receives a second post which includes "the morning paper — paper that obliterated the day before" and a criss-cross from "an old friend at Scarborough" (128) implies the hovering past and invading future. The end of the pageant brings people to withdraw from the open stage and confront reality. The lily pool becomes a shelter for the fish that hide themselves under the leaves because they are scared "by shadows passing" (121) and adumbrates the shelter against the air raids by the Lutfwaffe.

> The darkness increased. The breeze swept round the room. With a little shiver Mrs. Swithin drew her sequin shawl about her shoulders.

> She was too deep in the story to ask for the window to be shut. 'England,' she was reading, 'was then a samp. Thick forests covered the land. On the top of their matted branches birds sang . . .'
> The darkness of England is again conveyed by a letter.
> Lucy turned the page, quickly, guitily, like a child who will be told to go to bed before the end of the chapter.
> 'Prehistoric man,' she read, 'half-human, half-ape, roused himself from his semi-crouching position and raised great stones.'
> She slipped the letter from Scarborough between the pages to mark the end of the chapter, rose, smiled, and tiptoed silently out of the room. (129)

The letter from Scarborough suggests the return of the past German air raid in Scarborough in World War I as one of the first air-raid English towns to be victimized (Usui 7). The letter from Scarborough which was slipped "between the pages to mark the end of the chapter" of history plays a role to predict the second coming, yet it is ignorantly buried in ancient times. This action is a deprecation of the "phoney war." The very end of *Between the Acts* is, however, the very moment to plunge into the most terrifying future event in human history by means of travelling back to the past.

> Isa let her sewing drop. The great hooded chairs had become enormous. And Giles too. And Isa too against the window. The window was all sky without colour. The house had lost its shelter. It was night before roads were made, or houses. It was the night that dwellers in caves had watched from some high place among rocks. Then the curtain rose. They spoke. (129-30)

IV. Conclusion

The house has lost its shelter, and Pointz Hall is transformed into a lost paradise where both the social and cultural shelter and the domestic sacred space are abandoned. Woolf's suicide note is finalized in consummating the surging human existence that is confronted with the unescapable danger and chaos of being attacked and destroyed in the air raids. Woolf who writes her pacifist novel during the wartime leaves not only her role with Miss La Trobe (Wirth-Nesher 197), but also entrusts her codes, mocking the wrongly-input ideological facets of the British Empire, to one country house, Pointz Hall.

Notes

This paper includes a short paper entitled "In Search for Space: A Conflict between Blitz and Pageant in *Between the Acts*" which was presented at the 66th General Meeting of the English Literary Society of Japan at Kumamoto University in May, 1994, and a part of "In Quest for Herstory: Virginia Woolf's Novels and Sir Joshua Reynolds's Portraits" which was delivered at the 4th Annual Conference on Virginia Woolf at Bard College, New York, in June, 1994. This paper was originally published in *Doshisha Studies in English* 72 (March 2000): 25-48.

1 Mitchell A. Leaska names *Pointz Hall*, the draft of *Between the Acts*, "the longest suicide note in the English language" (451). As for Woolf's subjective anxiety, Galia Benziman makes an interesting comment that "Woolf treats her English community as a subject in possession of a body as well" (54). By comparing Woolf with Darwin who "offered one of the most famous violations of anthropocentrism in modern thought," Sam See states that Woolf "extends this violation to a civilization whose efforts at domination betray, and threaten to destroy its members' collective 'lower form.'" (641).

2 See some photos in Gardiner (31) and a series of Henry Moore's "Shelter" drawings such as "Shelter Drawing (1940), "Study for the Grey Tube Shelter"

(1940), and "Shelter Drawing: Woman Eating Sandwich" (1941).
3 "The whole operation took three days and the totals moved out from big cities all over Great Britain were 827,000 school age children, 103,000 teachers and social workers, 524,000 mothers and babies, 7,000 disabled people, and 13,000 expectant mothers. Some 48% of the school children of London were in this total" (Ellis 16).
4 See the Queen's House, Greenwich, 1616-35 (Chambers 81).
5 See Anthony House, Cornwall, 1710-21 (Ginger 58).
6 See "View of the park from the terrace of Woburn Abbey, Bedfordshire, as proposed by Humphrey Repton" (*Girouard, A Country House Companion* 164).
7 According to Ford, those who sat for their portraits wanted to be recognized "as something: as a country gentleman, perhaps, with gun and faithful dog, posing against the backdrop of his own fertile estate" (134).
8 Penny remarks that the "occasion for commissioning many of these fanciful female portraits was an engagement, that brief, envied, interval of ambiguous identity, free from filial obligations and unafflicted with domestic responsibilities, when thinking was most liable to be wishful and compliments were unusually hyperbolic" (29).
9 See "A formation of six No.9 Squadron Spitfires in October 1938" (Mahon 6).
10 As for the rape incident, see Jane Marcus (76) and Patricia Laurence (240).

Works Cited

Abbott, Reginald. "Rough with Rubies: Virginia Woolf and the Virgin Queen." Ed. Sally Green. *Virginia Woolf: Reading the Renaissance*. Athens: Ohio UP, 1999. 65-88.

Ackerman, James S. *The Villa: Form and Ideology of Country Houses*. Princeton: Princeton UP, 1990.

Beer, Gillian. *Virginia Woolf: The Common Ground*. Edinburgh: Edinburgh UP, 1996.

Benziman, Galia. "'Dispersed Are We': Mirroring and National Identity in Virginia Woolf's *Between the Acts*." *Journal of Narrative Theory* 36.1 (Winter 2006): 53-71.

Chambers, James. *The English House*. New York: Norton, 1985.

Ellis, Chris. *Winston Churchill's Britain at War Theme Museum*. N.p., n.d.

Ford, Boris, ed. *The Cambridge Cultural History of Britain*. Vol.5. *Eighteenth-Century Britain*. 1991. Cambridge: Cambridge UP, 1992.

Gardiner, Juliet. *The People's War*. London: Collins & Brown, 1991.

Gillespie, Diane Filby. *The Sisters' Arts: The Writing and Painting of Virginia Woolf and Vanessa Bell*. Syracuse: Syracuse UP, 1988.

Ginger, Andrew. Country *Houses of England, Scotland, and Wales*. London: George Phillip, 1991.

Girouard, Mark. *A Country House Companion*. New Haven & London: Yale UP, 1987.

——. *Life in the English Country House: A Social and Architectural History*. 1978. Trans. Shizuko Mori Hughes. Tokyo: Sumai-no-Tosho Shuppankyoku, 1989.

The Illustrated London News 1939. London: British Ferries, 1989.

Jackson, Robert. *The London Blitz*. London: The Museum of London, 1990.

Laurence, Patricia. "The Facts and Figure of War: From *Three Guineas* to *Between the Acts*." Ed. Mark Hussey. *Virginia Woolf and War: Fiction, Reality, and Myth*. Syracuse: Syracuse UP, 1991. 225-45.

Leaska, Mitchell A. *Pointz Hall: The Earlier and Later Typescripts of 'Between the Acts.'* New York: University Publications, 1983.

Macksey, Kenneth. *Invasion: The German Invasion of England, July* 1940. London: Greenhill, 1990.

Mahon, Carol, et al. *Duxford*. London: Imperial War Museum, 1992.

Marcus, Jane. *Virginia Woolf and the Languages of Patriarchy*. Bloomington: Indiana UP, 1987.

McWhirter, David. "Woolf and the Tragicomedy of History." *English Literary History* 60 (Fall 1993); 787-812.

Ponting, Clive. *Whitehall: Tragedy and Farce*. London: Sphere, 1986.

Pridmore-Brown, Michele. "1939-40: Of Virginia Woolf, Gramophones, and Fascism." *PMLA* 113 (1998): 408-21.

See, Sam. "The Comedy of Nature: Darwinian Feminism in Virginia Woolf's *Between the Acts*." *Modernism / Modernity* 17.3 (Sep.2010: 639-667.

Simkins, Peter. *Cabinet War Rooms*. London: Imperial War Museum, 1983.

Usui, Masami. "The German Raid on Scarborough in *Jacob's Room*." *Virginia Woolf Miscellany* 35 (Fall 1990): 7.

Walker, John. *Portraits, 500 Years*. New York: Harry N. Abrams, 1983.

Wirth-Nesher, Hana. "Final Curtain on the War: Figure and Ground in Virginia Woolf's *Between the Acts*." *Style* 28.2 (Summer 1994): 183-200.

Woodcock, George. *Who Killed the British Empire?: An Inquest*. London: Jonathan, 1974.

Woolf, Virginia. *Between the Acts*. 1941. Harmondsworth, Middlesex: Penguin, 1992.

——. "Thoughts on Peace in an Air Raid." *The Death of the Moth and Other Essays*. 1942. New York: Harcourt, 1970. 243-48.

Zwedling, Alex. *Virginia Woolf and the Real World*. Berkeley: U of California P, 1986.

Chapter 2

A Paradox of 'A House of History's Own': in Virginia Woolf's *Orlando* and *A Room of One's Own*

I. Introduction

In *Orlando* and *A Room of One's Own*, Woolf attempts to reconstruct a paradox of 'a house of history's own' in order to encode the neglected and unarticulated voices of women "in the pursuit of truth" (*AROO* 27) which was overwhelmed by all the male forces issued throughout centuries since the establishment of feudal England. In order to underline the textual and political discourse that ignored, trivialized, and marginalized women's history, experience, and abilities, *Orlando* and *A Room of One's Own* connote the paradox which is embedded in the ideological aspects represented by the architectural embodiments as men's houses which were erected and established in the British Isles as men's land.

The comparative studies on *Orlando* and *A Room of One's Own* have received some attentions. In 1968, Herbert Marder first points out that *Orlando* and *A Room of One's Own* "represent a summing up of Virginia Woolf's feminist ideas as of the late twenties" (24) and considers those two as "companion volumes" (26). In 1980, Maria DiBattista regards *Orlando* as "a fanciful vindication of the rights of literary women," and notes that it "remained for *A Room of One's Own* to convert fantasy into dogmatic prescription" (147). J.J. Wilson, moreover, calls a set of these novels "these two soeurs junelles [twin sisters]" (183). Sandra Gilbert remarks that *Orlando* is "a text complementary to *A Room of One's Own*" (21). More recently, Kari Elise Lokke is convinced that *Orlando* "brilliantly embodies the seemingly contradictory political and aesthetic theories of *A Room of One's Own* in a vision of the comic sublime" (236). Although these critics point out the parallelism between *Orlando* and *A Room of One's Own*, regretfully enough, there have been no extensive and thorough critical comparative studies on those works. In analyzing Woolf's revolt against the British Empire as a house of men's own manipulated in those works, it is necessary to examine the shared controversial facets which motivate Woolf to pursue her search for a room of one's own.

Orlando was published on October 11, 1928, "the day on which the novel's last chapter takes place and Orlando arrives at the present time" (Lyons xliv); whereas *A Room of One's Own* finalizes its statement on October 26, 1928. In completing these apparently different kinds of works at the same time, Woolf's internal conflict reaches to the same point where "the androgynous mind" (*AROO* 97) is an inevitable factor, and a purely private space with financial independence becomes a key for a woman writer to establish herself and survive in the twentieth century. Tracing the reign of Elizabeth I to Woolf's contemporary era, *Orlando* and *A Room of One's Own* embody the multilayered and integrated paradox of self-search embedded within the male-created British history. The paradox also exists in a series of striking transitions of space-search;

from an attic room of the great house in the seventeenth century, a drawing room of a London townhouse in the eighteenth century, a sitting room of a domestic house in the nineteenth century, to a locked room of one's own in a house of everyone's own in the twentieth century. These striking transitions can be observed and explored in the relationship between literature and architecture. The representative architectures generate the power which contributes to creating the British history. Focusing on both Knole in *Orlando* and Oxbridge in *A Room of One's Own*, it is significant to discover the paradox which Woolf places in a relationship between literature and architecture within a house of history's own.

II. A Paradox in a Relationship between Literature and Architecture

It is important to locate the exploration in assuming that women writers were excluded from both spaces — the house of men's own and the university of men's own — which accommodated the male-dominated political, social, legal, and economical power throughout British history. A paradox exists in a relationship between literature and architecture in a highly diversified transition from Orlando in the great house, through Judith Shakespeare possessing neither a house nor a room, through Mary Beton and Mary Seton and their mothers without any right of inheritance and possession of property, to Mary Carmichael in a bed-sitting room. A set of parallels — between Orlando and Judith Shakespeare and between Orlando and Mary Carmichael — assign a crucial effect of sexual politics on the interrelation between women's literature and men's architecture. Both *Orlando* and *A Room of One's Own* engrave the Tudor Age as the ground of the English monarchy and patriarchy where the male-centered power controlled literature and where the female creative power was entirely marginalized. The freedom and privilege of being involved in literature is founded upon the political and economical power of the British monarchy and its society that plays a role as the patron of literature and learning.

Orlando's possession of a great house manifests this privilege of enjoying literature; while Judith Shakespeare's lack of her house is foregrounded in the women's structural and institutionalized poverty that deprives them of the freedom and priority of an access to literature. At the beginning of *Orlando*, Orlando at sixteen is deeply involved in his creative activities of writing poetry and drama in his attic room of the great house in the Elizabethan Era and becomes a patron of Nick Green during the reign of King James. On the other hand, Woolf's fictional figure, Judith Shakespeare "before seventeen," in *A Room of One's Own*, has no way of presenting her talents which are equal with those of her brother William Shakespeare; consequently, she is beaten by her father, leaves her father's house, migrates to London by herself, becomes a mistress of Nick Green and pregnant, and commits suicide without any literary work or even one word left. Orlando as a son of a noble man is shaped by the historically male-dominated policy-making and control of the policy processes. Judith Shakespeare as a daughter of the middle-class educated man, however, links accounts of battered women's experiences to constructions of battering and structural issues and concludes how women's political and institutionalized weakness results in sexual subordination and eternal silence.[1]

The parallelism between Orlando and Judith Shakespeare, both of whom confront and contrast Nick Green, also symbolizes a tension between a well-situated yet distorted male view of literature and a dislocated yet well-oriented female view of literature. Women's potential is, however, entirely sacrificed for the male-controlled misjudgement upon literature. Nick Green is "an imaginary writer" who is "partly based on the Elizabethan hack writer, pamphleteer, poet and playwright, Robert Greene (1558-92), notorious for his envy of Shakespeare" (*O* 243). Judith Shakespeare's challenge to Nick Green is enormously more provocative than Orlando's challenge to Nick Green. The betrayal of Orlando and Judith Shakespeare by Nick Green, therefore, embodies the overall destructive force inhering in literature which excluded the voices of unknown people and which approved the known male poets who were financially supported and evaluated by the men of power.

The intermediate procedure from the parallel between Orlando and Judith Shakespeare to that between Orlando and Mary Carmichael is followed by Woolf's interrogation of gender and the legally institutionalized discourse that is questioned by Mary Seton. It is generally known that Orlando's loss of the right of an heir to the great house caused by her sex change in the eighteenth century reflects Vita Sackville-West's loss of Knole when the title and the house were "entailed to pass through the male line," to her father's younger brother Charles after her father's death in 1928 and then to her cousin Eddy in 1962 (Robert Sackville-West 94). Woolf's sympathy to Vita without Knole is also said to have motivated Woolf to write *Orlando*. Woolf's compassion, moreover, centers on problematic women's legal situations as well as the institutions that frame those situations.

> Moreover, it is equally useless to ask what might have happened if Mrs. Seton and her mother and her mother before her had amassed great wealth and laid it under the foundations of college and library, because, in the first place, to earn money was impossible for them, and in the second, had it been possible, the law denied them the right to possess what money they earned. (*AROO* 24)

The women's legal and economical oppressions are identical before 1882 when the husband is prohibited from disposing the wife's property. The women's legal oppression and poverty as its consequence deprives women of possessing all the houses ranging from a private house like Knole to a house of education and learning like Oxbridge. Orlando as a woman in the eighteenth and nineteenth centuries is a Mary Seton who represents the weaker vessel that suffers the unequal and subordinate position determined by the legal institution.

The parallel between Orlando and Mary Carmichael adds further dimensions and complexities in the course of establishing women's literature. Orlando's privilege of having an attic room where he writes a pile of poems is, next, situated against Mary Carmichael's lack of "desirable things, time, money, and idleness" (*AROO* 93) in a bed-sitting room where she, as an unknown woman, is writing her first novel in the twentieth century. This tension is ironically resolved in Lady Orlando's reencounter with Nick Green, now Sir Nicholas, as "the most influential critic of the Victorian age" (*O* 193), at the beginning of the twentieth century. "The Oak Tree" which was first written in 1586 is transformed into a new version after three hundred years' revisions. Woolf criticizes the fact that the fate of 300-year-old "The Oak Tree" has to depend upon the fame and power of Sir Nicholas and of the publishing company as another men's house. Orlando as an unknown young woman writer in the seventeenth century is a Judith Shakespeare without a house, a room, and all the other kinds of privileges. Orlando in the twentieth century is a Mary Carmichael with a small space which allows her to concentrate on writing her first book, *Life's Adventure*. Both Judith Shakespeare and Mary Carmichael portray the women whose talents, abilities, and even the real selves were suppressed under the enormous power of all the houses such as the British monarchy, the father's house, and the husband's house, and the publishing house. The title of Orlando's work, "The Oak Tree," has lost its original meaning and the manuscript consists of Orlando's 300-year life of adventure, that is, formerly unrecorded, untold, and unknown stories in the history of literature. The lost part of literature is discovered, revived, and articulated in voices sprung from small rooms whose walls "are permeated by their [women's] creative force" (*AROO* 87) by the twentieth century. The parallel between Orlando and Mary Carmichael illustrates another feminist discourse in the contextual analysis of the architectural and literary embodiments as the capsulated history.

Knole and Oxbridge that lock out women are located against "A Room of One's Own," as a refuge which liberates women from all the restrictions, conventions, and powers. A new space is reborn with Orlando's "The Oak Tree" and Mary Carmichael's *Life's Adventure* as well as with Vita without Knole and Jane Ellen Harrison of Newnham College outside of Cambridge. Both Knole as a house of men's own and Oxbridge as a university of men's own are engraved as the foreground of the women's neglected life and lost self. The women's self-search which is questioned, examined, and ultimately accomplished both in *Orlando* and *A Room of One's Own* crucially originates in challenging the foundation and establishment of male space which reflects that of architecture itself. The architecture that houses the ideology as the political, social, economical, and legal disclosure is illustrated within a frame of literature. The paradox in a relationship between literature and architecture is what Woolf intends to mold in her own self-search that launched in her revolt against her father's house, library, and room, and that continued as women's objection against the British society as a house of history's own.

III. A House of Men's Own in Orlando

As an heir of the great house, Orlando possesses all the privileges to occupy a man's own space ranging from the banqueting hall to the attic room. The banqueting hall is a public place where Orlando welcomes Queen Elizabeth and her party; on the contrary, the attic room is a purely private space where Orlando is indulged into writing poetry and drama. Orlando's prolificness proven by "no more perhaps than twenty tragedies and a dozen histories and a score of sonnets" (*O* 18) embodies Orlando's intermixed public and private luxuries. The luxuries both in public and in private are primarily grounded upon Orlando's social and financial status as a nobleman with a great house which is based on Knole.

Orlando's possession of the great house represents the establishment of the British monarchy of the Tudor Age. In *Orlando,* Elizabeth I in her late years "made over formally, putting her hand and seal finally to the parchment, the gift of the great monastic house that had been the Archbishop's and then the King's to Orlando's father" (*O* 17). Though there is no official record, it is generally believed that Elizabeth I gave Knole to her cousin and councillor, Thomas Sackville. Vita remarks in Knole that in June 1566 "Queen Elizabeth had presented him [Thomas Sackville] with Knole, but the house was then both let and sub-let, it was not until 1603 that he was able to take possession" (50). These remarks and beliefs are, however, constructed by more subtle and complicated incidents that had influence on the shifts of the political power. The historical background and changed owners of Knole is complex and intriguing enough to retell the structural and interactional elements of the British monarchy as the most dominant institution.

The foundation of Knole — the park, the gatehouse, the tower, even an interior of Knole — connotes the early history as the house for the people of power especially during the transitional period from 1456 to 1566. This 100-year period witnesses the most remarkable changes of Knole in respect of the political power struggle. The enclosure of the park is the first foundation of Knole's position and meaning in the British history. The earliest record of Knole is set in 1456 when Thomas Bourchier, Archbishop of Canberbury bought the manor of Knole from Sir William Feinnes, Lord Say and Sele and expanded as a domestic place till his death in 1486. It was thus in 1456 when the park was first enclosed by Bourchier "to indulge a passion, popular among the nobility, for hunting" (46).

The park in *Orlando* embodies the timeless and transcendental space which embraces Orlando's self after his / her 360-year life that began with a solitary moment of a young noble man.

> And it was at this moment, when she had ceased to call 'Orlando' and was deep in thoughts of something else, that the Orlando whom she had called came of its own accord; as was proved by the change that now came over her (she had passed through the lodge gates and was entering the park).
>
> The whole of her darkened and settled, as when some foil whose addition makes the round and solidity of surface is added to it, and the shallow becomes deep and the near distant; and all is contained as water is contained by the sides of a well. So she was now darkened, stilled, and become, with the addition of this Orlando, that is called, rightly or wrongly, a single self, a real self. (*O* 216)

The park is located as the essential ground to produce the self because it contains the soil to produce the nature such as trees and plants, and the nature to breed the living creatures such as deer. These basic elements of the park that represents the medieval game forest and landscape remains for centuries in Knole because Knole, with a few exceptions, did not undergo the improvement of the park to create the picturesque landscape in the eighteenth century. Consequently, Knole is characterized by "the timelessness" of the park where in the twentieth century Orlando can enjoy the fluidity of the natural landscape; "All this, the trees, deer, and turf, she observed with the greatest satisfaction as if her mind had become a fluid that flowed round things and enclosed them completely" (*O* 216-17). When Orlando visits the great house, it is no more possessed by Orlando. In 1947, Knole was taken over by the National Trust though the Sackvilles' home was allowed to remain there.[2] Knole as a private property finalizes its status when it faces the financial difficulty due to the rising taxes (Robert Sackville-West 93).[3] The park which is enclosed in the foundation of Knole marks the fundamental element of the space that transcends the chronological time and remains as the spiritual locale beyond the boundary between the public and the private.

The conflicting yet striking element of Knole in its foundation is registered in its political and social transformation of the house due to the change of its owners. Along with the change of the owners, Knole is reborn with new additional buildings whose roles affect and alter the meaning of Knole. After Knole has three successors of Archbishop, John Morton (1487-1500), William Warham (1504-1532), and Thomas Granmer (1532-), it was "voluntarily" given to Henry VIII (Robert Sackville-West 53-54). In 1534, Henry VIII succeeded in breaking with Roman Catholic and became the supreme head of the English Church; as a result, the abbeys and cathedrals were converted into the great houses, "not to the glory of God, but for the glorification of the men who lived in them" (Chambers 49). Knole was one of sixty royal residences that Henry VIII had acquired by his death. Henry VIII's strong intention to build and enlarge the great houses results from his desire to present his political power over his subjects. It is recorded that Henry VIII spent a large amount of money on new buildings, such as the central gatehouse (now the main entrance), the Green Court and the buildings around it, the King's Tower, and the west front (Robert Sackville West 54). Knole with the new additional buildings and an extended structure as a royal residence controlled by Henry VIII internalizes the political backbone of the British monarchy whose anatomy is firmed as the keystone of the British Empire.

It is apparent that Knole is equivalent to the other magnificent palaces and houses that Henry VIII built during his reign and *Orlando* delineates those landmark architectures connected with Henry VIII. The equivalence and similarity is proven in the style and tastes of the architecture. The Green Court of Knole which was erected to lodge Henry VIII's attendants is, for example, similar to a courtyard at Hampton Court and the quadrangle of an Oxford college which were built during the same period (Robert Sackville-West 54). Along with the great houses, the establishment and demolishment of the palaces emerged as vital to the process of ordering and reordering the English monarchy in the Tudor Age. Orlando's appointment is informed at Whitehall which was formerly Archbishop York's residence, taken from Cardinal Wolsey by Henry VIII, and reformed as a royal palace. Cardinal Wolsey was the son of a grazier and innkeeper who was elevated to Henry VIII's Lord Chancellor. When Wolsey was made Archbishop of York, he resided at Hampton Court and finished building lodgings for Henry VIII in 1525. Since Wolsey fell from favour, he was forced to relinquish his ownership to Henry VIII, who added a third courtyard to Hampton Court (*Hampton Court Palace* 6-7; Chambers 54). Henry VIII also built such palaces as Bridewell and St. James Palace in addition to those in Greenwich and Richmond that Henry VII had established. Orlando visits Elizabeth I at Richmond before her death, and experiences King James I's coronation at Greenwich in 1603. The British monarchy's feudal power is confirmed both in the palaces which Henry VII and Henry VIII built and the great houses which Henry VIII encouraged to enlarge and improve.

Knole which was reborn with additional buildings in a new expanded form constitutes the strengthened power of the British monarchy. The transformation from the religious dwelling to the royal residence outlines the overall consequence of the Reformation that determines the solid ground of the British monarchy and its rulers.

The second transformation of Knole within the British monarchy's power strife delineates the struggling yet expanding power of the British monarchy and its subjects during its transitional era. After Henry VIII's death in 1547, Knole was passed to his son, Edward VI at ten, from Edward to his guardian, John Dudley, Duke of Northumberland, and to Queen Mary, from Mary to Cardinal Pole, Cranmer's successor as Archbishop of Canterbury in 1553. Knole's short role as a religious dwelling caused by Queen Mary's Catholic revival is engraved as the conflicting dilemma between the striving Catholicism and the empowering Anglican Church. After Mary's death, Queen Elizabeth throned in 1558 granted Knole to Northumberland's son and her favourite, Robert Dudley, later Earl of Leicester, in 1561, yet Leicester returned Knole to Elizabeth in 1566. The intermediate stage of Knole evidences the most crucial stage of establishing the monarchy until Elizabeth I is enthroned and England is ruled under the most influential authority.[4]

The final landing of Knole into Elizabeth I's hands after a series of owner changes due to the shifts of the political authorized power transfigures Knole into one of the vast mansions in Britain because of Elizabeth's political strategies and the Sackvilles' devotion to the monarchy. Elizabeth I's visit to Orlando's great house is described as an inevitable ritual and obligation for Orlando to undergo. The sudden alarm with a trumpet which "came from the heart of his own great house" (*O* 15) makes Orlando acknowledge the importance of entertaining Elizabeth I. Orlando's long way from the park through "the vast congeries of rooms and staircases to the banqueting-hall" which contains a five-acre distance recalls a model of the expanded and remodelled great house subordinated by the Tudor monarchy. Unlike Henry VIII who founded the great buildings, Elizabeth I was "no builder; but she was a great inspirer of building in others" (57-58). The reason why Elizabeth I encouraged noblemen and gentlemen to build their great houses and she would frequently visit those houses is that the her intention to control the upper class by replacing "the rule of force by the rule of law" (Girouard 84) and her frequent visits made the house owners spend money so that she could diminish their overpowered situations. As Elizabeth I's visit was usually accompanied by 150 officials and attendants (Chambers 58), the great house owners had to extend their houses into the ones which could accommodate and entertain them. By this Elizabeth I's strategy, the Tudor political power was more strictly established and the foundation of the English monarchy was affirmed. At the same time, the vast mansions were superbly built, repeatedly reformed, and virtually enlarged so as to entertain and satisfy Elizabeth I.

The interrelationship between Elizabeth I and the Sackvilles as for the lease and the ownership of Knole is connected with the power structure between the Queen of England and her subjects entirely controlled by Elizabeth. In *Orlando*, the parallel between the "old," "worn," and "bent" Queen and the young nobleman "with finest legs" is inscribed in that in age, sex, and rank in the last period of the Elizabeth I's reign. Orlando's devotion to his grandmother-like Elizabeth I and her affection to him enable him to gain an emerald ring as a symbol of her triumph over him, a highest office of Treasurer and Steward as an embodiment of the closest relationship with Queen, and the Garter as the highest order of English knighthood in the English feudalism.

The Sackvilles' involvement in the royal court alters Knole's destiny which ends with possessing 356 rooms. In 1566 when Dudley returned Knole to Elizabeth I, Thomas Sackville inherited a large fortune and a country house at Buckhurst from his father, Richard. Because of Richard's remarkable success in the timber and iron business, the Sackvilles had already acquired great estates in Sussex and Kent. Thomas Sackville, trained as a lawyer like Richard and a poet himself, gained more estates and titles from Elizabeth I. In 1567, he was made Baron Buckhurst, one of only two completely new peerages created by Elizabeth I (Robert Sackville-West 56). Thomas Sackville, however, faced financial difficulties after he served as ambassador to France in 1571-72. As he needed to rebuild his fortunes, he manipulated his position and gained profits by assigning the lease of Knole to a local landowner, John Lennard, in 1574-1604. During this period, Thomas Sackville's political power dramatically increased as he was rewarded as a Privy Counsellor in 1586, a Knight of the Garter in 1589, Cancellor of the University of Oxford in 1591, and Earl of Dorset in 1604. Like Orlando, Thomas Sackville was appointed to the most significant position, Lord Treasurer by Elizabeth I in 1599. As Lord Treasurer, Thomas Sackville was responsible for the sale of Crown lands so that he could negotiate the sale of the freehold of Knole directly to himself and bought back the lease on Knole in 1604. At this time, Thomas Sackville became the freehold owner of Knole. Because of his position as Lord Treasurer, moreover, Thomas Sackville initiated reforming and remaking Knole in order to transform it into a great house in 1604 when he was 69 years old, one year after Elizabeth I's reign was over. The Sackvilles' ownership of Knole which is confirmed after Thomas Sackville's thirty-seven-year service to Elizabeth I manifests the surviving power of the Queen's subject during the most crucial period of the British monarchy.

During the early history of Knole, the dramatic changes of the politics which alter its owners and consequently the house itself embody a house of history's own. *Orlando* outlines the establishment of a house of history's own in the British monarchy. The early history of the house, however, turns only a phantom for Orlando in the twentieth century; "There stood the great house with all its windows robed in silver. Of wall or substance there was none. All was phantom. All was still. All was lit as for the coming of a dead Queen" (*O* 227). The British history that was registered and engraved in the great house symbolized by Knole plays a role to juxtapose the foundation and establishment of the political power of the British monarchy.

IV. A University of Men's Own in *A Room of One's Own*

In *A Room of One's Own*, Woolf states Oxbridge and the British Museum embody other houses of the men's power. The establishment and improvement of both architectures represent how the male-centered political power has contributed to the powers of education and academics. Since both Oxford and Cambridge were founded by the thirteenth century, they have played roles as centers of learning. The early history of Oxbridge from the Medieval Age to the Tudor Period manifests a series of conflicts manipulated by political powers.

Like Knole, Oxford and Cambridge whose origins were traced back to the medieval age were improved especially during the Tudor Period and continued to exclude women in Woolf's contemporary era. As Woolf makes Mary Seton remark in *A Room of One's Own*, Emily Davies was confronted with enormous budget difficulties in establishing women's college formerly in Hitchin in 1869 and in moving it at Girton in Cambridge, in 1873 (21-22). Anne Jemima Glough, who attended the first meeting of Davies's Schoolmistresses' Association, founded Newham College to house the women in 1874 (Hussey 182). Though Girton was founded when "it was only after a long struggle and with the utmost difficulty that they got thirty thousand pounds together" (*AROO* 22), the facilities were minimum and poor. The women throughout the history were deprived of possessing, inheriting, and controlling the money; on the other hand, their fathers and husbands monopolized the property and even possessed the freedom and authority to use it "to found a scholarship or to endow a fellowship in Balliol or Kings" (*AROO* 24). In order to illustrate the women's poverty and its influence upon women's potential and life, Woolf exhibits an etching of Oxbridge from its foundation to its establishment.

Woolf resents that Oxbridge, which was improved with the solid financial support of the kings and queens of the monarchy especially in the sixteenth and seventeenth centuries, was extended with another financial source of the newly-established "tithes" at the age of faith, and was expanded with endowment to "more chairs, more lectureships, more fellowships" (*AROO* 11) and "the libraries and laboratories; the observatories" (*AROO* 12). Since its establishment in the Medieval Age, Oxbridge has been the privileged sanctuary to nourish male-centered power, especially in religion, education, politics, economics, and law.

The early history and establishment of Oxford and Cambridge, therefore, embodies another story of establishing a house of man's own in respects of religion and monarchy in British history. Neither of the universities were founded as academic institutions from the very beginning. Along with the enthusiastic pursuit for learning in Europe, England had several schools for pupils of Catholic theology and Oxford was developed from a small community of several schools to a larger body in 1221. This rapid change was largely caused by two incidents. As the University of Paris, the center for education in Europe, banned foreign students in 1167, English students needed their own university in England. The English priests, moreover, lost contact with Europe because of Henry II's strife with Becket of Canterbury. Both the students and the priests needed to found their own school. The early Oxford schools became the first central place for learning and the tithe barn at Holywell was already an important source of income for the college by 1300 (Catto). The ground of Oxford as the center of Catholic masters and pupils connotes the Englishmen's first pursuit of 'a university of their own' under the strong influence of Catholicism.

The establishment of both Oxford and Cambridge possesses the male-centered violence as a hidden agenda within the seemingly high society of education and scholarship. It is important to notice that the reason why Cambridge developed from a small community of pupils related to nearby wealthy abbeys is that a large number of pupils called "gowns" emigrated from Oxford to Cambridge. This emigration was caused by a series of conflicts between the gowns and the townspeople in Oxford. Its initial incident is that one pupil killed his mistress and escaped early in December 1209, and town people hanged the other two students who lived in the same house (Southern 26).[5] Between 1210 and 1214, Oxford was deserted by the masters and pupils, and some masters moved with their pupils to Cambridge. After this crisis, ironically, Oxford was transformed into a well-organized university with "privileges to guard, revenues to administer and special rights to maintain" (Southern 26). In order to accommodate a number of pupils gathered at Cambridge,

Hugh de Balsham founded Peterhouse by contributing St. Peter's Church. Located in marsh, as Woolf says (*AROO* 11), Cambridge, thus, became a second body of scholars, priests, and gowns in 1226. Both Oxford and Cambridge were directly connected with and well supported by religion in its foundation and both universities retained the functions of a seminary until 1850 (Searby 1). The historical fact that Cambridge was founded as the result of the man's supreme dominance and violence upon the woman within the male sanctuary narrates the truth that an unknown woman's voice is entirely erased and her life was sacrificed for protecting and legalizing the authorized position of Oxbridge.

Oxbridge's second stage of improvement and expansion represents the interconnected male-centered power of religion and monarchy. As Woolf states, both universities expanded with the establishment of new colleges "in the age of faith," and their curriculums and systems were reformed during "the age of reason" (*AROO* 11). Their financial source was mostly endowments from priests during the pre-Reformation era, kings and queens such as Henry VIII and Elizabeth I during the Reformation, and wealthy merchants and professionals since the beginning of the seventeenth century. Consequently, the connection between the universities and the embodiments of the political, economical, and social forces became strong so that the universities became part of the British monarchy and the Anglican Church.

Especially after abbeys diminished, universities became the object of endowments. The amount of endowments which was spent for education, especially to grammar schools and Oxbridge, occupied 27 percent in total of endowments between 1480 and 1660. Those endowments were used for three purposes: the first one was to establish scholarships at grammar school for those who would go to Oxbridge; the second one was to increase the amounts of fellowships and establish new fellowships; and the third one was to found new colleges (Green 20-21). King's College which was founded by Henry VI in 1441 added King's Chapel which was completed by Henry VIII in 1515. The tradition of King's College whose admissions were only for Eton graduates continued till 1861. As the result of the Reformation, Henry VIII transformed the former abbeys to colleges as well as to great houses; Christ Church at the site of Cardinal College at Oxford and Trinity College at the former site of King's Hall and Michaelhouse at Cambridge in 1546. Trinity College, which had sixty fellows in those days, has been the greatest college both in quality and quantity at Cambridge till now. Elizabeth I also contributed to Jesus College at Oxford and founded the university rules of Cambridge in 1570, which were not changed for the following 300 years. After two new colleges were founded at the end of the sixteenth century, the new colleges were not founded until the nineteenth century at Cambridge. As a number of large colleges increased, Oxbridge formed Gothic styles with the "courts" (at Cambridge) or the "quadrangle" (at Oxford) which Woolf tries to pass through at the beginning of *A Room of One's Own*.

Woolf's visit to Oxbridge in *A Room of One's Own* is a journey to the origin of both universities, especially of how they were founded as the learning center of male-dominant theology and improved as the house of the academics by the two enormous forces, the British monarchy and the Anglican Church.

V. Conclusion

Woolf's creating a paradox of a house of history's own both in *Orlando* and *A Room of One's Own* signifies her strong intention to cast a light on the issue of women's inarticulate voices and their unrecognized selves. As fraternal twin sisters, *Orlando* and *A Room of One's Own* share their biological father who imprisons his daughters within a house of his own erected by the political force of the British monarchy; while they inherit the genetic code from their biological mother who is oppressed and neglected under the power of the house. The genetic code that *Orlando* and *A Room of One's Own* transmit from Judith Shakespeare is passed on through Woolf to an Orlando and a Mary Carmichael as a single true self.

Notes ■

The abridged form of this paper was presented for the Panel, "Woolf and History" (Chair, Masami Usui) on June 9 (Fri.) 8:30-10:00 at the 10th Annual Conference on Virginia Woolf: "Virginia Woolf Out of Bounds" which was held from June 8 through June 11, 2000 at the University of Maryland at Baltimore County, Maryland, U.S.A. This paper was originally published in *Doshisha Studies in English* 73 (March 2001): 57-78.

1 Abel points out that Judith Shakespear's "vulnerability resides in her body, not (in contrast to Three Guineas) in her sexuality" (101). Responding Abel's theory, Celia R. Caputi Daileader makes a further discussion on a racial issue in Woolf's presentation of Gipsies and the Moors (63-65).

2 Vita's sorrow was enormous when she signed a document to give Knole away to the National Trust (cited from *Spectator, Knole* 215).

3 According to Robert Sackville-West, Vita's uncle, the 4th Lord Sackville and Major-General Sir Charles worried about the future difficulty to maintain Knole after paying the death duties and entered into discussion with the National Trust in 1935 (95).

4 Abbott remarks that Woolf "empowers herself as a female artist, and, as a female artist manipulating the image of a powerful historical figure" that Woolf imposes on Elizabeth I (77-78).

5 Green remarks that the reason of a migration to Cambridge was "a quarrel

between the students and the townfolk, the first of many such, caused, so it was alleged, by the execution of a scholar in revenge for the murder of a townswoman by another student" (14).

Works Cited

Abel, Elizabeth. *Virginia Woolf and the Fiction of Psychoanalysis*. Chicago: U of Chicago P, 1989.

Abbott, Reginald. "Rough with Rubies: Virginia Woolf and the Virgin Queen." *Virginia Woolf: the Renaissance*. Ed. Sally Green. Athens: Ohio UP, 1999. 65-88.

Brown, Jane. *Vita's Other World: A Gardening Biography of V. Sackville-West*. New York: Viking, 1985.

Catto, J. J., ed. *The History of the University of Oxford*. Vol. I: *The Early Oxford Schools*. Oxford: Clarendon, 1984.

Chambers, James. *The English House*. New York & London: Norton, 1985.

Daileader, Celia R. Caputi. "Othello's Sister: Racial Hermaphroditism and Appropriation in Virginia Woolf's *Orlando*." *Studies in the Novel* 45.1 (Spring 2013): 56-79.

DiBattista, Maria. *Virginia Woolf's Major Novels: The Fables of Anon*. New Haven: Yale UP, 1980.

Gilbert, Sandra M. "Woman's Sentence, Man's Sentencing: Linguistic Fantasies in Woolf and Joyce." Marcus, *Virginia Woolf* 208-24.

Girouard, Mark. *Life in the English Country House: A Social and Architectural History* .1978. New Haven & London: Yale UP, 1979.

Green, V. H. H. *The Universities*. London: Pelican, 1969.

Hampton Court Palace: Souvenir Guide Book. Hampton Court: Hampton Court, n.d.

Hussey, Mark. *Virginia Woolf A to Z*. New York: Facts On Files, 1995.

Lokke, Kari Elise. "Orlando and Incandescence: Virginia Woolf's Comic Sublime." *Modern Fiction Studies* 38.1 (Spring 1992): 235-52.

Lyons, Brenda. "A Note on the Test." Woolf, *Orlando* xliv-xlvi.

Marcus, Jane, ed. *New Feminist Essays on Virginia Woolf*. Lincoln: U of Nebraska P, 1981.

——, ed. *Virginia Woolf and Bloomsbury: A Centenary Celebration*. Bloomington: Indiana UP, 1987.

Marder, Herbert. *Feminism and Art: A Study of Virginia Woolf*. Chicago: U of

Chicago P, 1968.

Oates, J. C. T. *Cambridge University Library: A History*. Cambridge: Cambridge UP, 1986.

Sackville-West, Robert. *Knole, Kent*. London: The National Trust, 1998.

Sackville-West, Vita. *English Country Houses*. 1941. London: Prion, 1996.

——. *Knole and the Sackvilles*. 1922. London: The National Trust, 1991.

Searby, Peter. *A History of The University of Cambridge*. Vol. III: 1750-1870. Cambridge: Cambridge UP, 1997.

Southern, R. W. "From Schools to University." Catto 1-36.

Weightman, Gavin. *London River: The Thames Story*. London: Collins, 1990.

Wilson, J. J. "Why is Orlando Difficult?" Marcus, *New Feminist* 170-84.

Woolf, Virginia. *Orlando*. 1928. London: Penguin, 1993.

——. *A Room of One's Own*. 1928. London: Penguin, 1993.

Chapter 3

Animal-Assisted Therapy in Virginia Woolf's *Flush, A Biography*

I. Introduction

Virginia Woolf's *Flush, A Biograpby* has rarely been criticized because it is usually considered as Woolf's least important book since it is a mock-biography of Elizabeth Barrett Browning's cocker spaniel, Flush.[1] It is, however, important to notice that Woolf's pursuit for inventing her own style of biography can be witnessed in three biographies, *Orlando, A Biography* (1928), *Flush, A Biography* (1933), and *Roger Fry: A Biography* (1940). It is, therefore, significant to reinvestigate *Flush* as an embodiment of Woolf's search for her own voice and self by replacing it in the other voice under the name of biography of a dog. In *Flush*, the woman poet's marginalized self is retrieved in her companionship with her dog in a process of animal-assisted therapy.

Especially, *Orlando* and *Flush* embody Woolf's intention to heal her mind after she established a unique form of literature. Woolf began to write *Orlando* in 1927 after completing *To the Lighthouse*; while she began to write *Flush* in 1931 after completing *The Waves* and while continuing writing *The Pargiters*. Woolf plunged into sketching *Orlando* and *Flush* in order to heal her mind after the enormous and heavy works of compiling *To the Lighthouse* and *The Waves* respectively.

> *Flush* is only by way of a joke. I was so tired after *The Waves*, that I lay in the garden and read the Browning love letters, and the figure of their dog made me laugh so I couldn't resist making him a Life. I wanted to play a joke on Lytton — it was to parody him. But then it grew too long, and I don't think its up to much now. But this is all very egotistical. (*The Letters of Virginia Woolf* 4 161-62)

By repeatedly manipulating the word, "joke," in the following letters regarding her new biography, *Flush*, Woolf disguises her serious attitude toward her new creative force. While she was indulged into writing *Flush*, she realized that the little book had become "too slight & too serious" (*The Diary of Virginia Woolf* 4 134) and it would take more efforts and time than she had first expected. *Flush* is considered as another experimental work whose importance Woolf discovered while she sought for a healing effect by writing it. *Flush* expresses Woolf's challenge of creating the inarticulate narrative voice sprung within the equal human-to-dog bond and companionship.

II. The Dual Therapy: Barrett Browning's Flush and Woolf's Pinker

What motivated Woolf to write *Flush* is as important as what healed her in her writing. It is known that Woolf created *Orlando* for her lesbian lover, Vita Sackville-West, and wrote *Flush* for Barrett

Browning. Woolf's compassion to both Vita and Barrett Browning as women artists motivated her to seek for their voices. The significant yet hidden tie between *Orlando* and *Flush* is, moreover, that the cover model of the first edition of *Flush* by Hogarth Press is known as Pinker (or Pinka), Woolf's own cocker spaniel who was presented by Vita in 1926 during a period of their most intense relationship between 1925 and 1928 (See the cover picture of Pinker as Flush in a penguin edition of *Flush*). When Pinker was given to Woolf when she spent the night on July 26, 1926, with Vita at Long Barn, Woolf suffered from what Leonard called "'a whole nervous breakdown in miniature'"(Reid 293).

In Flush's case, Mary Russell Mitford, an essayist, novelist, and playwright, had an admiration of and compassion to Barrett Browning and gave Flush to her. In "Married Poets," Mitford describes how "intimacy ripened into friendship" between them and illustrates the physical features of Barrett Browning: "On a slight, delicate figure, with a shower of dark curls falling on either side of a most expressive face, large tender eyes richly fringed by dark eyelashes, a smile like a sunbeam, and such a look of youthfulness, ..." (170). Mitford's description of Barrett Browning is similar to Woolf's one of both Barrett Browning and Flush in *Flush*: "Heavy curls hung down on either side of Miss Barrett's face; large bright eyes shone out; a large mouth smiled. Heavy ears hung down on either side of Flush's face; his eyes, too, were large and bright: his mouth was wide" (20). Mitford, then, records Barrett Browning's physical and psychological difficulties especially after she "broke a blood-vessel upon the lungs" ("Married Poets" 170). Mitford's strong sympathy to Barrett Browning is expressed in her understanding of Barrett Browning's agony over her brother's tragic death, her confined life during her winter stay at Torquay, her devotion to literature, and her ultimate confinement in her father's

London house.

> Returned to London, she [Barrett Browning] began the life which she continued for so many years, confined to one large and commodious but darkened chamber, admitting only her own affectionate family and a few devoted friends (I, myself, have often joyfully traveled five-and-forty miles to see her, and returned and the same evening, without entering another house); reading almost every book worth reading in almost every language, and giving herself, heart and soul, to that poetry of which she seemed born to be the priestess. ("Married Poets" 172)

The reason why the writer Mitford gave Flush to the invalid poet Barrett Browning is proven the same as that the writer Vita gave Pinker to the invalid writer Woolf.

Flush is overlapped with Pinker as Flush came into Woolf's mind while she shared her life with Pinker. It was observed that friends of Leonard and Virginia in 1933 "could readily draw the parallel between Flush Browning and Pinker Woolf" (Szladits 504). In some photos taken in the 1930's, Pinker is in the middle of Virginia, Leonard, and their friends and close relatives (Spater and Parsibs 133, 139, 141; Alexander). Woolf's diary entries on Pinker between 1927 and 1935, moreover, divided into two distinct sections: the early period between 1927 and 1929; and the later period between 1933 and 1935. Between 1927 and 1929, Woolf mentions about Pinker frequently as her walks (*D3* 146; *D3* 186), her sleep in the chair (*D3* 166; *D3* 184), the lice (*D3* 175), and her bearing four puppies (*D3* 196). Between 1933 and 1935, Woolf mainly reports Pinker's decline of health such as eczema (*D4* 162) and weak eyes (*D4* 195), and finally her death (*D4* 317). During the period between 1930 and 1932, however, Woolf remarks primarily on her progressive *Flush* instead of mentioning Pinker. It is also significant to note that the relationship between Woolf and Vita was over in 1935 when Pinker died unexpectedly. Woolf's own dog, Pinker, is switched into her half-biographical and half-fictional dog, Flush, both in her writings and in her psychology because Woolf s life with Pinker is identified with Barrett Browning's life with Flush.

Pinker plays a child-like role for the Woolfs in the psychologically matured period of their marriage and professional life. Though Quentin Bell defines that Woolf was "not, in the fullest sense of the word, a dog lover" (175), both Virginia and Leonard were terribly depressed when Pinker ended her eight-year life unexpectedly and mysteriously one day before their homecoming from their travel to Germany, Holland, Austria, and Italy.

> Holidays are very upsetting. And its cold & grey. And my hand shakes. And I want some regular hours & work. And it'll take at least a weeks agony to get back into the mood. And I shall slip back by reading about in the book, & dreaming after tea; & perhaps, if nature allows, taking a walk. L. very depressed too, about poor dear Pink. 8 years of a dog certainly mean something. I suppose — is it part of our life thats buried in the orchard? That 8 years in London — our walks — something of our play private life, thats gone? And — odd how the spring of life isn't to be tapped at will. (*D4* 318).

Pinker as a token of love between Vita and Virginia turns into a companion both for Virginia and Leonard. Virginia's letters to Ethel Smyth and Vita at the beginning of June 1935 also represent the Woolfs' agony over Pinker's death: to Smyth, "This you'll call sentimental — perhaps — but then a dog somehow represents — no I cant think of the word — the private side of life — the play side"

(*D*4 396); and to Vita, "That very nice of you, about giving L. a dog. But at the moment I think he feels too melancholy" (*D*4 400). The Woolfs' intense sense of loss due to Pinker's death on May 30 is proven in their gain of a new cocker spaniel of the same breed and color as Pinker's, Sally, a month later, on June 30 (Spater and Parsons 142). Bell's remark on Virginia as the one with an "odd and remote" affection to animals and Leonard as "a systematic disciplinarian" (175) is a misjudgment upon the childless couple in their late middle ages. Shown in two sets of photographs of Virginia and Leonard (Lehmann; Spater and Parsons 96) taken at Monks or Monk's House, the Woolfs as a childless couple discover and embrace the importance of having a mutual companion dog in their life that confronts a series of crises yet that still cultivates intimacy, reliability, and understanding within the common private space.

Considering these factors, Woolf presents Flush as a companion dog for animal-assisted therapy for Barrett Browning, by way of observing and embracing Pinker who cures Woolf's own mind and reflects her as she suffers from a series of repeatedly occurred mental breakdowns, struggles with her own creative activities, and makes an effort of transforming her love affair with Vita which was actually over in 1928 into their close friendship which continued until 1935. Though spread and motivated in the United States, the dog-assisted therapy traces back to 1792 in the York Retreat, a mental hospital in York, Britain, and was also encouraged by Florence Nightingale in 1859 who "observed that pets were perfect companions for patients who were confined to longterm stays due to illness" (Janssen 40; Burch 4). The contemporary definition of animal-assisted therapy is, as Nightingale connotes, that animals help the patients "to promote improvement in human physical, social, emotional, and / or cognitive functioning" (Janssen 40).[2] Used in various types of patients, animal-assisted therapy expects a number of goals where animals can "ease loneliness," "improve communication," "foster trust," "reduce the need for medication by providing a diversion from pain," "improve cognitive functioning," "improve physical functioning," "decrease stress and anxiety for patients and their families," "improve body image," "motivate" the patient "to participate in" his or her recovery (Miller & Connor 65-67). Neither specialized nor hospitalized, Barrett Browning in the former part of her life lived a confined life as an invalid whose physical, social, emotional, and cognitive functions were restricted and suppressed under her father's overprotection. Barrett Browning's confinement causes both physical and psychological strife and fatigue. Barrett Browning, therefore, needs the two programs of animal-assisted therapy that are regarded as the most common ones in psychotherapy and physical rehabilitation as Voelker remarks. Confined and suppressed, Flush as a companion dog suffers both physical and psychological strife and fatigue and desires the freedom and ideal life. Though usually focusing on "the human partner and the potential benefits from interaction with companion animals," the human-animal interactions, especially in animal-assisted therapy, have to be reconsidered from "the animal's point of view and its quality of life" (Hubrecht and Turner 267-68). As equal partners, both Barrett Browning and Flush have to undergo the paradoxical process of developing and establishing the harmonized relationship.

The meaning and effect of animal-assisted therapy in *Flush*, therefore, has to be observed in the dual aspects of Barrett Browning's establishment of the emotional bridge between the inner world and the outer world with an assistance by Flush: first, the encounter between Barrett Browning's agony enclosed in her back bedroom and Flush's sympathy over her agony; second, the resolution between Barrett Browning's liberated self from the back bedroom and Flush's domesticated self within human privacy.

III. The Encounter between Barrett Browning's Agony and Flush's Sympathy

The human-to-human relationship is transformed into a solid and individual-based relationship by establishing the reliable human-to-dog relationship. Presented as a companion dog by Mitford, Flush influences Barrett Browning's relationship with the others because Flush plays an important role to display his sympathy and emotions to Barrett Browning who has been confined as a sick gentlewoman by her patriarchal father in Victorian London. Barrett Browning's loneliness and super-sensitivity in her imprisonment deprives her of having opportunities of becoming social with the others. Even after Barrett Browning has her selected visitors such as Mitford, Mrs. Jameson, and Mr. Kenyon, Barrett Browning becomes exhausted as she "sank back very white, very tired on her pillows" in her privacy with Flush (*F* 30). Barrett Browning's strong sense of fatigue embodies the lack of energy to sustain her nerves as well as her physical strength. Flush assists Barrett Browning to confirm the reliability of human natural emotions and instincts during the course of verbal and nonverbal communication. As described at the beginning of *Flush*, spaniels "are by nature sympathetic" and Flush has "an even excessive appreciation of human emotions" (*F* 12). Flush's influence upon Barrett Browning not by language but by display of instincts is enormous enough to give her encouragement to confront the men with power such as Robert Browning, even the boss of the gang, Mr. Taylor, and ultimately her father Mr. Barrett.

Flush is the only private companion with whom Barrett Browning can share the natural emotions and personal secrets concealed in her confined life in her bedroom, especially regarding Barrett Browning's secret love to Robert Browning. The back bedroom that symbolizes confinement in Barrett Browning's life is, however, a purely private space where inward emotions can be born and shared among its inhabitants. The back bedroom as Flush's schoolroom witnesses the conflict and resolution of sharing the privacy between Barrett Browning and Flush.

> Such an education as this, in the back bedroom at Wimpole Street, would have told upon an ordinary dog. And Flush was not an ordinary dog. He was high-spirited, yet reflective; canine, but highly sensitive to human emotions also. Upon such a dog the atmosphere of the bedroom told with peculiar force. We cannot blame him if his sensibility was cultivated rather to the detriment of his sterner qualities. Naturally, lying with his head pillowed on a Greek lexicon, he came to dislike barking and biting; he came to prefer the silence of the cat to the robustness of the dog; and human sympathy to either. (*F* 32)

The first five years from his puppyhood to his adulthood consist of Flush's transformation from an untrained puppy to a well-trained house pet by overcoming the struggles. This transformation, moreover, empowers the private innermost emotions through the established sense of respect and reliability.

It is true that Flush's transformation is defined partly in a negative tone: "All his natural instincts were thwarted and contradicted" (*F* 25). Louis DeSalvo argues that Flush as a young male dog with "greater freedom" and "greater access to experiences, treated better than a young woman of the privileged class" has to be changed into an English-girl-like dog when he joins the Barrett household and becomes Barrett Browning's dog (286). Considering the long history of human-to-dog relationship that began in the undated ancient times, the dog's "contradicted" natural instincts can be regarded as ones that trace back to their undomesticated days over millions of years and it is impossible to extinguish their natural instincts and temperaments in the course of only thousands years (*Fox* 54). The "bond" born between Barrett Browning and Flush after Flush overcomes "another feeling, urgent, contradictory, disagreeable" (*F* 26) is, however, not that between confined English girls, but that between the master and the house pet.

As for the domesticated dogs in Britain, spaniels in general have a long history since they were taken to England from Spain through France possibly by Romans who brought various breeds to Britain (Smith 8 & 14). In the tenth century when the dogs were first recorded as guards for sheep in *The Enclosure and Redistribution of our Land* by W. H. R. Curtler, spaniels are referred with greyhounds (Smith 8). Spaniels are then mentioned as sporting dogs during the period of the Forest Laws that began in the eleventh century and became empowered under the control by British monarchy. Only spaniels and greyhounds were restricted as sporting dogs for centuries in Britain, and especially spaniels were developed into setters and evolved into seven varieties until 1892 when the Kennel Club registered them officially. As Caughie remarks that Flush has "all the markings of good breeding" (517), the history of spaniels in Britain represents that of domesticating, training, breeding dogs for the small-game retrieving in the field trials and ultimately for companionship. The encounter between Barrett Browning and Flush is, therefore, that between the human being and the dog in the field, the master and the subject in the forest, and the owner and the companion in the domestic space.

Trainings for the house pet are based on the disciples of taking advantages of dogs' natural instincts that include their group society regulations, their leader-to-subject relationship, and their hunting habits. Flush's natural temperament issued outside at Three Miles Cross embodies the dog's natural instincts of living, hunting, and pursing reproduction registered for some million years. To domesticate the dog in the most ideal way is not to destroy the dog's temperament but to retrieve the natural instincts in a way that they accord with humans. Flush at Three Miles Cross has an open space where he can live without a chain and walk with Mitford. The expedition in the nature reflected by Flush is actually described in Mitford's *Our Village*: "At noon to-day, I and my white greyhound, May-flower, set out for a walk into a very beautiful world, — a sort of silent fairy-land, — a creation of the matchless magician the boar-frost" (27). Flush's longing for the nature is retrieved by already-nourished instincts of domesticated dogs. Training Flush's self in Barrett Browning's back bedroom is a trial to retrieve the dog's natural instincts of living in a group in a cave in ancient times as Flush "felt that he and Miss Barrett lived alone together in a cushioned and firelit cave" (*F* 25). The relationship between Barrett Browning and Flush is that between the master and the domesticated dog, or that between the leader and the subject. The private companionship between Barrett Browning and Flush is grounded upon the strategy of sharing the life between the humans and the dogs.

The encounter between Barrett Browning's agony and Flush's sympathy is built upon the established relationship between them. The communication between Barrett Browning and Flush is, however, not a verbal communication but a transmitted inarticulate empathy between them.

> Flush was equally at a loss to account for Miss Barrett's emotions. There she would lie hour after hour passing her hand over a white page with a black stick; and her eyes would suddenly fill with tears; but why? 'Ah, my dear Mr Horne,' she was writing. 'And then came the failure in my health . . . and then the enforced exile to Torquay

> . . . which gave a nightmare to my life for ever, and robbed it of more than I can speak of here; so do not speak of that anywhere. Do not speak of that, dear Mr Horne.' But there was no sound in the room, no smell to make Miss Barrett cry. Then again Miss Barrett, still agitating her stick, burst out laughing. She had drawn 'a very neat and characteristic portrait of Flush, humorously made rather like myself', . . . (*F* 27)

Barrett Browning's unstable emotions as an invalid poet is observed, perceived, and sympathized by Flush. Barrett Browning's letter to Mr. Horne implies her agony over her physical and psychological unhealthy self and life, while Barrett Browning's drawing of Flush embodies her sense of humor. The contrast between Barrett Browning's opposing characteristics symbolizes the silenced self that Barrett Browning bear in her confinement.

Barrett Browning's revelation of her inarticulate conflicting characteristics to Flush is made because Flush is the only private dweller inside Barrett Browning and in her back bedroom. Barrett Browning's silenced self ultimately encounters the means of exposing her innermost emotions to the other self, Flush.

> The fact was that they could not communicate with words, and it was a fact that led undoubtedly to much misunderstanding. Yet did it not lead also to a peculiar intimacy? 'Writing,' Miss Barrett once exclaimed after a morning's toil, 'writing, writing . . .' After all, she may have thought, do words say everything? Can words say anything? Do not words destroy the symbols that lie beyond the reach of words? Once at least Miss Barrett seems to have found it so. She was lying, thinking; she had forgotten Flush altogether, and her thoughts were so sad that the tears fell upon the pillow. Then suddenly a hairy head was pressed against her; large bright eyes shone in hers; and she started.

...

So, too, Flush felt strange stirrings at work within him. (*F* 27-28)

This established bond between Barrett Browning and Flush confirms their nonverbal communication. To transmit the inarticulate emotions, feelings, and thoughts from Barrett Browning to Flush provides both of them with the curer-healer relationship.

Transmitting emotions from Flush to Barrett Browning is also important because Flush is dignified as a companion. The most intriguingly-conveyed episode of this transmission delineates Flush's evoked terror and anger over a "force," or an intruder between Barrett Browning and Flush. Flush's imagination of a hooded man as a force is turned into Flush's encounter with an actual intruder and force, Robert Browning. Flush's jealousy and anger is strengthened enough to bite Robert Browning twice in the Barrett's household. Flush's suppression of biting and barking as the outcome of the house-training is challenged in his instinctive aggression against the outsider. In her letters to Robert Browning, Barrett Browning employs Flush as a media of conveying her emotions to Robert Browning. Woolf, moreover, uses Barrett Browning's letters to Robert Browning in order to present a tension between Barrett Browning's vigor and self empowered by Robert Browning and Flush's annoyed self.

It is important to trace how the private companionship between Barrett Browning and Flush influences the birth and development of intimacy between Barrett Browning and Robert Browning. Flush's instincts to the male force that Robert Browning possesses is described in his instinct to the danger that the imaginary hooded man would bring about. During Barrett Browning's correspondence days and five meetings with Robert Browning, Flush observes Barrett Browning's "agitation," "vigor," "excitement," and a change with "her strength" and "improvement" and concludes that he "felt nothing but an intense dislike" for Robert Browning (*F* 41). It is also important to note that Flush is in the prime time as a male dog whose first intercourse was made at Three Miles Cross as hinted that "Love blazed her torch in his eyes; he heard the hunting horn of Venus. Before he was well out of his puppyhood, Flush was a father" (*F* 13) and later being remembered by Flush in his aging: "They [the young dogs] were chasing each other in and out, round and round, as he had once chased the spotted spaniel in the alley. His thoughts turned to Reading for a moment — to Mr. Partridge's spaniel, to his first love, to the ecstasies, the innocences of youth" (*F* 100). Flush's natural instincts to pursue female dogs are, however, suppressed in Barrett Browning's back bedroom. Robert Browning is illustrated as a love-stealer who intrudes upon the established relationship between Barrett Browning and Flush.

The encounter between Robert Browning and Flush alters the relationship between Barrett Browning and Flush, and ultimately the relationship among the three. Flush's sympathy encounters the final trial to accept Robert Browning as Barrett Browning's new companion. The resolution is made by Flush's eating Robert Browning's cake and this resolution is shared with Barrett Browning.

> He [Flush] would eat them now that they were stale, because they were offered by an enemy turned to friend, because they were symbols of hatred turned to love. Yes, he signified, he would eat them now. So Miss Barrett rose and took the cakes in her hand. And as she gave them to him she admonished him, 'So I explained to him that *you* had brought them for him, and that he ought to be properly ashamed therefore for his past wickedness, and make up his mind to love you and not bite you for the future — and he was allowed to profit from your goodness to him.' (*F* 48)

The final encounter between Barrett Browning's agony and Flush's sympathy bears the new companionship among Barrett Browning, Robert Browning, and Flush.

IV. The Resolution between Barrett Browning's Liberated Self and Flush's Domesticated Self

Flush as a domesticated and trained companion dog is confronted with a series of hardships so that it is also necessary to consider the partnership from Flush's point of view. The welfare of animals has to be reconsidered in animal-assisted therapy since animals might be stressed in their activities, suffer from inadequate housing, working conditions, and partnership (Hubrecht and Turner 267-70). The passage to the healthy animal-to-human relationship is reviewed in Flush's life that overcomes his own agony. Flush's agony connotes both the historical background of dogs in Britain and his own personal history from Three Mile Cross to Wimpole Street.

The history of dogs in Britain is that of human control of and power over dogs. Its turning point was in 1895 when the first dog show was held as an important step to "the improvement of the outward appearance of dogs," "the segregation of breeds," "the discovery of new ones," and the public awareness of and attention to "the management and care of their domestic pets" (Smith 45). Among British dogs, spaniels as well as greyhounds, lurchers, mastiffs and sheepdogs existed in early England (Smith 14). Because both spaniels and greyhounds were restricted as sporting dogs for centuries and spaniels were officially classified into seven varieties, as Woolf remarks at the beginning of *Flush*, by the Kennel Club in 1892 (Smith 26), spaniels have been considered as major important dogs in Britain. As Woolf identifies the seven different breeds of spaniels as the dignified aristocratic classes, each spaniel has evolved until "each spaniel has its own character and desirable qualities" as interbreeding is not permitted now (Caras and Findlay 310). It is however, in 1842 when Mitford gave Hush to Barrett Browning in *Flush*.[3] It was before The Kennel Club was founded in 1873 and the Spaniel Club was founded in 1886. Flush was, then, not officially registered as cocker spaniel yet described by its early name, "cocking spaniel."[4] The instinctive struggle that Flush repeatedly faces from his puppyhood to adulthood is the roles of spaniels, a hunting dog in the field, a domestic pet in the country area, and a companion dog in the confined urban space.

Flush's own history as well as the dog's history in the nineteenth century reach to the turning point of resolving the agony. The resolution between Barrett Browning's self liberated from her back bedroom in her father's house and Flush's self domesticated within her back bedroom is made through three steps: Flush's kidnap, Barrett Browning's secret marriage to Robert Browning, and their elopement and their new life in Italy.

Flush's kidnap by a notorious gang of pet theives and Flush's confinement in the den in Whitechapel becomes the double trials that Flush undergoes as a domesticated dog and that Barrett Browning goes through by her consistent attachment to Flush, her own sense of justice, and her provocative sense of courage and power. The confinement conditions are severe in inadequate housing, poor hygiene, and entire neglect. In addition to Robert Browning, Barrett Browning shows her strength to another male-force, Mr. Taylor, who kidnaps Flush and blackmails Barrett Browning. As a dog-stealer, Mr. Taylor represents the male-force outside the household like that of Robert Browning. It is usually argued that there is a contrast between Wimpole Street as the wealthy residential area of the high society and Whitechapel as the poor dangerous zone of the low society. Squier points out as the striking ideological background of Whitechapel in the nineteenth century, "the savage butchery of five Whitechapel prostitutes by Jack the Ripper in 1888" (130). Squier interprets that this Whitechapel brutal murder reflects another conflict between men and women and Barrett Browning herself "extends the Whitechapel conflict from class to sex" (130). Flush was, however, kidnapped in September 1846 and the dog-stealing was actually a good business for the underground gangs as Barrett Browning indicates in her letter.[5] The danger and crisis that the dogs as house pets faced in Victorian London is a hidden aspect that both dogs and their owners had to challenge.

Though the animal abuse may connote the woman abuse as the weaker vessel in the society, the cruelty of animal abuse is not simply a metaphor of woman's oppression but a reality that Flush faces as a dog. The biographical truth is that Flush was kidnapped three times. In September 1843, for example, Barrett Browning writes that "Flush was rescued, but not before he had been wounded severely; and this morning he is on three legs and in great depression of spirits" and Flush had been targeted by the dog-stealers for a long time (154). In *Flush*, the kidnap experience becomes the trauma during the rest of Flush's life as it is remembered before his death.

> And then he lay for a time snoring, wrapt in the deep sleep of a happy old age. Suddenly every muscle in his body twitched. He woke with a violent start. Where did he think he was? In Whitechapel among the ruffians? Was the knife at his throat again?
>
> Whatever it was, he woke from his dream in a state of terror. He made off as if he were flying to safety, as if he were seeking refuge. (*F* 101)

The kidnap experience is molded in *Flush* as a well-cared and protected house pet in the urban Victorian society. Not a fictional figure, Mr. Taylor lived as the boss of the gangs in notorious Whitechapel and Flush was a victim that was abused and violated by the gangs.

Flush's experience of living in the worst conditions in the gangs' den implies the long neglected history of abusing animals in the Victorian society. Though the dogs were popular in Victorian England, they were used as fighting dogs especially in the ratting sports at pubic houses (Mayhew 3: 6-9). Because the dogs were popular, moreover, the dog stealing was a good business and there were some methods of stealing dogs owned by ladies and gentlemen who could pay them back.

> They [robbers] steal fancy dogs ladies are fond of — spaniels, poodles, and terriers, sporting dogs, such as setters and retrievers, and also Newfoundland dogs. . . . Their mode of operation is this: — In prowling over the metropolis, when they see a handsome dog with a lady or gentleman they follow it and see where the person resides. So soon as they have ascertained this they loiter about the house for days with a piece of liver prepared by a certain process, and soaked in some ingredient which dogs are uncommonly fond of. They are so partial to it they will follow the stranger some distance in preference to following their master. The thieves generally carry small pieces of this to entice the dog away with them, when they seize hold of it in a convenient place, and put it into a bag they carry with them. (Mayhew 4: 326)

The dog stealing business which was carried out in such methods mostly by professional thieves was accompanied by letting "the owners have them [their dogs] back for a certain sum of money," "generally from 1*l*. to 5*l*" (Mayhew 3: 326). A more intriguingly way was applied by a dog-finder who stole a dog, advertised it at a public house, announced the the dog was found, and restored to its owner "on payment of expenses" and one dog-finder called Chelsea George earned the average 150*l*. yearly (Mayhew 2: 52). Flush and Barrett Browning are victims of this dog-stealing business which was prevalent in Victorian London that could not prevent ladies and gentlemen from being frequently involved in the thefts, robbery, and other underground business.

What both Flush and Barrett Browning undergo by way of this dog-stealing involvement is the challenge to the wholesome conditions and circumstances that both the dog and its owner need to possess. As for Flush, the dog-stealing experience is the most painful one in his life. According to the United Kingdom Farm Animal Welfare Council, the animals have to be housed in conditions with five freedoms: freedom from thirst, hunger, and malnutrition; freedom from discomfort; freedom from pain, injury, or disease; freedom to express normal behavior; and freedom from fear and distress (Hubrecht and Turner 269). These five freedoms against which Flush stays in the Whitechapel den are registered as important elements both by Barrett Browning and Flush.

The energy and power that Barrett Browning presents in rescuing Flush means that against the male power of the underground world. Her courageous hunting of Mr. Taylor represents her inner strength to Flush and to herself. As Woolf connotes in *Flush*, Barrett Browning's exploration in Whitechapel enables her to illustrate the underground of the Victorian society in her novel-poem, *Aurora Leigh* in 1857 (63).[6] In depicting women's conflicts in this poem, Barrett Browning is herself "a principal actor in the work of healing" as a woman poet against the Victorian society, its authorized literature, and its canon of criticism (David 118). At the same time, Barrett Browning is a liberated fighter who articulates the silenced selves of the weak in the society. She is empowered to face the dog-banditti by herself because of her affection to Flush and Robert Browning. The relationship between Barrett Browning's liberated self and Flush's domesticated self is developed into the equal partnership with equal welfare that is sprung and reassured in Flush's kidnap.

As Flush's kidnap became a trial both for Barrett Browning and Flush, the secret marriage ensures the close relationship between them and the common boundary freed from the patriarchal force that Mr. Barrett place upon them. The secret marriage is informed silently to Flush who has a chance to witness the marriage ring which was worn and hidden by Barrett Browning. This marriage brings Flush another reunion, or partnership among the three instead of between the two. The marital relationship between Barrett Browning and Robert Browning changes the partnership between Barrett Browning and Flush. This newly established partnership between Barrett Browning and Robert Browning embodies their freedom from the Victorian father, Mr. Barrett, and from his power to control his daughter's life. Squier, however, draws an interesting comparison between Mr. Taylor and Mr. Browning: as "their parallel experiences during Flush's kidnapping make clear, both Flush and his mistress are equally subject to the wills of the men around them, whether the lawless Mr. Taylor or the lawful Mr. Browning" (131). Mr. Barrett is the most powerful male force with which Barrett Browning is fatally confronted because he is a freedom-stealer as a patriarchal authority within the household. In the new partnership, Flush is also freed from the Victorian patriarchal force to which he has to surrender, obey, and be silenced as he is scared by "a force" of Mr. Barrett (F 31). The newly-established partnership between Barrett Browning and Robert Browning gives the intense sense of freedom and reliability to the already-established partnership between Barrett Browning and Flush.

The most significant resolution is carried out when all of the three, Barrett Browning, Robert Browning, and Flush, escape from Britain and settle in Italy that is free from Victorian convention, customs, and social values as Barrett Browning remarks that "Fear was unknown in Florence; there were no dog-stealers here and, she may have sighed, there were no fathers" (*F* 76). The change of the circumstances due to the elopement to Italy influences the partnership among Barrett Browning, Robert Browning, and Flush. The human-to-society relationship is also nourished, improved, and evolved by leading a balanced life associated with the society. The human-to-dog relationship recovers as the equal and well-balanced one. Gillian Beer remarks that "Flush, like Elizabeth Barrett, like Adeline Virginia Stephen, is a prisoner always on the edge escape in Victorian bourgeois society" (102). Both Barrett Browning and Flush can escape from their confined lives that restrict their physical activities, damage their psychological freedom, and burden their social values.

The new life in Florence that enables Barrett Browning to transform from an invalid gentlewoman to a vigorous person results in her matured and fulfilled life both as a poet and as a woman. Becoming "a different person altogether," Barrett Browning gains her physical strength as she "rattled off in a ramshackle fly to the borders of a lake and looked at mountains" (*F* 73). Casa Guidi, her settlement space with Robert Browning in Florence, is a bare, large, and open space where Barrett Browning can breathe the free air. This settlement provides her with another important gift, her pregnancy and birth of her boy-baby, Penini. The late pregnancy and birth which is accompanied with the danger to both mother's and baby's lives is what Barrett Browning undertakes as the most significant turning point in her life. Barrett Browning's liberated self is confirmed in her physical and psychological recovery and stability outside the British patriarchal society and values.

Flush in Florence, like Barrett Browning, embraces the sexual and spiritual freedom, and even democracy as a "new conception of canine society" (*F* 75), though he confronts Barrett Browning's change, Penini as the newcomer to the companionship, and his own aging problems.

> The moment of liberation came one day in the Cascine. As he raced over the grass 'like emeralds' with 'the pheasants all alive and flying', Flush suddenly bethought him of Regent's Park and its proclamation: Dogs must be led on chains. Where was 'must' now? Where were chains now? Where were park-keepers and truncheons? Gone, with the dog-stealers and Kennel Clubs and Spaniel Clubs of a corrupt aristocracy! Gone with four-wheelers and hansom cabs! With Whitechapel and Shoreditch! He ran, he raced; his coat flashed; his eyes blazed. He was the friend of all the world now. All dogs were his brothers. He had no need of a chain in this new world; he had no need of protection. (*F* 75)

Flush's liberation during the prime time of his life nourishes his sense of independence, responsibility, and self-esteem after a recovery from the trauma that he has been confined in the Barretts' house. During this period, Flush's experiences are enlarged enough to embrace the free spirit, accept the democracy among dogs, overcome "rage and jealousy and some deep disgust" to Penini. Flush's sexual liberation that is "in search of something denied him all these years" (*F* 76) is recovered enough to chase female dogs through the night. Flush's sexual desire and its fulfillment is accompanied with Barrett Browning's one that is proven in her pregnancy after the first anniversary of her wedding day. Flush's maturity is also witnessed in his own awareness of his newly-established self and a new concept of values. Flush's companionship with mongrels, his physical freedom without a chain, his nursing Penini, his bareness after his coat was clipped, and his brotherhood with people and dogs in Florence are what Flush embraces till the end of hip life. The dignity of Flush's life and self is affirmed as an equal companion in the human society.

The paradox between Barrett Browning and Flush is ultimately resolved when the equal companionship between them is assured and their revolt against the Victorian force is accomplished. Their empowered selves construct the empire of their own with the strong sense of attachment, reliability, respect, and ultimate companionship.

V. Conclusion

Flush presents to us the significant yet often-neglected topic of a human-to-animal companionship in the modern society. Silenced and marginalized selves in a woman poet and a dog are retrieved in the common space where they are confronted with the invisible force and authority that threaten and injure their genuine talents, abilities, social interaction, interpersonal communication, and attachment to the others. The internal anxiety that haunts both Barrett Browning and Flush is reduced and remedied until the intense sense of independence is born to support their self-esteem and improve their cooperation between them. Animal-assisted therapy is carried out in a well-balanced condition both for Barrett Browning and Flush and the quality of life, the common goal of animal-assisted therapy, is enhanced and guaranteed. In *Flush*,

Woolf creates an ideal human-to-animal companionship, especially for the woman artist whose marginalized self is struggling to fight against the invisible enormous force.

Notes

This paper was originally published in *Doshisha Studies in English* 74 (March 2002): 61-91. In this book, I cut all figures.

1. As for contemporary critical articles on *Flush*, there are a few excellent works, such as Pamela L. Caughie's "Flush and the Literary Canon: Oh where oh here has that little dog gone" and her *Virginia Woolf and Postmodernism: Literature in Quest and Question of Itself* (Urbana: U of Illinois P, 1991); Rachel Blau DuPlessis's "'Amor Vin — :' Modifications of Romance in Woolf," ed. Margaret Homans, *Virginia Woolf A Collection of Critical Essays* (Englewood Cliffs, NJ: Prentice Hall, 1993), 115-35; and Ruth Vanita's "'Love Unspeakable': The Uses of Allusion in *Flush*," ed. Vara Neverow-Turk and Mark Hussey, *Virginia Woolf Themes and Variations* (New York: Pace UP, 1993), 248-57. As for recent studies, see Hovanec, Kendall-Morwick, and Crag Smith.
2. It is based on the definition by Delta Society, a non-profit organization of animal-assisted therapy in the United States, and it leads to enchanting quality of life for the patients (See Hines and Fredrickson 24-26).
3. According to Flint, Woolf mistook the year when Flush was first actually given to Barrett Browning and it was in 1840 when Flush was first taken to Barrett Browning (118-19).
4. Flint makes a note about its reference in a letter from Miss Mitford to Mrs. Partridge on July 3, 1846 (119).
5. In *Flush*, Woolf writes that "Mr. Taylor was said to make an income of two or three thousand a year out of the dogs of Wimpole Street" (53); on the other hand, Barrett Browning writes, in her letter to Robert Browning on September 2, 1846, that "They [banditti] make some three or four thousand a year by their honorable employment" (Karlin 304). In Flush's first kidnap in 1843, Barrett Browning confesses in her letter of September 19 to H. S. Boyd that the dog-banditti "had been 'about stealing Flush these two years,' and warned us plainly to take care of

him for the future" (155).
6 See Woolf's "Aurora Leigh."

Works Cited

Alexander, Peter F. *Leonard and Virginia Woolf A Literary Partnership*. Hemel Hempstead: Harvester Wheatsheaf, 1992.
Barrett Browning, Elizabeth. *The Letters of Elizabeth Barrett Browning*. Ed. Frederick Kenyon. 2 vols. London: Smith, Elder, 1897.
Beer, Gillian. *Virginia Woolf: The Common Ground*. Edinburgh: Edinburgh UP, 1996.
Bell, Quentin. *Virginia Woolf: A Biography*. 2 vols. New York: Harvest, 1972.
Burch, Mary R. *Volunteering with Your Pet: How to Get Involved in Animal-Assisted Therapy with Any Kind of Pet*. New York: Macmillan, 1996.
Caras, Roger, and Michael Findlay. *The Penguin Book of Dogs*. 1980. Harmondsworth: Penguin, 1983.
Caughie, Pamela L. "Flush and the Literary Canon: Oh where oh where has that little dog gone?" 1991. McNees II 514-32.
David, Deirdre. *Intellectual Woman and Victorian Patriarchy: Harriet Martineau Elizabeth Barrett Browning, George Eliot*. London: Macmillan, 1987.
DeSalvo, Louis. *Virginia Woolf: The Impact of Childhood Sexual Abuse on her Life and Work*. Boston: Beacon, 1989.
Flint, Kate. Editor's Notes. Virginia Woolf. *Flush*. Ed. Kate Flint. Oxford: Oxford UP 1998. 116-32.
Fox, Michael W. *Inu no Shinrigaku [Superdog]*. Trans. Kenji Kitagata. 1990. Tokyo Hakuyo-sha, 1994.
Hines, Linda, and Maureen Fredrickson. "Perspectives on Animal-Assisted Activities and Therapy." Wilson and Turner 23-39.
Hovanec, Caroline. "Philosophical Barnacles and Empiricist Dogs: Knowing Animals in Modernist Literature and Science." *Configurations* 21.3 (Fall 2013): 245-69.
Hubrecht, Robert, and Dennis C. Turner. "Companion Animal Welfare in Private and Institutional Settings." Wilson and Turner 267-89.
Janssen, Maridith A. "Therapeutic Interventions: Animal Assisted Therapy Programs." *Palaestra* 14.4 (Fall 1998): 40-42.

Karlin, Daniel, ed. *Robert Browning and Elizabeth Barrett: The Courtshi, Correspondence 1845-1846.* Oxford: Clarendon, 1989.

Kendall-Morwick, Karalyn. "Mongrel Fiction: Canine *Bildung* and the Feminist Critique of Anthropocentrism in Virginia Woolf's *Flush*." *Modern Fiction Studies* 60.3 (Fall 2014): 506-26.

Lehmann, John. *Thrown to the Woolfs: Leonard and Virginia Woolf and the Hogart Press.* New York: Holt, 1978.

Mayhew, Henry. *London Labour and the London Poor.* 4 vols. 1849-1850. London: Frank Cass, 1967.

McNees, Eleanor, ed. *Virginia Woolf: Critical Assessments.* Vol. 2. Robertsbridge, East Sussex: Helm Information, 1994.

Miller, Julie, and Katherine Connor. "Going to the Dog . . . for Help." *Nursing* 30.11 (Nov. 2000): 65-67.

Mitford, Mary Russell. "Married Poets." Recollections of a Literary Life; or Book *Places, and People.* 1852. New York: AMS, 1975. 169-84.

——. *Our Village.* 1824. New York: Woodstock, 1990.

Reid, Panthea. *Art and Affection: A Life of Virginia Woolf.* New York & Oxford: Oxford UP, 1996.

Smith, A. Croxton. *British Dogs. Britain in Pictures* 21. 1945. Tokyo: Hon-no-tomosha, 1997.

Smith, Crag. "Across the Widest Gulf: Nonhuman Subjectivity in Virginia Woolf's *Flush*." *Twentieth-Century Literature* 48.3 (2002): 348-61.

Spater, George, and Ian Parsons. *A Marriage of True Minds: An Intimate Portrait of Leonard and Virginia.* New York & London: Harcourt, 1977.

Squier, Susan Merrill. *Virginia Woolf and London: The Sexual Politics of the City.* Chapel Hill: U of North Carolina P, 1985.

Szladits, Lola L. "The Life, Character and Opinions of Flush the Spaniel." 1970. McNees 504-10.

Voelker, Rebecca. "Puppy love can be therapeutic, too." *JAMA* 274.24 (Dec. 1995): 1897+.

Wilson, Cindy C., and Dennis C. Turner, eds. *Companion Animals in Human Health.* Thousand Oaks, CA: Sage, 1998.

Woolf, Virginia. "Aurora Leigh." Ed. Michele Barrett. *Women and Writing.* New York: Harvest, 1979. 133-44.

——. *The Diary of Virginia Woolf.* Ed. Anne Olivier Bell. Vols 3 & 4. New York: Harcourt, 1980 -1982.

—. *Flush, A Biography*. 1933. Harmondsworth: Penguin, 1983.
—. *The Letters of Virginia Woolf*. Ed. Nigel Nicolson and Joanne Trautmann. Vol 4. New York: Harcourt, 1979.

Chapter 4

In Quest for Herstory: Virginia Woolf's Novels and Sir Joshua Reynolds's Portraits

I. Introduction

In Virginia Woolf's novels, Sir Joshua Reynolds's portraits are embedded as icons of a cultural heritage as well as ironical symbols of human conditions in the concentrated and deepened space of rooms within the house-space. The women's portraits, especially, create a myth which uncovers the hidden aspect of long-neglected *herstory*. The women's selves that were engraved underneath the women's exterior beauty and already-constructed image should be examined and correctly interpreted. Woolf manipulates Reynolds's portraits of women in her rereading and recreation of women's quest for space and self.

In Woolf's novels, the idealized image of Reynolds's portraits of women is definite and strong enough to be remembered, and it becomes a commanding metaphor of the conventional beauty. In *The Voyage Out*, Clarissa Dalloway is dressed in white with a long necklace "astonishingly like an eighteenth-century masterpiece

— a Reynolds or a Romney" (*VO* 38). As an interior, moreover, Reynolds's portraits are favored even by a young college student and owned in a purely private man's room: in *Jacob's Room*, Jacob Flanders has "photographs from the Greeks, and mezzotint from Sir Joshua — all very English" in his Cambridge dorm room (31). Reynolds's portraits of women outline the idealized image of women which can be occupied and possessed in the private space even in the modern British society. In *Mrs. Dalloway*, a Sir Joshua picture is hung on the wall in the Dalloways' townhouse in London. In Between the Acts, two portraits, both a lady's and a gentleman's, are decorated in the dining room and another lady's in the staircase of Pointz Hall.

The *Voyage Out*, *Jacob's Room*, *Mrs. Dalloway*, and *Between the Acts* reproduce what Reynolds's portraits of women symbolize in patriarchy. The British tradition of displaying portraits of ancestors and family members in the aristocratic and established gentlemen classes started along with the foundation and abundance of the British country house as a comfortable dwelling space after the civil wars were over and the British monarchy and feudal system were established.

> It was not until the long and triumphant premiership of Robert Walpole, from 1721 to 1742, that the English aristocracy as a whole recovered the prosperity and self-assurance destroyed in the Civil War. It was then that the culture of the squirearchy received the definite form that was destined to become the distinguishing characteristic of English life. (Walker 166)

After the influence from Continental art, English painting began to be established in the eighteenth century, that is, "a period of exquisite taste in applied art and domestic architecture, and the portraits of the time should be considered in connection with the room that they were to adorn" (Walker 168). It is also the period when the "growth of institutional patronage" "perpetuated the expectation that the portrait should enhance the formal status of the individual" gained by political success and class (Moore and Crawley125). Along with the construction of men's sphere, the women's domestic sphere evolved into the poetic discourse of women. In such a golden era of portraiture, Reynolds appeared and developed the tradition of British portraiture after such eminent painters as Van Dyck, Peter Lely, Godfrey Kneller from Holland, Michael Dahl, and William Hogarth.

Woolf places a cultural interpretation on Reynolds' portraits that counterpoint a woman and a man in different frames and, therefore, embody a tension between history and *herstory*. Man's portrait represents patriarchy as it connotes his power, authority, and dignity. On the contrary, woman's portrait, which is frequently accompanied with man's portrait and which is mostly commissioned by her father or husband, is overshadowed by man's portrait in respect of his value as a socially proper heir. Though being frequently praised for their external and physical beauty, women's portraits reproduce what was neglected and untold in the process of establishing the British feudal society and its patriarchal values that confined women to men's public and private spheres.

II. The Signifier of Portraits

The portrait is, generally, "the representation of an identifiable individual," as John Walker defines it (7). It is not simply grounded upon "a likeness," but the resemblance should "reflect the true personality of the sitter" (Walker 9) and still should be "recognizable" (Walker 7). It should be recognized "as something" which symbolizes the social rank, status, role beyond the individual, as Boris Ford remarks (134). For Reynolds, "the *difference* between the individual appearance and a 'general idea'" was such a predominant issue that he constructed "a persona" inhabited by the sitter and recorded his or her presence (Barlow 224-25). However intentionally Reynolds might adopt his ideal theory to his portraiture, Roger Fry names Reynolds' theory as "an applied aesthetics" (x). The portrait is also commissioned because of its "permanence"; the "physical appearance of human beings is constantly changing; decay is continuous, disappearance ultimate" (Walker 11). There rises, moreover, a question of duality in the portrait, that is, the real personality and "the mask" (Ford 134), along with that of the precisely-copied appearance and the intentionally-modified and technically-retouched form. As soon as the portrait is turned into merely an interior, the mask or modified formation can be intensified and a persona faces a crisis to be destroyed underneath the generalized creation of art.

More than a permanent recognizable individual with a social role, the portrait connotes the larger views of an era such as the conventions, tastes, and social changes. Susan Morris remarks, moreover, portraits are "the gossip columns, newsflashes, party political broadcasts and family albums of the past — of the age before photography, radio, television, modern printing techniques, computers and all the host of other technologies which record and transmit images or ideas today" (3). And even as computer graphics have become popular, we react to the portraits of the different eras and even go to see the originals in art museums. In her essay, "The Royal Academy," Woolf remarks that within "the precincts, everything appears symbolic, and the state of mind in which you ascend the broad stairs to the picture galleries is both heated and romantic" (89). Moreover, we can purchase and possess the originals if we are rich, or decorate the engravings or the prints in our houses and even in our offices if we lead a modest life. As an icon of cultural heritage, the portrait is also reborn as part of an interior of the private house-space which is inhabited, occupied, or shared by those who are connected through common ideological codes.

As time passes, the portrait loses its ideological significance and is often separated from the place where the portrait is originally decorated. In such a procedure, the portrait gains more attention solely as an interior of the new space. In this new space, whether it is a private house or a public place, the woman's portrait or its reproduction is highly demanded and consequently selected. In short, there rises a paradox when the original portrait or its reproduction is selected as an interior. The woman's portrait is preferred to the man's portrait. As for a difference between Reynolds's portraits of women and those of men, Woolf remarks in "Scottish Women" that the public "will pay thrice as much for an engraving from Sir Joshua, if the subject is a woman, as it will pay for a picture of equal merit, if the subject is a man" (211). The evaluation of Reynolds's portraits of women is, in this sense, primarily based on their external beauty and elegance because they are suitable for decorations. In the grant style, John Steegmann insists that Reynolds believed that "women and children should be idealized rather than particularized, that they should be abstract rather than real and individual" (127).

The woman's portrait in this respect connotes its owners' and its observers' private preferences rather than their interest in the ideological meaning of the portrait. In choosing and observing the paintings, however, it is essential to encode what is connoted underneath their visual attractiveness and to investigate what is silenced within their frame. In reading the observers' psychology at the National Gallery and the National Portrait Gallery, Woolf points out in "Pictures and Portraits":

> Let us wash the roofs of our eyes in colour; let us dive till the deep seas close above our heads. That these sensations are not aesthetic becomes evident soon enough, for, after a prolonged dumb gaze, the very paint on the canvas begins to distil itself into words — sluggish, slow-dropping words that would, if they could, stain the page with colour; not writers' words. ("Pictures and Portraits" 164)

The myth behind the portrait is examined in order to preserve the quality of the original production and to reinterpret the silenced stories with a new perspective. Woolf recreates what is hidden behind the aesthetic reproduction of one's life, gives the voice to the silenced self, and revives the frozen self within the frame of art. The woman's oppressed life restored within the frame of art is retold in contrast to the man's established life in Woolf's literature in respect of the prediction of the dual future engraved in a pair of infant sister / brother portraits in *Mrs. Dalloway* and the conclusion of the dual fate symbolized in pair of young lady / gentleman in *Between the Acts*.

III. The Predicted Future in Children's Portraits in *Mrs. Dalloway*

In *Mrs. Dalloway*, "the Sir Joshua picture of the little girl with a muff" (191) is hung on the wall in the landing between the front door and the stairs in the London townhouse, which is the Dalloways' private residence. This engraving is chosen purely as one of the interiors of the house, although this house is altered from a private residence into a public place during the party. In a public yet shared space, this engraving plays an important role within a sphere of silent communication between the occupants of the space. This painting is illuminating as a sign of monstrous conflict between Clarissa Dalloway and Doris Kilman regarding Clarissa's daughter, Elizabeth Dalloway, at seventeen, on the surface level and ultimately womanhood and self-search.

The portrait of a girl with a muff is entitled *Lady Caroline Scott as 'Winter'* believed to have been exhibited at the Royal Academy in 1777. This portrait is, interestingly, paired with that of her brother, *Charles, Earl of Dalkeith*. These portraits, which are the same size, were commissioned by their father, the 3rd Duke of Buccleuch, and hung together at Bowhill (Penny 276). Bowhill, located in Selkirkshire of Scotland, is the home of the Duke of Buccleuch and Queensberry KT, which is nationally and internationally known for its extensive estate of hills, valleys, and park and for its outstanding collection of arts by Canaletto, Claude, Raeburn, Reynolds, Gainsborough, and Ruysdael ("Bowhill House and Country Park"). *Lady Caroline* is still now one of the represented works by Reynolds in the Bowhill collection.

There is a contrast between *Lady Caroline* and *Charles, Earl of Dalkeith* in respect of signifiers embedded in the portraits. The *Lady Caroline* is framed in cold and monotonous scenery with the snowy ground, the dead trees, and the gloomy sky, while the *Charles, Earl of Dalkeith* is posed in a bright and colorful "composition" "with the rich green grass and blue sky of summer" (Penny 276). Those two opposite compositions suggest the two fatal future lives of a woman as a weaker vessel and of a man as the heir of patriarchy, respectively.[1] The portraits of the little girl and the little boy convey more details of their conflicting fates. With her face and eyes looking straight ahead and her cheeks rosy against the cold weather,

Lady Caroline stands still with two companions, a robin hopping at her feet on the snowy ground and a terrier that looks back at her. She is dressed in a cape, with a red muff clutched tightly in front and her large hat pulled over her eyes. As for a muff or mittens, Penny quotes from Aileen Ribeiro that "girls 'were encouraged to wear long mittens (which were more practical than gloves) in order that their hands and arms should remain soft and white'" (279). This description implies protection, closure, and silent acceptance of women's destiny.[2] At the same time, the strong impression is observed in the girl's straight eyes that look into the audience and the lips that are a little apart as if she is about to speak. In this way, this portrait gives us an impression of her self-determination, strong will, and straightforward attitude toward life itself.

On the other hand, the Earl of Dalkeith leans forward with his hand on an owl's head and is accompanied by a big spaniel that looks up at the owl. According to Penny, the owl symbolizes learning and the spaniel "perhaps alludes to the sporting life" (276) as the aristocrats' and gentlemen's privileged leisure. Those facets imply a promised future for a man who can enjoy both educational opportunities and outside activities, and ultimately dominate the social code and values. Born in 1772 as the eldest son of the 3rd Duke of Buccleuth, the sitter succeeded as the 4th Duke of Buccleuch in 1812 and died in 1819. He and his wife, Harriet, daughter of the 1st Viscount Sidney, had a good friendship with Sir Walter Scott who refers to "sweet Bowhill" in *The Lay of the Last Minstrel* and dedicated it to him (Penny 276). Bowhill was originally the seat of the Douglas family and became the home of the Scotts. The original building founded in 1708 does not leave any remains, yet the present house dated back in 1812 when the Earl of Dalkeith succeeded the title and many additions were made during the nineteenth century as the base of the Scott family in preference of Dalkeith ("Bowhill"). The history of the house corresponds with the sitter's succession of the title. The features enclosed in the portraits underline the biographical and historical elements as well as symbolical and metaphorical contents.

The women's biographies, however, should be written to reevaluate how "words pierce beneath paint" because there was "a rage" in the ladies of the eighteenth century who sat for Sir Joshua, as Woolf insists in "Sweetness — Long Drawn Out" (117-18). The conflict between the outer figure and inner self is what Clarissa and Miss Kilman are confronted with in their silent observation of the *Lady Caroline*. This flat creation is deepened, multiplied, and embossed so that it can deconstruct and reconstruct the stories behind the painting. Painting, as Diane Gillespie analyzes, enables people to "communicate something about their self-images and values" (218).

Clarissa's internal conflict, which reflects the fate of a lady embedded in the *Lady Caroline*, is recognized in her torn self between her ecstasy of triumph and her hollow psychology of depression.

Indeed, Clarissa felt, the Prime Minister had been good to come. And, walking down the room with him, with Sally there and Peter there and Richard very pleased, with all those people rather inclined, perhaps, to envy, she had felt that intoxication of the moment, that dilatation of the nerves of the heart itself till it seemed to quiver, steeped, upright; — yes, but after all it was what other people felt, that; for, though she loved it and felt it tingle and sting, still these semblances, these triumphs (dear old Peter, for example, thinking her so brilliant), had a hollowness; at arm's length they were, not in the heart; and it might be that she was growing old, but they satisfied her no longer as they used; and suddenly, as she saw the Prime Minister go down the stairs, the gilt rim of the Sir Joshua picture of the little girl with a muff brought back Kilman with a rush; Kilman her enemy. (*MD* 191)

The difference in class, social status, and physical attractiveness between Clarissa and Miss Kilman primarily causes them intense feelings of hatred, as seen in Miss Kilman's expression of her rage in connecting Clarissa as a leisured lady with the *Lady Caroline* as a privileged luxury fitted for a private townhouse of the upper-middle class. In Clarissa's consciousness, however, the same portrait distinguishes the Prime Minister as an embodiment of patriarchy from Miss Kilman as a suppressed self. At the end of the party when she sees the Prime Minister descending the stairs, Clarissa is haunted by the *Lady Caroline*, recognizes enemies inside herself, and reaches an understanding of women's common agony. At this moment, Clarissa distinguishes herself from the Prime Minister and connects herself with Miss Kilman. In addition to this, Sir William Bradshaw, as another embodiment of patriarchy, proves to be distinct from Clarissa and Kilman, both of whom share the same feelings of rage.

The predicted future of infant portraits depicts the fate determined by the difference in sex and gender. The men's biographies that are enclosed within their portraits represent the history of men's own raging from the patriarchal values to the political power to strengthen the British Empire. *Mrs. Dalloway* underlines the dual representation of Reynolds's portraits of children whose destiny is determined by the succeeded sexual politics of the British Empire. The protected enclosure of women's space is predicted in the portraiture of the girls whose personal record is primarily the marriage record as the most important reference for women in the male-oriented society.

IV. The Concluded Fate in Lady / Gentleman Portraits in *Between the Acts*

In *Between the Acts*, the tension between *herstory* and history is more suggestive yet more apparent in two portraits in the dining room of Pointz Hall, which embraces the public and open space both for family members and their guests, and one unknown lady's portrait at the staircase.[3] It is important to note the dual aspect of portraits that the man's portrait is the Olivers' ancestor, while neither of the women's portraits is their ancestress. The man's portrait has the ancestor's name, story, title, record, and even its voice; on the other hand, the women's portraits lead the audience to silence, leaving no name, title, and voice.

> Two pictures hung opposite the window. In real life they had never met, the long lady and the man holding his horse by the rein. The lady was a picture, bought by Oliver because he liked the picture; the man was an ancestor. He had a name. He held the rein in his hand. He had said to the painter:
>
> 'If you want my likeness, dang it sir, take it when the leaves are on the trees.' There were leaves on the trees. He had said: 'Ain't there room for Colin as well as Buster? Colin was his famous hound. But there was only room for Buster. It was, he seemed to say, addressing the company not the painter, a damned shame to leave out Colin whom he wished buried at his feet, in the same grave, about 1750; but that skunk the Reverend Whatshisname wouldn't allow it.
>
> He was a talk producer, that ancestor. But the lady was a picture. In her yellow robe, leaning, with a pillar to support her, a silver arrow in her hand, and a feather in her hair, she led the eye up, down, from the curve to the straight, through glades of greenery and shades of silver, dun and rose into silence. The room was empty.

Empty, empty, empty; silent, silent, silent. The room was a shell, singing of what was before time was; a vase stood in the heart of the house, alabaster, smooth, cold, holding the still, distilled essence of emptiness, silence. (*BA* 24)

The "ancestor" of Pointz Hall, has his name, and even his horse and dog have their names, Buster and Colin respectively. It is an identifiable individual with a social rank and its tastes; it is recognized as a country gentleman because of his horse and "famous hound."

The horse and hound in British portraiture became important in employing the motif of the hunt in the seventeenth century, when the sensitivity and attention to animals was born (Strong 64-65). As shown in the earliest example of the portrait with the hunting motif in *Henry, Prince of Wales a la Chasse* (1604) by Robert Peake the Elder, the hunt "provided a motif for the portrait with its assertion of land possession" (Strong 64). The horse is, moreover, employed in the battle scene where the men are recognized as heroes, as shown in Reynolds's *Colonel George Coussmaker* and The *Prince of Wales* (later George IV). The dog in British portraiture is, moreover, significant not only as a domesticated working animal for hunting but also a faithful pet represented in Nathaniel Bacon's *Self-Portrait* (1625) as it is pointed out that royalty, "together with the aristocratic and gentry classes, reveled in their dogs," especially greyhounds, hounds, and spaniels, and proved in the proverb, "'he cannot be a gentleman who loveth not a dog — (Strong 61). The portraits of dogs symbolize that the aristocrats' and gentlemen's dogs enjoyed much higher status and privileged life than their servants, while their ownership was "by law confined only to persons above a certain social level" (Strong 61).

According to Ford, those who sat for their portraits wanted to be recognized "as something": as a country gentleman, perhaps, with gun and faithful dog, posing against the backdrop of his own fertile estate" (134). To the guests, Mrs. Manresa and William Dodge, Bartholomew (Old) Oliver tells "the story of the pictures," especially the fact that his ancestor "left it on record that he wishes his dog to be buried with him" and Lucy Swithin says that she always feels "he's saying: 'Paint my dog'" (*BA* 31). The ancestor's portrait has a strong power and influence on the descendants as an essential part of the family history and a proof of the ideology.

On the other hand, the woman's portrait in the dining room is merely "a picture" without a name and a rank. It is recently purchased by Bartholomew simply because he prefers the picture and it is also liked by Dodge. The painter of this portrait is never affirmed though Bartholomew once investigated it with a specialist:[4]

> ... "'A man — I forget his name — a man connected with some Institute, a man, who goes about giving advice, gratis, to descendants like ourselves, degenerate descendants, said ... said ...'" He paused. They all looked at the lady. But she looked over their heads, looking at nothing. She led them down green glades into the heart of silence.
> 'Said it was by Sir Joshua?' Mrs. Manresa broke the silence abruptly.
> 'No, no,' William Dodge said hastily, but under his breath. (*BA* 32)

Bartholomew's voice cut in the middle represents the distinct silence around this portrait that connotes no precise record, story, and history connected with this picture.

This lady's portrait is, moreover, different from the man's portrait because the lady is painted as Diana, goddess of the hunt, as Gillespie concludes by a proof of the arrow (211). There is a myth of a woman's unidentifiable portrait with a mythological allusion, which Reynolds preferred, though this is not recognized as a Reynolds's portrait.[5] Reynolds employed Diana to this effect in his portraits of *The Duchess of Manchester as Diana*.[6] As in Reynolds's *Duchess of Manchester*, James McArdell's *Lady Anne Dawson*, Francis Cotes's *Lady Stanhope and Lady Effingham as Diana and her Companion*, the portraiture of Diana, partially different from Woolf's depiction of the long lady, has an arrow and an ornament forming a crescent moon in hairs. The lady in white or ivory drapers and feathers in hairs leaning against the pillar resembles both *Georgiana, Duchess of Devonshire* and *Jane Fleming, Countess of Harrington*. As for fanciful women's portraits represented by Diana, Penny remarks that the occasion was "an engagement, that brief, envied, interval of ambiguous identity, free from filial obligations and unafflicted with domestic responsibilities, when thinking was most liable to be wishful and compliments were unusually hyperbolic" (29). Though Gillespie says that the long lady is "an ironically appropriate companion for the ancestor with horse and dog," the effect and meaning of applying mythological allusions to an unmarried lady was fashionable in Reynolds's days, and it definitely represents a young lady not capturing, but soon being captured in the institution of marriage and the marital conventions. Reynolds improved symbolic conventions to embody a woman's status, especially a noble breeding and, more significantly, portraits of women of noble breeding "were hung (and listed in the catalogue) without their names in Royal Academy shows" (Perry 21). The mythological allusion and the anonymousness of ladies' portraits underline the cultural/social icon of the women as the weaker vessel.

This pair of portraits represents the gender difference. The man's portrait was commissioned, preserved, and maintained as proof of the country gentleman; the woman's portrait was "bought" as a supplemental decoration along with the man's portrait. Though both are being decorated in a public and shared space in the country house, the man's portrait contains more public significance than the woman's counterpart. Gillespie remarks that those portraits "establish two poles against which to measure the situations and characters in the book. One painting causes the viewers to generate words, and the other to be silent" (212). Moreover, the man's portrait symbolizes history, whereas the woman's portrait is excluded from the mainstream of man's story.

In *A Room of One's Own,* Woolf emphasizes the lack of women's biographical and bibliographical reference and record in contrast with the established source of men's lives.

> . . . There are no yard measures, neatly divided into the fractions of an inch, that one can lay against the qualities of a good mother or the devotion of a daughter, or the fidelity of a sister, or the capacity of a housekeeper. Few women even now have been graded at the universities; the great trials of the professions, army and navy, trade, politics, and diplomacy have hardly tested them. They remain even at this moment almost unclassified. But if I want to know all that a human being can tell me about Sir Hawley Butts, for instance, I have only to open Burke or Debrett and I shall find that he took such and such a degree; owns a hall; has an heir; was Secretary to a Board; represented Great Britain in Canada; and has received a certain number of degrees, offices, medals, and other distinctions by which his merits are stamped upon him indelibly. Only Providence can know more about Sir Hawley Butts than that.
>
> When, therefore, I say 'highly developed', 'infinitely intricate' of women, I am unable to verify my words either in Whitaker, Debrett, or the University Calendar. (*AROO* 85)

In contrast with the ancestor's portrait and its established biography and empowered history, the nameless woman's portrait lacks all kinds of "measures" and consequently leaves only the silent posture over her neglected and unrecorded story.

Another portrait of a lady on the top of the main staircase of Pointz Hall as a nameless and unidentified individual emphasizes the lack of women's history. Described as "an ancestress of sorts," the portrait is appreciated from the bottom to the top: "A length of yellow brocade was visible half-way up; and, as one reached the top, a small powdered face, a great head-dress slung with pearls, came into view" (*BA* 7). Among Reynolds's portraitures of women with similar costumes and hair styles, *Lady Bampfylde* exhibited in 1777 possesses the most elaborate characteristics. With "the plumed coiffure" that was introduced by Mrs. Abington in 1774 and became popular in late 1770's (Penny 273) and white muslin dress in the transparent and pale background, *Lady Bampfylde* embodies the baroque style (Penny 278). This portrait might have commemorated her marriage to Charles Warwick Bampfylde, the 5th Baron (Penny 277). The layered draperies and exaggerated hairstyle symbolize the heaviness, over-protection, and immovability that literally confine women in prison of marriage life and restrict them within conventional habits and behaviors.

The lady's name and the name of the painter are again never affirmed even though she is the acquaintance of or somehow related with the Olivers.

'This,' she [Mrs. Swithin] said, 'is the staircase. And now — up we go.'

She went up, two stairs ahead of her guest. Lengths of yellow satin unfurled themselves on a cracked canvas as they mounted.

'Not an ancestress,' said Mrs. Swithin, as they came level with the head in the picture. 'But we claim her because we've known her

— O, ever so many years. Who was she?' She gazed. 'Who painted her?' She shook her head. She looked lit up, as if for a banquet, with the sun pouring over her.
'But I like her best in the moonlight,' Mrs. Swithin reflected, and mounted more stairs. (*BA* 43)

In contrast to this lady's portrait, there is a drowned lady's story in Pointz Hall that is not conveyed to the guests, but handed down to the house's servants.

It was in that deep center, in that black heart, that the lady had drowned herself. Ten years since the pool had been dredged and a thigh bone recovered. Alas, it was a sheep's, not a lady's. And sheep have no ghosts, for sheep have no souls. But, the servants insisted, they must have a ghost; the ghost must be a lady's; who had drowned herself for love. So none of them would walk by the lily pool at night, only now when the sun shone and the gentry still sat at table. (*BA* 28-29)

The drowned lady who is identical in her name, Lady Ermyntrude, has neither detailed story nor history. Both the lady's portrait in the staircase and the drowned lady's anecdote connote the hidden or unrecorded biography of women's fatal lives. The paleness in both portraitures symbolizes the unhealthy and oppressed condition of women.

The place where this portrait is hung is on the top of the staircase, whereas the engraving of "a little girl with a muff" in *Mrs. Dalloway* is at the bottom of the stairs. Generally, the second floor is more private as shown in Pointz Hall, which has six or seven bedrooms upstairs. The portrait is, however, between the public and the private because it is not in one of the rooms upstairs, but on the top of "the principal staircase" (*BA* 7) that leads both family members and guests to the more private space in the British country house. Like the Dalloways' townhouse, the country house provides both private and public activities for its inhabitants and guests.

This gradually captured view of the portrait from the bottom to the top of the staircase is experienced by William Dodge as a guest when Mrs. Swithin as a hostess shows him around the house, as if observing the painting in the art gallery. Though Mrs. Swithin insists that the lady is not an ancestress but the family's acquaintance, the ambiguity, on the contrary, remains in Mrs. Swithin's statements in a question form: "Who was she?" and "Who painted her?" (*BA* 68). Before presenting the pageant which satirizes British history outside the house, the portraits are questioned and measured as its counterparts within the house-space. Such a presentation ironically suggests Woolf's definition of history. The presence of the nameless lady's portrait does not mean the absence of an ancestress but implies the complete ignorance or neglect of an ancestress.

The anonymity of the artist is also questioned rather than insisted upon. The uncertainty concerning this lady's portrait is reversed into the certainty of history as a metaphor of the male-centered public sphere. Although being uncertain, Mrs. Swithin's attitude toward this portrait is more intuitive and personal as is the portrait placed in a more private space than the dining room. Unconsciously placed outside the frame of history, the portrait bears the silent communication and agreement between the lady's portrait and Mrs. Swithin.

Both the portrait of the "long lady" in the dining room and the would-be ancestress's portrait on the top of the principle staircase are silenced selves without rooms of their own in the enclosed house-space of British society. As Isa and Mrs. Swithin exist under the name of Oliver and under the shelter of Pointz Hall, the portraits of ladies are alienated from their personal accounts so that they cannot be evaluated and appreciated properly and openly. Woolf attempts to give voice to the eighteenth-century women's silenced portraiture by having the women of the twentieth century disclose and discern the long-neglected and forgotten women's *herstory*.

V. Conclusion

Woolf's re-creation of women's quest for space and self is accomplished when women correspond to the portraits of women in their silent communication even through conflicts. The women in both childhood and adulthood in Reynolds's portraits signify the women's imprisonment in men's history that includes both private and public lives. The long neglected *herstory* is revealed and its absence is underlined in the women's portraits. Even though women's biographical stories are unrecorded in men's history, women can read their own stories and this reading empowers women of Woolf's contemporary.

Notes

The original version of this paper entitled "In Quest for Herstory: Virginia Woolf and Sir Joshua Reynolds's Portraits" was presented at the 4th AnnualConference on Virginia Woolf in Annadale-on-Hudson, New York, in 1994. The research for this paper was accomplished partly by the Research Grant of Fukuhara Award in 1994. This paper was originally published in *Doshisha Studies in English* 75 (March 2003): 111-135. In this book, I cut all figures.

1 The similar yet more apparent example of a pair of portraits of brother and sister can be witnessed in Reynolds's children's portraits: *Master Crewe as Henry III* commissioned and exhibited in 1776 and *Miss Crewe* left unfinished because of her death at age eight in 1775. They are children of Miss Frances Ann Greville,

who married John Crewe in 1766 and died at age 37 in 1765. Portrayed by Reynolds nearly forty times, she became a great leader of the Whig party and was known as one of the beauties of her time (Penny 200-01). *Master Crewe* is John, the eldest son and later 2nd Lord Crewe (1772-1835), who appears as Henry VIII, a favorite character in the eighteenth century with two Cavalier King Charles Spaniels, the most popular pets among aristocrats, as if he represents the political success of Britain. On the other hand, *Miss Crewe* is Frances, the elder daughter who unfortunately died young. *Miss Crewe* is similar to *Lady Caroline* in the dark cape and a large cap, and in the barren landscape. Penny interprets that Reynolds's portraits of children are "highly original creations which owe little to earlier masters; the subjects are seen with a sympathetic but, at the same time, sharp eye, the paint is handled with directness and fluency and the resulting design is — and this is especially true of *Miss Crewe* — powerful by any standards" (270).

2 Like *Miss Crewe* and *Lady Caroline*, *Lady Caroline Howard* depicts the metaphor of women's fate both in dress and in landscape. Born in 1771, Lady Caroline Howard, daughter of the 5th Earl of Carlisle and his countess, Margaret Leveson, was about seven in 1778 when she sat and the painting was exhibited, and married John, the 1st Earl of Cawdor, in 1789. Different as it is in the rose-plucking pose and low-placing of the figure, *Lady Caroline Howard* wears the black cape with a large cap protecting her in the cold pale sky. Penny quotes from Aileen Ribeiro that Lady Caroline Howard's "mitts are of cream silk lined with white silk" (278).

3 In the larger space-theme in *Between the Acts*, the meanings of male and female portraits are discussed in Usui's "Woolf's Search for Space in *Between the Acts*" (35-37).

4 According to Gillian Beer in her note, the lady's picture is painted by Thomas Gainsborough (1727-88), a contemporary and rival of Reynolds (*BA* 134). Reynolds "was very conscious of Gainborough's move towards a more naturalistic style in his full-length portraits of the 1760's and, always competitive, took up some of his designs and motifs and endeavoured to surpass them" (Hayes 98), especially his usage of sumptuous drapers of ladies' dresses and expansive landscape background seen in *Jane Fleming* (Strong 218).

5 For example, Reynolds's *Mrs Hale as 'Euphrosyne'* exhibited in 1766, *Lady Sarah Bunbury Sacrificing to the Graces* exhibited in 1765, *Mrs Siddons as the Tragic Muse* signed in 1789, and *Thais* exhibited in 1781 depict women in the classical, metaphorical, and / or literary allusions.

6 Steegmann points out that in the portrait of *Lady Worsley at Harewood House* she "obviously called for a repetition of the Diana motif, but where he expected to the usual type of Yorkshire fox-hunting woman he found a witty and highly-civilised beauty; so Lady Worsley is painted as her gay and charming self, not in semi-classical draperies but in anextremely elegant riding-habit" (125-6).

Works Cited

Barlow, Ernest Van. "The Portrait's Dispersal: Concepts of Representation and Subjectivity in Contemporary Portraiture." *Portraiture: Facing the Subject.* Ed. Joanna Woodall. Manchester and NY: Manchester UP, 1997. 219-38.

"Bowhill." 17 Sep. 2002
<http://www.boughtonhouse. org.u1c/httn/others/bowhill.htm.>

"Bowhill House and Country Park." *AboutBritain. Com.* 17 Sep. 2002
<http:www.aboutbritain.com/Bowhill.htm.>

Ford, Boris, ed. *The Cambridge Cultural History of Britain.* Vol. 5. *Eighteenth-Century Britain.* 1991. Cambridge: Cambridge UP, 1992.

Fry, Roger. Preface and Introduction. *Discourses.* By Sir Joshua Reynolds. London: Seely, 1905. v-xxi.

Gillespie, Diane Filby. *The Sisters' Arts: The Writing and Painting of Virginia Woolf and Vanessa Bell.* Syracuse: Syracuse UP, 1988.

Hayes, John. *The Portrait in British Art: Masterpieces Bought with the Help of the National Art Collections Fund.* London: National Portrait Gallery, 1991.

McNeillie, Andrew, ed. *The Essays of Virginia Woolf.* 3 vols. New York: Harcourt, 1987.

Moore, Andrew, and Charlotte Crawley. *Family and Friends: A Regional Survey of British Portraiture.* London: HMSO, 1992.

Morris, Susan. *A Teacher's Guide to Using Portraits.* 1989. London: English Heritage, 1992.

Penny, Nicholas, ed. *Reynolds.* New York: Harry N. Abrams, 1986.

Perry, Gill. "Women in Disguise: Likeness, the Grand Style and the Conventions of 'Feminine' Portraiture in the Work of Sir Joshua Reynolds." *Femininity and Masculinity in Eighteenth-Century Art and Culture.* Ed. Gill Perry and Michael Rossington. Manchester and NY: Manchester UP, 1994. 18-40.

Steegmann, John. *Sir Joshua Reynolds.* London: Duckworth, 1933.

Sir Strong, Roy. *The British Portrait 1660-1960*. Woodbridge, Suffolk: Antique Collectors, 1991.

Usui, Masami. "Woolf's Search for Space in Between the Acts." *Doshisha Studies in English* 72 (2000): 25-48.

Walker, John. *Portraits: 5,000 Years*. New York: Harry N. Abrams, 1983.

Woolf, Virginia. *Between the Acts*. 1941. Harmondsworth: Penguin, 1992.

——. *Jacob's Room*. 1922. Harmondsworth: Penguin, 1992.

——. *Mrs. Dalloway*. 1925. Harmondsworth: Penguin, 1992.

——. "Pictures and Portraits." McNeillie 3: 163-66.

——. *A Room of One's Own*. Harmondsworth: Penguin, 1992.

——. "The Royal Academy." McNeillie 3: 89-95.

——. "Scottish Woman." McNeillie 1: 211-15.

——. "Sweetness — Long Drawn Out." McNeillie 1: 117-20.

——. *The Voyage Out*. Harmondsworth: Penguin, 1992.

Chapter 5

Against "Once a Lady Athlete, Always a Lady Athlete" in Virginia Woolf's *Three Guineas*

I. Introduction

"Once a lady athlete, always a lady athlete" represents how definitely women were excluded from the fair evaluation of their athletic abilities as well as of their serious attitude toward sports even in the early twentieth century. In *Three Guineas*,[1] Virginia Woolf insists on the importance of women's emancipation in sports in order to prevent the war. Woolf presents this issue in a political context where men's power suppresses women's power in educational, professional, and socio-cultural spheres.

Woolfs *Three Guineas* has been read and evaluated as a woman writer's political pamphlet opposed to the sexual, racial, and political wars in the early twentieth century when the world was confronted with the crisis of the coming Second World War. Woolf's intense opposition and even hostility to the patriarchal institutions such as the government, the church, the university, and even the private house filled with its history, fame, and all the privileges is turned into her strong desire to explore the possibilities of the new house, that is, the anti-patriarchal institution.

> Take this guinea then and use it, not to burn the house down, but to make its windows blaze. And let the daughters of uneducated women dance round the new house, the poor house, the house that stands in a narrow street where omnibuses pass and the street hawkers cry their wares, and let them sing, 'We have done with war! We have done with tyranny!' And their mothers will laugh from their graves, 'It was for this that we suffered obloquy and contempt! Light up the windows of the new house, daughters! Let them blaze!' (83)

The new house that embodies the new space for women's liberation from the traditionally restricted activities and spheres is metaphorically created in Woolf's literary text which intriguingly discloses the anti-war and anti-imperial statement.

One of the most striking yet ironical examples that Woolf imposes upon her anti-war and anti-imperial statement is the emerging and rolling wave of women athletes as challenging outsiders in education, profession, and ultimately social consciousness. It is what Woolf calls "an outsider's experiment" or "an extraordinarily interesting experiment" that will be "of great value to the cause of peace" and also "may well bring about a psychological change of great value in human nature" (116). Woolf's examination of women and athleticism in a pacifist context explains how a diagram of sex / gender and athleticism became determined by the Victorian values, and how those diagrams were contested between two world wars during the rise and fall of the British Empire and the threatening approach of the Nazis and the Fascists both in national and international sport spheres.

II. Diagram of Men and Athleticism

Sports were especially evaluated in the mid-nineteenth century as one of the most important subjects at the boys' public schools to educate and train the middle, upper-middle and upper class boys into gentlemen, and the leading subjects of the British Empire (Mangan *Athleticism*). The educational effect of sports fitted for the emerging Victorian middle-class ideology especially played a significant role to the steady rise of the Empire from the nineteenth to the twentieth century. Sports in this transitional period signify the important elements to construct and accomplish the national authority as the collected force in such interrelated contexts of imperialism, colonialism, and industrialism.

As for the cost of men's education that English families have spent since the thirteenth century, Woolf analyzes:

> For your education was not merely in book-learning, games educated your body; friends taught you more than books or games. Talk with them broadened your outlook and enriched your mind. In the holidays you traveled; acquired a taste for art; a knowledge of foreign politics; and then, before you could earn your own living, your father made you an allowance upon which it was possible for you to live while you learnt the profession which now entitles you to add the letters K.C. to your name. (4-5)

Male advantage and privilege in monopolizing education, leisure, and professional training shapes the model of the upper-class education.[2] Their luxury is supported by the financial background, social status, and political power that sprang from the country estate and its seats, and is also supported by national and colonial capitalism.

It was during the Victorian period that this male luxury reached the peak in proportion to the rise of the British Empire. The newly established middle and upper-middle classes that consist of professionals and merchants in the mid-nineteenth century desired their sons to be educated into gentlemen in public schools (Mangan *Athleticism*). The Victorian society also needed a number of young subjects to contribute to the political and economic strength and stability of the country. Sports were evaluated as an appropriate trial ground for the future national military service in mid-Victorian England. The increase of the number of boys' public schools and the harsh rivalry among them, especially between the old boys' public schools and the new counterparts, transformed the curriculum and discipline into more physically-oriented ones, that is, those marked by "athleticism and manliness"; this "fusion of moral rectitude and physical robustness," consequently, "had become essential hallmarks, and supported a huge, voracious and self-perpetuating games machinery centered on rowing, cricket and football" (McCrone 60). The team-play for the purpose of winning the games is an essential scheme for men to survive in the society for their own country. Eminent Thomas Arnold at Rugby regarded organized sport as "a key means of asserting control and moulding character, while at the same time allowing boys some measure of self-government" (Cunningham 115). Sports as a core of the survival force which was virtually nourished in boys' young days were highly expected to be employed outside the educational institutions. The Victorian era embraces this strong inclination toward sports as the important subject to train both men's strong bodies and minds.

The steady ground of sports in boys' public schools helps the widely-spread popularity and its institutionalization that eventually breaks borders of generation, class, and its sphere within the men's world, and even transforms amateurs into professionals. At the beginning of the Victorian era, cricket and golf were organized and played under certain rules, rowing was not properly acknowledged as sport yet called boating, and football and hockey were "tests of strength rather than skill," and lawn tennis was just newly invented; most of those sports began to be well-organized with the establishment and development of organizations, clubs, rules, awards, cups, techniques, equipments, and even costumes (McCrone 12). The mid-Victorian headmasters of public schools, represented not only by Arnold at Rugby but also the other reformers at Harrow, Marlborough and Uppingham, made a great contribution to promote and organize the games according to J. A. Mangan (*Athleticism* xxiv). The connection between the public school and the university was easily made by the late-nineteenth century by what Mangan names a "process of circular casuality" where the "successful games player at school flourished in the same capacity at the university and then returned to school as lauded assistant master to set another generation of devotees along the same route" (*Athleticism* 126).

The harsh criticism on the increasing idle sport-minded students at Cambridge and Oxford delineates how popular university sports were both within and without the university spheres. Even though he is listed among the tutors known for their enthusiasm for sports at Cambridge, Leslie Stephen, Woolfs father and one of the leading Victorian literary figures, criticizes "the unintellectual games-playing public school boy" as "'an animal of whom one finds it difficult not to be rather proud'" in *Cornhill Magazine* in 1873 (Mangan, *Athleticism* 110) and also acknowledges "the dangers that the popularity of athletic sports posed to intellectual life at the universities" in 1870 (Bailey 126). In spite of those criticisms, their separation from traditional yet unmoral university recreations such as gambling, drinking, and horse races and their improvement in such virtuous characteristics as the sense of loyalty, endurance, toughness, courage, self-confidence, cooperation are generally evaluated as the consequence of their sport activities. Those traits on the playing fields are also often connected with those in imperial and colonial services. Men's pursuit for a victory or glory is thus grounded upon their physical and psychological involvement in fighting whose spirit is nourished in their sport-based education. Woolf harshly criticizes this male characteristic of a fighter:

> As it is a fact that she cannot understand what instinct compels him, what glory, what interest, what manly satisfaction fighting provides for him — "without war there would be no outlet for the manly qualities which fighting develops" — as fighting thus is a sex characteristic which she cannot share, the counterpart some claim of the maternal instinct which he cannot share, so it is an instinct which she cannot judge. (197)

This male characteristic to pursue the victory through the war is emphasized and exploited in the context of the Victorian imperialism and colonialism. It is remarked that the "ferocity of keenly-contested house matches helped create a hardened imperial officer class naively eager for colonial wars" and English playing fields had been generally acknowledged as "training grounds for imperial battlefields" (Mangan, *Athleticism* 138). It is also significant to notice that the university cup in boat race and cricket match received a wide popularity in public and also a national and then international attention in the press coverage (McCrone 24). The fact that university as the privileged and closed society gained the public interests and attentions by way of the growing popularity of amateur men's sports proves the infiltration of a diagram of men and sports into the country.

Another infiltration of a diagram of men and sports is witnessed in the middle and lower-middle class people's direct participation in sports. The Victorian industrialism made it possible to clear the ground for a shift from the nation-wide popularity of elite schools' sports to the emerging middle and lower-middle population's involvement in sports. In Victorian England, the first and most radically affected industrial society, the concept of leisure was developed and extended as the important element in people's physical and psychological lives, especially in the emerging middle and lower-middle classes (Bailey and Cunningham). In addition to various kinds of cultural activities held in pubs, churches, and newly-founded clubs and associations, sports became a most popular recreation and the new athleticism was born, cultivated, and reformed.[2] After public school students and graduates started to spread their enthusiasm for "the reformed canon of athletic sports through into adult life" in the 1860s, the entire nation turned to be obsessed with sports so that Gladstone in 1887 pointed out that "'athletics are becoming an ordinary incident of life'" (Bailey 124).

With a rapid emerging middle and lower-middle class people in the urban area, the decline of Victorian values, power, and stability had already threatened the ruling class. It was the Crimean War that "had the effect of bringing Englishmen face to face with the role of force and of fighting in industrial and urban communities" (Cunningham 117). The upper and upper-middle classes who had had privileges of enjoying traditional gentlemen's sports such as hunting, cricket, and horse-riding were easily accessible to the newly-developed sports as they had enough leisure time, space, facilities, and financial background. On the other hand, the rapidly increasing middle and lower-middle class city workers who emerged after the Industrial Revolution did not just follow the gentlemen's traditions but had to satisfy their needs, possibilities, and tastes. In his article entitled "Athletic Sports and University Studies" published in *Fraser's Magazine* in 1870, Leslie Stephen, who was keenly aware of an increasing urban middle-class population, encouraged them to be absorbed in physical education (Bailey 126). In a more political context, Charles Kingsley, in "Education and Health" in 1874, emphasizes that the large middle-class population's "necessary practice as a duty to one's country became more insistent after his conversion to Darwinism" (Bailey 126). The interaction among working and lower-middle-class people's changed lifestyles, the increase of sports population among them, and the establishment of the sports industry originate from industrialization and urbanization in the late Victorian period.

In order to rebuild the declining force of the British Empire at the end of the nineteenth century, moreover, sports and colonialism were politically interconnected by the establishment of amateur and professional sports in a national sphere and its transmission to a colonial sphere. The popularity of sports within the British Empire was transported to her colonies such as Australia, America, Canada, Caribbean, and India so that sports created another colonialism. Cricket, the most popular and widely-spread sport in the Empire, especially played a role to reestablish the relationship between the Empire and the colonies; however, there were both positive (national) and negative (anti-colonial nationalist) attitudes to the introduced product of the Empire (Cashman 259). The role of the professional, especially in cricket, enlarged from the nation-wide popular "spectator sport" for working-class men, women, and even children to the international popular sport during the period when William Clarke's All-England Eleven was founded in 1846. The other professional teams followed it so that England sent the first overseas tour of all professionals in 1859 (Cunningham 113). After the other sports such as rugby, football, and rifle-shooting did tours to South Africa, Canada, and Australia, "Empire sporting links" were established (Moore 147). This "Anglo-Saxon superiority" and the British Empire's invasion and occupation by sports in colonies, however, faced the more universal and international union and association of sports at the end of the nineteenth century. The establishment of "Empire sporting links" is the British Empire's last trial to reconstruct her declining power and situation in international politics and economics.

A diagram of men and athleticism was firmly founded as the key of encoding the harsh competitions in industrialism, imperialism, and colonialism that needed the physically and psychologically healthy male subjects and that liberated the rising classes from the traditional aristocratic boundaries. The male-centered unity, connection, and stable interrelation that were virtually established in introducing and improving sports among men of all classes both in domestic and colonial spheres are the essential circumstances to cultivate, develop, maintain, and even reconstruct the British Empire as the collective representative of patriarchy.

III. Diagram of Women and Athleticism

At the same time when a diagram of men and athleticism is established, that of women and athleticism is also defined. Throughout the history until our contemporary era, women have been excluded from and even opposed to athleticism which is predominantly a collective representative of masculinity. The athletes usually mean the male athletes because athletes are the foregrounds of fighters and the matches are the preview of wars. In Ancient Greek, it is obvious that "physical training and sports were closely related to the man's role in warfare" (Guttmann 7-8) and its tradition has been succeeded throughout Europe. It is, however, surprising to unveil that the same sports trainings "were sometimes associated by the ancients with the woman's role in human reproduction" (Guttmann 8). Throughout the history of Britain, it was the Victorian values that as a result culturally constructed the distinct line between the male and female characteristics and behaviors. These values are especially represented by its cultural norm of "The Angel in the House" as "a full expression of the idealization of womanhood that is central to the theory about woman's separate domestic sphere" (Hellerstein, Olafson, Hume, and Offen 134). In contrast, the idealized angel coexists with its seemingly juxtaposed byproducts such as the demon, the old maid, and the fallen woman in Victorian England (Auerback 63).

Women's physical conditions and characteristics that were mistakenly defined by the Victorian values largely influenced the meaning of sports to women. As for young women, especially, the "change from girlhood into womanhood was considered the greatest crisis in a female's life" and the doctors advised young women, especially during menstrual periods, that "great care had to be taken to make sure that fertility was not permanently jeopardized by unladylike behaviour and a squandering of vital energies" (McCrone 7). The Victorian young women were discouraged from practicing any kind of physical exercises and training to protect and maintain their feminine ideal and fertility so that they would be able to be engaged in what Woolf calls "the only profession open to women," that is, marriage. Even though women of leisure enjoyed hunting, riding, and archery in the early to mid-Victorian era, as is proven in some paintings and portraits of upper-class women, most women in the early to mid-Victorian era were expected or even forced to remain indoors (McCrone 6-7). Even in a contemporary study on female athletes, the female athletes' outsiderness is rooted in the unchanged recognition where "the traits associated with athletics, such as strength, power, and competitiveness, have been assigned to the masculine gender and stand in direct contrast with the traits traditionally appropriate to the female gender, weakness, powerlessness, and cooperation" (Peper, quoted from the S. L. Bem and Kaplan, 13).

The rise, development, and establishment of sports in the context of Victorian ideology further emphasize sex-segregation; whereas it also influences and motivates women to be involved in physical trainings and leisure. Women's advanced educational opportunities, professional pursuit, and political involvement are associated with and influenced by one another. Women's pursuit to and gain of rights in sports, which are also directly or indirectly connected with those three women's emancipation movements, however, was not argued as the main controversial issue. "Unlike the fight for legal and political rights," as McCrone points out, "there was no organized campaign to promote women's sport, and its development was somewhat removed from the centres of feminist controversy" (14). Yet, already in late-Victorian England, *Punch* presented a large number of cartoons featuring women's sports "as part of a larger process of emancipation and social change that threatened the sexual status quo" (McCrone 260). The caricature published in *Punch* in 1910 describes the cynical connection between golf and votes for women with its phrase, "No Strokes for Women" (McCrone, Plate 14). It is also pointed out that the the physically exposed and manlike women "threatened the stability of society" and their masculine endeavors were "physical manifestations of suffrage" (Behling 192). Sports as an embodiment of patriarchy are long-neglected subjects that have to be argued within a context of women's emancipation movement. Woolf makes an intriguing comment on women's liberation from the private house into the male spheres including the sports ground:

> It forced open the doors of the private house. It opened Bond Street and Piccadilly: it opened cricket grounds and football grounds; it shriveled flounces and stays; it made the oldest profession in the world (but Whitaker supplies no figures) unprofitable. . . . The fathers, who had triumphed over the strongest emotions of strong men, had to yield. (138)

So far as the private house implies all the male-dominant privileges, this statement connotes that women's emancipation in sports is closely related with the development and establishment of all faces of women's emancipation: women's higher education, women's profession, and also women's right to vote.

The most apparent connection between women's sports and women's educational opportunities is proven in the girls' elite day and public schools, state schools, and emerging women's colleges from the middle to the end of the nineteenth century. Women's education rapidly developed because industrialization produced a number of middle-class population and their strong desire for daughters' education. It led to the need for the overpopulated middle-class women's financial independence, and affected the social consciousness of women's emancipation. It is Emily Davies, the founder of the fist women's college, Hitchin College, in 1869 (later moved to Girton at Cambridge in 1873), that insists on the necessity of women's physical exercise for both physical and mental health and makes a comment that "'women are not healthy . . . it is a rare thing to meet with a lady of any age who does not suffer from headaches, languor, hysteria, or some ailment showing a want of stamina'" (McCrone 26). However urgently women's education and subsequently physical education were desired, the path to equal educational opportunities was a hard path, as Woolf figures out in a contrast between the enormous efforts to raise money to establish women's colleges and the historically affluent men's public schools and Oxbridge:

> First, there is the fact that the great majority of the men who had ruled England for the past 500 years, who are now ruling England in Parliament and the Civil Service, have received a university education. Second, there is the fact which is even more impressive if you consider what toil, what privation it implies — and of this, too, there is ample proof in biography — in fact of the immense sum of money that has been spent upon education in the past 500 years. (24)

Women's education that suffers a shortage or even the lack of funds and understanding is juxtaposed with men's education that can take advantage of affluent funds. In contrast to wealthy Oxford and Cambridge, both Girton and Newnham suffered the want of funds. Davies, who advocated the necessity of women college students' physical exercise such as walking and swimming at Hitchin and then sports such as rackets, fives, croquet, badminton, gymnastics, and lawn tennis at Girton, could only have an insufficient and controversial gymnasium built in 1877 (McCrone 26).

The establishment of girls' day schools and public schools in the mid- to late nineteenth century is directly connected with the establishment of women's physical education and sport. Though there appeared some official sponsorship to promote women's education such as the Schools' Inquiry Commission on the Education of Girls (1868) and the Association of Headmistresses of Endowed and Proprietary Schools (1874), individual headmistresses draw the outline of women's physical education and sports in two different ways. One of them is rather conservative enough to support the Victorian values. Calisthenics or Swedish gymnastics were originally introduced to Britain by a Swedish trainer and educator,

Martina Bergmen-Osterberg. Swedish gymnastics improved women's health and maintained a ladylike behavior.[3] In addition to military drill, Swedish gymnastics were primarily introduced to working class young women because they are inexpensive and easily accessible and learned, and also effective enough to satisfy the social needs of those women (Hargreaves 68-69). Gymnastics were easily accepted because it is an indoor exercise, and also it was believed that even at Newnham gymnastics were useful not only for the maintenance of health but also "the production of a good carriage" (McCrone 35). Even an eminent reformer of girls' physical education, Dorothea Beale, headmistress of Cheltenham Ladies' College from 1858, was insistent to oppose competitive sports and even prohibited prizes and matches against other schools (Hargreaves 63). On the other hand, Frances Mary Buss, headmistress of the North London Collegiate School from 1850, made a great individual contribution to introduce an advanced program of physical education as well as a wide range of sports and activities along with establishing a large gymnasium. Buss included sanitation, ventilation, hygiene, and health teachings in physical education and required the students to receive regular physical examinations. This systematic and practical physical education for women to have knowledge and record of women's health as well as to maintain health is the first step toward women's progress of self-care and self-control within a socially-accepted context of sports.

Unlike physical education as a unique form of women's education, sport in girls' public school was modeled after that of boys' public school even though girls' public schools underwent hardships. Each school had a different kind of programs of competitive sports, yet they began to allow almost the same games as those played at boys' public schools: for example, hockey, cricket, tennis, lacrosse, basketball, rounders, fives, bowls, croquet, quoits, golf, hails, swimming, skating, archery, etc. House and school matches became popular in the late nineteenth century as happened in boys' public schools in the mid-Victorian era. The women players, however, had to face a gap between the predominantly masculine form and activities of sports and their feminine ideal image of the future angel in the house: "Your girls play like gentlemen, and behave like ladies" was expected and preferred (Hargreaves 68). Women's participation in sports as well as women's intellectual achievements were initially promoted in establishing women's colleges. Women's teams and players in Cambridge and Oxford were confronted with the deeply-rooted and consistent sex-segregation in male-dominant sport spheres such as the gymnasium, grounds, and fields.

Against a diagram of men and athleticism, a diagram of women and athleticism signifies women's challenge to gain the sporting rights both in national and international levels beyond the domestic and international political and economical competitions. The deeply-rooted Victorian idealized image of women and its consequences is the starting point for their endless race.

IV. Contest of Diagrams of Sex / Gender and Athleticism

This diagram faced a challenge in a political context in the 1920s and 1930s when British imperialism was confronted with Italian and German Fascism and when women's athleticism had already begun to be developed and reformed yet was struggling to gain its legitimate status in the international sports scenes such as the Olympic Games.

In *Three Guineas*, Woolf quotes two articles regarding women and sports as the controversial issue in the 1930s. One of them entitled "National Fitness Movement" which appeared in *The Times*,

September 24, 1937 describes the conflict of the increasing women athletes:

> Speaking of the work of the great voluntary associations for the playing of certain games, Miss Clarke [Miss E. R. Clarke of the Board of Education] referred to the women's organizations for hockey, lacrosse, netball, and cricket, and pointed out that under the rules there could be no cup or award of any kind to a successful team. The gates for their matches might be a little smaller than for the men's games, but their players played the game for the love of it, and they seemed to be proving that cups and awards are not necessary to stimulate interest for each year the numbers of players steadily continued to increase. (116)

This report embodies the continuing discrimination against the women's sports organizations in respect of rules, games, and awards; at the same time, it describe the increase of women players and their consistent and strong will and spirit toward sports. This phenomenon underlines a dual aspect of the surroundings of women athletes in the 1930s even after the first step of women's emancipation movement was completed.

Another article that Woolf quotes from the August 15, 1936 issue of *Daily Herald* argues against women's segregation from sports more definitely.

> Official football circles here [Wellingborough Northants] regard with anxiety the growing popularity of girls' football. A secret meeting of the Northans Football Association's consultative committee was held here last night to discuss the playing of a girls' match on the Peterborough ground. Members of the Committee are reticent.... One member, however, said today: "The Northants Football Association

is to forbid women's football. This popularity of girls' football comes when many men's clubs in the country are in a parlous state through lack of support. Another serious aspect is the possibility of grave injury to women players." (117)

This statement expresses the socially structured prejudice against women athletes and can be counted as a most striking example of sex-segregation in sports because women's football has made quite a difficult path up to the twentieth century. With an "incorporated constant opposition" and a late progress compared with the other European and American counterparts, British women's football gained popularity, the Women's Football Association was founded in 1969, and by the end of 1992 / 3 season it consisted of 450 clubs and over 10,000 members (Hargreaves 251). Since the WFA was taken over by the (men's) Football Association and controlled by the male-dominant strategies, women's football has been struggling to regain its complete legitimacy.

In order to lead to the anti-war and anti-imperial statement in the late 1930s, Woolf's text of examining how to use three guineas should imply the gradual revelation of the wrong-input ideology. This ideology reflects how to consider, evaluate, and employ sports, and also determines the sex-segregation of sports. To understand why Woolf was against the women athletes' suppression in a political context, it is necessary to trace why and how male athletes were born, trained properly, and established well, and why female athletes were born, yet ignored, harassed, and even banned especially in a transitional period from the Victorian era to the early twentieth century. The era when Woolf made a political statement was a crucial turning point which witnessed an opposition to imperialism and Fascism both of which emphasized competitive sports against individualized, socially liberated, and internationalized sports, and which witnessed the changing and struggling women's emancipation and participation in sports both in national and international scenes.

Woolf's illustration of the diagram of women and athleticism in *Three Guineas* expresses the foreground of seemingly-opposed political forces in domestic and in foreign spheres. What Woolf calls "educated men's daughters" have to be against British imperialism in a domestic sphere, and at the same time against the Nazi and the Fascists:

> The daughters of educated men who were called, to their resentment, "feminists" were in fact the advance guard of your own movement. They were fighting the same enemy that you are fighting and for the same reason. They are fighting the tyranny of the patriarchal state as you are fighting the tyranny of the Fascist state. (102)

British women's political emancipation and suffrage movement was as equally intensified as the British Empire's war against the Nazis and the Fascists. While British subjects were wrongly cultivated and controlled to establish the political, economic, and social security and strength of the Empire with their unconsciously obsessed nationalism, German and Italian citizens were also more systematically and structurally transfigured into the fighters who aimed at invading the other nations and races by force and destroyed what they believe are inferior to them.

Georgian England, even at its start in 1910, was a conflicting era when the decline of the British Empire's political, economic, colonial superiority and control was prolonged, the old aristocratic society was substituted for the newly-established professionals' society, and the emergence of the Nazis and the Fascists threatened the Empire as the long-ruling tycoon of Europe. Because of this apparently weakened condition of the Empire, there appeared an agreement "that the physical condition of the rank-and-file needed to be improved if the Empire was to be properly defended" (Birley 19).

The Fascist doctrines are grounded upon the harsh dictatorship as the collective form of aggression, violence, and control of the roles and meanings of sexes and races: Woolf indicates that "abroad the monster has come more openly to the surface. He is interfering now with your liberty; he is dictating how you shall live; he is making distinctions not merely between the sexes, but between the races" (102). The Nazis as the emerging monster in the early 1930s formulated the slogan "Strength through joy" in combining "physical culture and ideological indoctrination within a wholly revamped system of sports federation and youth organizations like the *Hilterjungend* and *Bund Deutscher Mädel*" (Guttmann 184). In the early stage, the Nazis expressed the strong objection to modern sports because they were "organized on the basis of universalistic criteria" and also already were "an international phenomenon" (Guttmann 183). *The Deutsche Turnerschaft* founded by the extreme nationalism largely influenced the Nazis at first; they were opposed to modern sports' individualism and egotism represented by British athleticism and refused to participate in the first modern Olympic game as the liberal and international stage (Guttmann 183).

In the newly-established youth organizations, under the leadership of Hitler, however, young men were encouraged to practice sports in order to train and develop "toughness and combativeness" and young women were trained "to prepare themselves for motherhood" (Guttmann 184). In 1938, the *Glaube und Schonheit* was organized as the next step from *Bund Deutscher Mädel*, so that the one straight line of the path to the strong-minded and physically healthy women as the ideal of German women was established.

At the outbreak of World War II, furthermore, the Fascist women, modeled after the Spartan women, were expected to achieve the qualities of Aryan mothers of the future fighters. In 1941, the official training began to improve toughness and courage in girls' physical education and sports; moreover, women's university and professional spheres required them to take physical education classes or join the sport recreation programs in order to maintain their physical strength and psychological stability to bear healthy and mighty Aryan children (Guttmann 185). The Nazis' commitment to extreme nationalism, racism, and cunningly-concealed sexism was eventually transformed into the most inhuman doctrines and a mass murder of human nature.

Similar to the Nazis, the Italian Fascists placed sports as the significant means to develop both psychological and physical strength and strictly "prepare young men for service to the state" (Guttmann 181). Benito Mussolini was known and even preferred to be evaluated as "the one most determined to project an image of superb vitality and exuberant physical strength" or "an example of perfectly harmonious physical and intellectual development" (Guttmann 180). In 1922 when the Fascists gained power and began to control schools, physical education became practically compulsory in Italy and consequently Italy's schools were demanded to "produce vigorous athletes" (Guttmann 181). As far as the Fascists emphasized masculine strength and physique, women were expected to become healthy and industrious wives and mothers according to the Fascist doctrines and also to the Roman Catholic values (Guttmann 181). Even to the well-performing women athletes, the feminine image and characteristics were required. So, the Fascist regime restricted women from participating in the 1932 Olympics in Los Angeles while they sent 101 excellent male representatives of Fascism to the game and ultimately won twelve gold, twelve silver, and eleven bronze medals then (Guttmann 182). The Fascist approach to athleticism by overpraising and overevaluating men's strength as the potential fighter's aggression and force endangered the balanced characteristics of human nature.

Both the Nazis and the Fascists represent the most radical example of the ideology-controlled evaluation and emancipation of human bodies and minds by way of operating the extreme male aggression and the wrong-input ideology to promote the war and justify the mass murder of human nature. Woolf's keen observation and consistent criticism of the global danger brought in by the wave of totalitalialism is based on her strong commitment to pacifism.

When international politics faced the most crucial challenge in national politics at the emergence of the Fascists as masculine trained and controlled fighters, the international sports sphere was also confronted with the trials in different national sports spheres. The competition between men and women in national and international games, cups, awards as well as clubs and associations embodies a crucial change of sex-segregation in sports. The women's spheres began to be enlarged in the early twentieth century and women athletes began to win over the male athletes on the fields. The Olympic Games that had excluded women from participating in the games as players before the twentieth century is a most striking example of sex-segregation in sports in an international level. Among the gradual yet slow changes in the early twentieth century, there are some notable yet still unstable examples (Guttmann 163-64). The 1900 Games in Paris included both women's golf and women's tennis, the 1904 Games in St. Louis admitted only women's archery, the 1908 Games in London extended to women's tennis, archery, figure skating, and the 1912 Games in Stockholm raised an argument by adding women's swimming. The 1916 Games in Berlin was not held because it was during World War I.

The Antwerp Games in 1920 as the first postwar game again set to limit women to only tennis, swimming, and diving, but the 1924 Games in Paris included fencing. Even if women athletes went through an unstable yet gradual path to the Olympic Games as the highest competitive international ground of sports, there was a strong opposition to women and athleticism in the 1920s. When the International Olympic Committee agreed on allowing five track and fields for women for the 1928 Games in Amsterdam, they required the Féderation Sportive Féminine International to change their title name from the Women's Olympic Games into the International Ladies Games (Lucas 250).

Along with the historical data showing how women began to appear in the Olympic Games in the early twentieth century, it was the time when feminine traits confronted masculine traits in competition and image. It is, first of all, important to note that some published records express how women athletes began to defeat their male counterparts. In 1938, Gelene Mayer "unexpectedly" defeated the men's champion in the U. S. national fencing title, so that immediately the U. S. fencing organization banned a competition between men and women and revoked Mayer's title because a possible physical contact prevented men from fighting with women to their best of abilities (Cahn 210). This incident manifests the impossibility of the fair judgment on competition between men and women in sports on the ground that feminine traits needed to be magnified and masculine traits needed to be minimized in mixed race competition. On the contrary, male journalists tended to portray women athletes' great achievements in only women games especially in the 1920s and 1930s by comparing them with their male counterparts under such titles, "Is There a Weaker Sex?" and "The Slightly Weaker Sex," and even evaluate the leading women athletes' success in contrast to the losing male athletes' superiority and strength (Cahn 209). At the same time, the pattern of women athletes being portrayed as unwomanly or what Cahn calls "mannish" women by a sportwriter in 1930 is dominant in mass media even in the 1960s (207). Modern women's remarkable achievements and competition in sports threaten the male pride and self-confidence supported by their dominant sense of male superiority and female inferiority.

The diagram of women and athleticism invented in the early twentieth century is an essential mirror to reflect sex-segregation among the emerging women athletes and Woolfs reporting her contemporary events related with this issue contains the unavoidable Victorian ideology that influenced the introduction, establishment, reformation, and contests of athleticism.

The contest between two diagrams regarding sex / gender that distinguished sports faced the crucial moment in the 1930s when the world was about to pursue the wrong-led ideology. Woolf is convinced that the progress of women's emancipation in sports has to be made without any influence of political power.

V. Conclusion

Woolf states that to "prevent war" can be carried out "by protecting the rights of the individual; by opposing dictatorship; by ensuring the democratic ideals of equal opportunity for all" (100). Women's entire gain of legitimacy in sports as the most definite representative of patriarchy makes it possible for Woolf's contemporaries to be opposed to any kind of war. No matter how hard and controversial the argument on women and athletes is, it is an inevitable step to prevent the propagation of patriarchal values, ideas, and states. Sports are, thus, a hidden metaphor for pacifist

Woolf to advocate competitive sports, their aggression, and all the wrong-input meanings. Reading Woolf's *Three Guineas* in a multilayered context of sex, gender, sport, and politics connotes a significant message that her readers can discover and encode in a process of tracing what was not officially recorded, not privately conveyed, and even not recognized.

Notes

This paper was originally published in *Doshisha Literature* 48 (March 2005): 35-59.

1 "Once a Lady Athlete, Always a Lady Athlete" is from the title of the article published in *Vanity Fair* in August 1933, by Paul Gallico who makes a fictional story of a young male reporter "infatuated with a female golfer" (Behling 194-95).
2 As for the leisure in Victorian England, see Bailey.
3 The first and most-widely accepted theory of women's physical education in the late nineteenth century is the noncompetitive gymnastics which were introduced by a Swedish trainer and educator, Martina Bergmen-Osterberg. Her method is based on the Swedish system that was invented by Per Hwneik Ling of the Royal Gymnastics Institute of Stockholm and that was "designed to develop every part of the body" (Guttmann 110). Her contribution to the growth and establishment of British women's physical education includes her role to educate and train teachers as the Superintendent of Physical Education for London's public schools between 1881 and 1886 and her establishment of the Hampstead Physical Training College in 1885 (later Bergman-Osterberg Physical Training College in 1895). One of her students, Rhoda Anstey who founded the College of Physical Training and Hygiene for Women Teachers in 1897 also founded the Gymnastic Teachers' Suffrage Society. See also Black and Im.

Works Cited

Auerbach, Nina. *Woman and the Demon: The Life of a Victorian Myth*. Cambridge: Harvard UP, 1982.

Bailey, Peter. *Leisure and Class in Victorian England: Rational Recreation and the Contest for Control, 1830-1885*. London: Routledge, 1978.

Behling, Laura L. *The Masculine Woman in America, 1890-1935*. Urbana and Chicago: U of Illinois P, 2001.

Birley, Derek. *Playing the Game: Sport and British Society, 1910-45*. Manchester and New York: Manchester UP, 1995.

Black, Naomi. *Virginia Woolf as Feminist*. Ithaca: Cornell UP, 2004.

Cahn, Susan K. *Coming on Strong: Gender and Sexuality in Twentieth-Century Women's Sports*. New York: Free, 1994,

Cashman, Richard. "Cricket and Colonialism: Colonial Hegemony and Indigenous Subversion?" Mangan 258-71.

Cunningham, Hugh. *Leisure in the Industrial Revolution, c. 1789-c. 1880*. London: Croom, 1980.

Guttmann, Allen. *Women's Sports: A History*. New York: Columbia UP, 1991.

Hargreaves, Jennifer. S*porting Females: Critical Issues in the History and Sociology of Women's Sports*. London and New York: Routledge, 1994.

Hellerstein, Erna Olafson, Leslie Parker Hume, and Karen M. Offen, eds. *Victorian Women: A Documentary Account of Women's Lives in Nineteenth-Century England, France, and the United States*. Stanford: Stanford UP, 1981.

Im, Jeannie. "Gift Subscriptions: Underwriting Emergent Agencies in Virginia Woolf's *Three Guineas* and Agnes Smedley's *Daughter of Earth*." *Modern Fiction Studies* 59.3 (Fall 2013): 569-90.

Lucas, John A, and Ronald A. Smith. "Women's Sport: A Trial of Equality." *Her Story in Sport: A Historical Anthology of Women in Sports*. Ed. Howell, Reet. West Point, NY: Leisure, 1982. 239-65.

Mangan, J.A. *Athleticism in the Victorian and Edwardian Public School: The Emergence and Consolidation of an Educational Ideology*. 1981. London: Frank Cass, 2000.

——, ed. *Pleasure, Profit, Proselytism: British Culture and Sport at Home and Abroad 1700-1914*. London: Frank Cass, 1988.

McCrone, Kathleen. *Sport and the Physical Emancipation of English Women, 1870-1914*. London: Routledge, 1988.

Moore, Katharine. "The Pan-Britannic Festival: A Tangible but Forlorn Expression of Imperial Unity." Mangan 144-62.

"National Fitness Movement: Happiness from Good Health." *The Times* 24 Sep 1937: 14.

Peper, Karen Ann. *A Content Analysis of Women's Perceptions of the "Female Athlete": The Relationship between Perceived Value Congruity and Language Choice*. Ph.D. Diss. Wayne State U. 1988.

Woolf, Virginia. *Three Guineas*. 1938. New York: Harcourt, 1966.

Chapter 6

Julia Margaret Cameron as a Feminist Precursor for Virginia Woolf

I. Introduction

Both Julia Margaret (Pattie) Cameron and her great niece Virginia Woolf advocated opening the door to a more unconventional and unique world of art as women whose values were restricted and determined by Victorianism. Cameron's biographer, Victoria C. Olsen, remarks about Cameron's uniqueness in the art world as well as in a family circle: "Cameron's work had been the subject of revived interest among turn-of-the-century art photographers, but also her life had been mostly the object of family legends as anecdotes about her passed from generation to generation" (3). Cameron's eccentricity, fame, and also unusual career as a photographer in Victorian England were transmitted from generation to generation especially among her close relatives such as the Pattles and the Stephens, and eventually the Bloomsbury Group. Woolf, as a relative and also writer of the twentieth century, shared a distinct and keen consciousness of creating art with Cameron beyond two generations.

As artists, both Cameron and Woolf had to strive against the male-centered world of art so that they trained themselves outside art and academic institutions. In the process of educating themselves, Cameron and Woolf nourished their keen sense of observing human inner selves and attempted to describe them in photography and fiction respectively. Because of those similarities, Woolf admired Cameron, and compiled a play, *Freshwater: A Comedy*, in 1923. As a familiar figure among Stephen relatives and friends, Cameron was an attractive subject for Woolf to recreate in the form of drama as a way of giving voice to her photographs. For Woolf, Cameron had an unusually strong personality as Gerhard Joseph notes in introducing Woolf's description of Cameron in "Julia Margaret Cameron," Introduction of *Victorian Photographs of Famous Men and Fair Women* (44).[1] Paying more attention to Cameron as an artist, in 1926, Woolf and Roger Fry worked together in order to publish that selection of photographs by Cameron by the Hogarth Press. In 1935, moreover, Woolf revised her original 1923 script of *Freshwater* for a family and friend performance at Vanessa Bell's studio. This revision represents, as Lucio P. Ruotolo remarks, "how Virginia had researched the subject of her great-aunt Julia Margaret Cameron" (vi). In this sense, there existed a closer collaboration between Cameron and Woolf and this collaboration represents Woolf's commitment to creating her own world of art in three stages: women as prisoners, outsiders, and eventually artists.

II. Women as Prisoners of Victorianism

In the Victorian and Edwardian societies, women were both physically and psychologically imprisoned in male-centered values, customs, life-styles, and viewpoints. Consequently, Victorian idealism had a paradox which reflects the limitations of its excessive idealism. At the same time, both Victorian idealism and its limitations were exported to and transplanted in Anglo colonial spheres such as India and Ceylon, where Cameron with her sisters, including Woolf's mother, spent their lives. In this shared environment, women attempted to unite together or share common interests with the other outsiders, especially in artists' communities. As Olsen points out, Cameron had a strong tie with her sisters and also established friendship with the other artists at Little Holland House in Kensington, where her sister, Sarah Prinsep, hosted a salon, after returning to England in 1848, whereas Woolf kept an unbreakable tie with her sister Vanessa (Stephen) Bell and furthermore, became deeply involved in the Bloomsbury Group. It was, however, in Freshwater, the Isle of Wight, where Cameron established her own artists' colony and overcame the boundaries of Victorianism; whereas it was in Bloomsbury where Woolf liberated herself from her father's ghost and Victorian and Edwardian values.

As the most striking symbol of Victorianism, the idealized image of women was rooted in all households, classes, communities, and also colonial spheres. Cameron challenged this image in her visual art, whereas Woolf did so in her verbal art. When Coventry Patmore's *The Angel in the House* was published between 1854-6, it influenced a cultural norm of Victorianism. After his conversion to Catholicism, moreover, its ideology was strengthened in the 1880s when Patmore revised *The Angel in the House* and his idea was more definitely addressed by Gerard Manley Hopkins who had asked Patmore to "reconsider his slackness in regard to the gender hierarchy in marriage" in *The Angel in the House* (Munich 82).

Based upon hierarchy, Christian marriage depends on woman's

subservience to her lord as man is subservient to his Lord. Correspondence between wife and sinner, lord and Lord, is a system facilitating allegorical representation. Wives' politeness compared to religiosity rather than to true belief. Since domestic hierarchy is analogous to the Church's temporal authority, a wife's mere courtesy compares to the undermining of the Church. (Munich 83)

Dedicated to Coventry Patmore, Cameron's portraiture of Emily Peacock entitled *The Angel in the House* was taken in Freshwater in May, 1873 (Weaver, *Julia Margaret Cameron 1815-1879* 129: Figure 1). It is quite evident that the cultural icon of Patmore's *Angel in the House* was so universal that it became the theme of other arts in Victorian England. Patmore's *Angel in the House* is, however, known for its irony in that Patmore's wife and model of *The Angel in the House* had already passed away because of hardships in life when the poem was published. Cameron's photograph implies this irony as is witnessed in the uncertain and undetermined expressions of the woman whose external appearance fits the image of *The Angel in the House*, yet whose internal self lacks the satisfaction and determination as if she wished to be liberated from the role and expectations imposed upon her.

The irony embedded in *The Angel in the House* is transmitted to another irony conveyed by the other angel photographs by Cameron. Along with Cameron's *Angel in the House*, there is a series of angel-women portraits of Mary Ann Hillier entitled *The Angel at the Sepulchre* (1869-70) and *The Angel at the Tomb* (1869-70), and those angels display more ironical implications. Even though these angel-women portraits present to us different themes on a surface level, they possess similar tones and meanings. Victorian implication of "The Angel in the House" is an idealized womanhood. However, the biblical original of the other angel is not female but male (Ford

55). The biblical angel is generally considered a male figure and the guardian angel plays a significant role in male-centered Christian churches. As for Christian marriage, moreover, its hierarchy is based on the theory that woman is subservient to her "lord" or her husband as man is to his Lord (Munich 83). Transcending the sex difference, however, the image of purified angel was virtually transformed into that of woman in Victorian England. Transcending the sex difference, again, the image of purified woman was switched into that of the guardian angel in Cameron's photography.

In addition to the transformation of sex, the models of those portraits have ironical backgrounds. Not precisely identified, Emily Peacock, with her sister Mary, was believed to be the neighbor's daughter, a frequent visitor of the Camerons in Freshwater, who modeled in Cameron's photo illustrations to Tennyson's *Idylls of the King* as Sylvia Wolf remarks (225). As in another portrait entitled *The Sisters* (1871), Peacock wears a dark dress with white furs around her neck. It is apparent that her traditional beauty and elegance is well suited to the image of *The Angel in the House*, yet it is ironical that her expressions are gloomy as in most of Cameron's women's photos. On the other hand, Mary Ann Hillier, the daughter of a shoemaker on the Isle of Wight, began to work as Cameron's parlor maid at age fourteen and remained Cameron's favorite maid and model till Cameron left for Ceylon in 1895 (Wolf 221). Hillier was considered less beautiful than another Mary and Cameron's frequent model, Mary Ryan (Ford 55). In *Annals of My Glass House* (1874), however, it is proven that Hillier's beauty attracted Cameron as she depicts her as "'one of the most beautiful and constant of my models, and in every manner of form has her face been reproduced, yet never has it been felt that the grace of the fashion of it has perished'" (Wolf 221). Consequently, Hillier was frequently posed as the Madonna and also as other religious figures.

Overall, however, both Peacock and Hillier were the models whose identifications were not necessarily important and whose personalities did not have to be mirrored through the lenses. Alison Chapman states that as Cameron herself in *Annals of My Glass House* "suggests that her camera has a distinctive and gendered agency of its own" and also confesses that, before those Victorian eminent male sitters, her "'whole soul has endeavoured to do its duty towards them in recording faithfully the greatness of the inner as well as the features of the outer man'" (52); consequently, Cameron had to "'arrest' great men' with her lens'" in her photographic portraits (53). Compared to Cameron's photographs of such great male figures with distinguished features and physiques as George Frederick Watts, Tennyson, Thomas Carlyle, and Charles Darwin, Cameron's women models represent the diversity and universality of women in Victorian England.

Overall, Cameron's *Angel in the House* implies the uncertain and unsatisfied expressions of woman in such respects as her more-natural-look hairs, ambiguous eyes, and partially-ajar lips. The "deep emotion" or "the inner-self or inner-truth" of Cameron's woman sitter, conveys "a shadow of conventionality" (Wynne-Davies 130). There exists women's concealed revolt against the external and determined image of their own. *The Angel at the Tomb*, more ironically, possesses the double image of women, "the pure and impure, the sacred and profane" because it represents the female guardian of the Holy Sepulchre on one hand and "the type of Mary Magdalene, whose principal attribute is her hair, with which she concealed her nakedness as a fallen woman and in her humility used to dry the feet of Christ" (*In Focus* 78). Cameron's female angel portraits played important roles in defining the woman because the angel's unconventional pose, unarranged natural flow of hairs, and also loose robe reflected the ironical image of the guardian angel.

Cameron's portraiture of angel women as prisoners shows the dual uniqueness in which there were both outer and internal imprisonments of women of different backgrounds.

Another challenge to break the imprisonment of *The Angel in the House* is discovered in one eminent actress, Ellen Terry. As for Woolf's use of Terry's "acting" in *Freshwater*, Penny Farfan makes an interesting examination on Woolf's acting theory and fiction "as an alternative to the historical entrapment of women in restrictive, male-determined roles" (4). In Act II of the 1935 version of *Freshwater*, Terry, a prisoner of Victorian patriarchy and a young wife of old Watts, is awakened to herself when her new lover attempts to persuade her to elope with him to Bloomsbury, which for Woolf is a symbol of freedom. Even though Terry in *The Story of My Life* refers to the happy moment of getting married to Watts at age of sixteen and her new life at Little Holland House as "a paradise, where only beautiful things were allowed to come," she soon realized that she was only lightly regarded as "the girl-wife of a famous painter" and they separated within a year (33). Terry's position as wife and model of a great Victorian artist nicknamed "Signor" represents the imprisonment of women and also their selves.

> Nell: And my name is Mrs. George Frederick Watts.
> John: But haven't you got another?
> Nell: Oh plenty. Sometimes I'm Modesty. Sometimes I'm Poetry. Sometimes I'm Chastity. Sometimes, generally before breakfast, I'm merely Nell.
> John: I like Nell best.
> Nell: Well that's unlucky, because today I'm Modesty. Modesty crouching at the feet of Mammon. Only Mammon's great toe was out of drawing and so I got down; and then I heard a whistle.

> Dear me, I suppose I'm an abandoned wretch. Everybody says how proud I ought to be. Thinking of handing in the Tate Gallery for ever and ever — what an honour for a young woman like me! Only — isn't it awful — I like swimming. (*Freshwater* 27)

For Cameron, too, Watts was such an influential mentor of art that she "spent much time in the misguided effort to explore the realm of fancy, and like the Academic painters of the period, whom she emulated, produced the worst kind of Victorian trash in pictures like *Pray God, bring Father safely home*" (Gernsheim, *A Concise History* 75).

Cameron's famous portrait of Terry entitled *Sadness* (1864), which was taken during her honeymoon at Freshwater, evidently "suggests the realization of a mismatched marriage" (*In Focus* 12). The shadowed face and leaned pose of the newly-wed young woman signify her intense sense of anxiety caused by a lack of physical and spiritual freedom, a lack of respect, and also a lack of understanding in her married life. At Little Holland House and Freshwater, Terry lost her own self and primarily played the role of the subject of art and also of male-expectation. In such an environment, Terry was deprived of all her own senses, abilities, and chances by Watts, who strictly prohibited her from speaking to others in her own way. Terry was, however, convinced later that "'the three I's,'" that is, "[i]magination, industry, and intelligence" are "all indispensable to the actress" (24) because the actress is not merely the subject to be described or drawn, but the artist. Terry actually wrote her own story, as its action is described by Woolf who praises Terry for her talents as an actress: "With her pen then at odds and ends she has printed a self-portrait" ("Ellen Terry" 174).

III. Women as Outsiders against Victorianism

Even though Cameron and Woolf belonged to different generations and lived in different eras, both of them as women had to overcome the invisible barrier of Victorian patriarchal society and resist Victorianism. In addition to comparative studies on Cameron's photographic illustrations for such Victorian masterpieces as Tennyson's *Idylls of the King*, there have been recent comparative criticisms on Cameron from twentieth-century modernist, feminist, and postcolonial perspectives (Aleksiuk, Chapman, Flesher, Hill, Reid, and Wussow). Wolf points out that Woolf's mother, Julia Jackson, who was Cameron's niece and favorite model, "provides a neat yardstick for cultural change: two generations to go from an age of idealism to an age of irony, from Tennyson to T. S. Eliot, from high Victorian to thoroughly modernist" (20-21). Since Cameron's photographs of her niece and Woolf's mother, Julia Jackson (or Julia Duckworth after her marriage to Herbert Duckworth), connect Cameron with Woolf, who also based Mrs. Ramsay on Julia in *To the Lighthouse*, the subject of Victorian women is shared by Cameron and Woolf. For both Cameron and Woolf, women were primarily prisoners of Victorian values and male-expectations symbolized by *The Angel in the House*.

Both Cameron and Woolf inscribed their revolt against women as prisoners of Victorianism in their art. Cameron's portraits of Julia Jackson — especially, *Mrs. Herbert Duckworth* (April 1867) and *My Niece Julia Full Face* (April 1867) — have more distinct features than Cameron's other portraits of women. Widely known as a beauty since her childhood, Julia was a constant model for leading artists such as Watts, Edward Burne-Jones, and Thomas Woolner (the Pre-Raphaelite sculptor), and also by eminent writers such as James Russell Lowell, George Meredith, and Henry James even after her second marriage to Leslie Stephen. Julia was definitely considered as the perfect image of idealized women in Victorian England. Regarding this important element of Victorian women, Woolf makes Watts, an eminent Victorian painter, remark: "[I]n the first place I wish to convey to the onlooker the idea that Modesty is always veiled; in the second that Modesty is absolutely naked" (*Freshwater* 17). Cameron's early portraits of Julia, two portraits entitled *Julia Jackson* (1865-66, and 1866), represent the veiled "Modesty." Regarding those portraits, April Watson suggests that Julia "appears as a symbol of eternal pulchritude and divine purity" (16) and also her beauty represents "angelic immortality" (17). It is more striking that both Cameron and Woolf attempted to break this veiled "Modesty."

Both visual and verbal portraitures of Julia by Cameron and Woolf signify how both artists unveiled the Victorian values. It was in 1867 when Julia at age twenty-one finally accepted Herbert Duckworth's proposal after turning down several proposals by well-established men, such as William Holman Hunt. It is mentioned that in Cameron's *Mrs. Herbert Duckworth*, which was taken just before her marriage, "[the] perfect framing of the bust is given great emphasis by Cameron's handling of light, which is carefully cast to accentuate the strength and beauty of the head" so that this quality and effect of this portrait is close to those of men rather than women (*In Focus* 58). This portrait just before marriage, which captures "her cool, Puritan beauty," remarkably depicts a distinct intensity and dignified human nature, especially in her straight and firm neck that leads to her determined expression. Joanne Lukitsh, furthermore, analyzes that "[the] dramatic contrasts of light and dark in [Julia] Jackson's profile and neck idealize her beauty, strength of character and intelligence" (*Five Great Woman Photographers* 68). Naomi Rosenblum also remarks that the portrait of Julia "combines strength and diffidence" (12). Though always admired and even adored for her external appearance and also idealized image of an angel in the house, Julia had the inner strength to confront women's sufferings and agony; first in her husband's unexpected early death, then her pregnant widowhood with two children, and finally her second marriage in which she was indulged by her husband in managing the household and raising her children (three in her first marriage and another four including Woolf in her second marriage).

Cameron's keen awareness of Julia's duality or struggle between two opposing characters inside her is proven in her photos of Julia.

> Only through acting other parts could women give at least symbolic expression to their own aspirations and emotions, at a time when simply being someone else's relative — a wife, mother or sister — was intended to be a woman's self-fulfilment. A clear expression of this double standard occurs in Julia Margaret's photographs of her niece, Julia Jackson. On the one hand Julia is regularly photographed under her own name, with all the attention to dramatic lighting and imposing costume that is afforded the 'lionised men.' On the other, she is also presented successively as Mrs. Herbert Duckworth and Mrs. Leslie Stephen, as though her own powerful personality were entirely subsumed within her husbands' [sic] identities. (Hopkinson 16)

Julia's powerful personality was similar to Cameron's as remarked by Anne Thackeray regarding her father's memory that Cameron was "'generous, unconventional, loyal and unexpected'" throughout her life (Melville 37). Julia's unconventional personality and her unexpected or even 'vicious' behavior were also remembered among her relatives and friends (Hopkinson 5). Cameron's compassion toward Julia drove her photographing women's intensive countenance like Julia's and also Cameron's own countenance.

Julia's inner strength was inherited by Woolf, who imposed her mother's strong personality upon her fiction, especially in *To the Lighthouse*.

> When she [Mrs. Ramsay] looked in the glass and saw her hair grey. Her cheek sunk, at fifty, she thought, possibly she might have managed things better — her husband; money; his books. But for her own part she would never for a single second regret her decision, evade difficulties, or slur over duties. She was now formidable to behold, and it was only in silence, . . . (*TTL* 14)

Mrs. Ramsay's internal strength and determination are always silenced by the voices, emotional expressions, and behaviors of the people around her, especially her egoistic husband, children, and their guests, most of whom are artists. In this second marriage to an eminent Victorian figure and author, surprisingly, Julia herself kept writing stories as well as diaries just as Mrs. Ramsay creates stories for her children. Julia's writings were, however, never paid attention to until the end of the twentieth century, because she was always the subject of art and also a diligent wife and muse for the Victorian patriarch Sir Leslie Stephen. However strong Mrs. Ramsay's inner self may be, her subjection to her husband — that is, Victorian patriarchy — imprisons her, and only the author Woolf can unveil what is hidden in the imprisonment of the idealized space of home.

As for the resistance to home and victimization within home in Victorian England, Woolf creates an internal monologue in a play of British history in *Between the Acts*.

> But Mrs. Lynne Jones still saw the home. Was there, she mused, as Budge's red baize pediment was rolled off, something — not impure,

that wasn't the word — but perhaps 'unhygienic' about the home? Like a bit of meat gone sour, with whiskers, as the servants called it? Or why had it perished? Time went on and on like the hands of the kitchen clock. (The machine chuffed in the bushes.) If they had met with no resistance, she mused, nothing wrong, they'd still be going round and round and round. The Home would have remained; and Papa's beard, she thought, would have grown and grown; and Mama's knitting? what did she do with all her knitting? Change had to come, she said to herself, or there'd have been yards and yards of Papa's beard, of Mama's knitting. (103).

Throughout the various historical changes, Victorianism finally became the past ideal that confronted "resistance." In "Professions for Women," Woolf states that what she had to do for her professional life is "killing the Angel in the House" inside her (105). Cameron and Woolf discovered the same theme in the same subject, Julia. Julia exists between Cameron and Woolf in the transformation of women from the mere subject and model of men's art to the creator of art herself. The women of the three generations centered in Victorian England formed a revolution against Victorianism, which deprived women of physical and spiritual freedom.

IV. Women as Artists

Owing to their imprisonment in Victorian society, women turned to be keen observers who can transmit their internal oppression into their profound compassion toward, and understanding of, outsiders. In *Freshwater*, Woolf recreates Cameron's philosophy: "Still, to the true artist, one fact is much the same as another. A fact is a fact; art is art; a donkey's a donkey" (16). Both Cameron and Woolf were keen observers and critics who could manipulate irony in their art. Comparing Cameron with Woolf, Natasha Aleksiuk remarks that the "visual and verbal irony thus generated may be used strategically to challenge gender and class stereotypes" (2). Olsen states that, for Cameron, Little Holland House in Victorian England played the same role as the Bloomsbury Group for Woolf, since Little Holland House "seems to have been a place where outsiders were made to feel comfortable and included, even powerful and influential" (107). To be outsiders means to become observers. On Cameron as a pioneer in the history of photography, Helmut Gernsheim points out that Cameron "had the real artist's gift of piercing through the outward appearance to the soul of the individual" (*A Concise History* 58). Wolf also insists that Cameron who wished to make portraits had a great interest in "the world within" even though she had lived in Ceylon and France and experienced different outer worlds and landscapes (31). On the other hand, Woolf repeated experimental writings to explore the human inner self and finally established her own style of the stream of consciousness. Both Little Holland House and Freshwater were conflicting spaces where women's inner selves were blindly neglected and consequently imprisoned, yet from where these women began to observe the hidden aspects of another imprisoned women and also to seek their possibilities. For transcending the limitations of portraits as visual biography and biography as verbal portraiture, both Cameron and Woolf seek universality in impersonations or mythology.

Outsiders' keen sense of observation was nourished not only within the newly-knitted artists' community in Britain but also in British colonial societies. The Anglo-Indian society where Cameron was born and mostly brought up had been established through the rapid growth of British industrialism and colonialism in the nineteenth century. Anglo-Indian society in that era can be defined as a microcosm of Victorian England, yet at the same time, it possessed a uniqueness of environment, landscape, and also behaviorism. Cameron was a colonial girl born of an English father and a French mother in Calcutta, India, was trained at home as a Victorian gentlewoman and in addition was sent to Versailles for further education. It is generally stated that Cameron's productive life as a photographer was over when she returned to Ceylon in 1875 and that she produced less work till her death in 1879 because of the lack of materials and also the loss of an artists' community. Among the few surviving India photos, however, another outsider's view of colonial India was discovered (Reid). Cameron's view as an outsider was inherited by Woolf who could not behave like a Victorian gentlewoman, attempted to become a professional writer, would often suffer mental breakdowns, and ultimately had a strong sense of exclusiveness in her own country.

In Cameron's case, she was not only a pioneer woman photographer but also lived beyond the nineteenth century since in England no woman professional photographer appeared after Cameron till more contemporary Susan Meisalas and Cindy Sherman because women were merely subjects and women's works were ignored (Davidov 390). Rosenblum made a brief yet significant survey of women and photography, and mentions that women had made the same start as men in producing pictures in 1893 when photography was introduced as the new medium, yet women's works were not so equally evaluated (11). Cameron, who was a gentlewoman of leisure, was given a camera at age 48 in 1863, yet was not precisely considered a professional photographer; however, her serious attitude toward photography both as a financial source and "aesthetic production" (Joseph 44) anticipates subsequent female artistic photographers.

Cameron's deep involvement in photography is depicted in *Freshwater*; how Cameron's will was strong enough for her to behave, unlike a Victorian lady, as a hunter. Cameron kills a tamed turkey because she needs its wings for her photography.

> Mrs. C. [re-entering]: Here's the turkey wings.
> Ellen: Oh, Mr. Cameron, have you killed the turkey? And I was so fond of that bird.
> Mrs. C: The turkey is happy, Ellen. The turkey has become part and parcel of my immortal art. New, Ellen. Mount this chair. Throw your arms out. Look upwards. Alfred, you too — look up! (*Freshwater* 13-14)

Cameron's obsession with her art is illustrated in this episode where her belief in the immortality of her art is strong enough for her to sacrifice the living thing. Cameron was known literally as "a lion hunter" because she was eager to make everybody around her, even travelers to the Isle of Wight, sit for her. Cameron's obsession with photographs foreshadows the coming wave of women artists in the twentieth century.

The seemingly artistic techniques that Cameron employed are often criticized as the accidental product of undeveloped camera technology, yet those techniques feature Cameron's unique ways. Regarding her soft-focus technique, Millard explains:

> She [Cameron] would, no double, have preferred technically perfect prints, but she was wholly able to accept, even to encourage, technical imperfections when they seemed to reinforce the effect she sought. Thus, many of the soft-focus images have a breadth they could not otherwise have achieved, as Roger Fry has pointed out. . . . In sum, each of Mrs. Cameron's images was *sui generic*, responsive only to

her vision of the moment and not part of an overall plan or the result of preconceived ideas about what a photograph should be. (198-99)

In spite of this comment, there are, as some other critics have noted, some proofs to represent a set of contrasts, the light and the shadow, perfection and imperfection, and the past and the present. Regardless of the early equipment and materials, the quality of Cameron's work can be favorably compared to that of the emerging artistic photographs in the twentieth century.

No only Cameron's taking photographs at first primarily as private and family activities but also her publishing a collection of those portraits beginning with *Mia Album* is an important stage of presenting photographs as aesthetic production which "can be seen as performing a different function in a viewer's narrative of past experiences" (Lukitsh, "Album Photographs on Museum Walls: *The Mia Album*" 30). In the same way as a fiction writer who writes manuscripts and eventually publishes a book, photographers are encouraged to compile the album and furthermore, publish a collection of their work as well as exhibiting photographs. Citing from cultural theorist Susan Stewart's idea of "how, within an exchange economy, ordinary objects — such as photographs — come to realize experiences of memory, time and space," Lukitsh states that [r]eflection upon the unities among the contents of the *Mia Album* extends to a consideration of the broader social significance of the activity of assembling photographs in albums" (29). In addition, Cameron's photography illustrations for Tennyson's *Idylls of the King* extend the possibilities of reconstructing the narrative and the visual imaginations. As for this effect, Marylu Hill makes an interesting comment on "doubled pastness" in Cameron's photos: "the past world of legend and the past world of legendary Victorians" (446). To present the private album to public as a collection of photographs is an essential step toward professionalism not only because it becomes a financial resource but also because it definitely receives reviews and criticisms. To seek the new role of photography is also important as it extends and deepens the possibilities of art.

In the case of literature, women had been excluded and their works had been nearly neglected until the new trend of fiction became popular at the end of the eighteenth century. Reading fiction became women's leisure, and therefore, women were employed as the subjects of writings and also writing fiction began to be seen as women's profession. However popular writing fiction became among women, as Woolf insists in *A Room of One's Own*, women poets and writers were not listed in great men of literature and women had been excluded from all kinds of creative activities until the twentieth century.

> For women have sat indoors all these millions of years, so that by this time the very walls are permeated by their creative force, which has, indeed, so overcharged the capacity of bricks and mortar that it must needs harness itself to pens and brushes and business and politics. But this creative power differs greatly from the creative power of men. (*AROO* 87)

Women's creative power actually began to be evaluated and established in the twentieth century, which in one respect embraces all the women forerunners in all art fields. Woolf's statement reflects not only her own position as a writer but also all the women artists, whether known or unknown, who had lived and already died. For Woolf, Bloomsbury was the first space where she could liberate herself from all the social and cultural conventions and restrictions and furthermore, where she could never be excluded from the other artists and intelligent young people around her. According to Ruotolo, Woolf urgently finished writing *Freshwater* since in 1923 it was "a welcome diversion in her struggle with 'The Hours' (*Mrs. Dalloway*)" (viii). In addition, Woolf revised the play to produce it in 1935 at Vanessa's studio with such cast as Vanessa as Julia Cameron, Leonard Woolf as Mr. Cameron, Duncan Grant as Watts, Adrian Stephen as Tennyson, and Angelica Bell as Ellen Terry (*Freshwater* npn). This extended Bloomsbury Group in the twentieth century, which represents a challenging space for the young and new artists and critics, was thus chosen as the most appropriate theatre company for *Freshwater*.

V. Conclusion

With their double stance of being prisoners and resistant, women could be reborn as creators who were willing to appreciate and express what was veiled under the Victorian values. Their new subject, technique, and also philosophy, which were sprung from their art work, represented their strong sense of commitment to their creative activities. Both Cameron and Woolf established the ground where women could pursue their professions and experiment with their art work and it implied a challenge to examine the internal self of woman. As artists, Cameron and Woolf, thus, shared the same intention in photography and literature, and their messages are united within our contemporary space.

Notes

This paper is completed as part of my project on "Woman Artists and Transnationalism" for the 2006-2009 Grant-in-Aid for Scientific Research (C) by the Japan Society for the Promotion of Science. I thank my colleague, Professor Randall D. Terhune, for reminding me of this topic in our conversation about a new book on Cameron. This paper was originally published in *Doshisha Studies in English* 80 (March 2007): 59-83.

1 Woolf describes Julia Margaret Cameron as having "'remarkably fine eyes, that flashed like her sayings, and grew soft and tender if she was moved. . . . But to a child she was a terrifying apparition, short and squat, with none of the Pattle grace and beauty about her [her Pattle sisters were great beauties], though more than her share of their passionate energy and willfulness. Dressed in dark clothes, stained with plump eager face and a voice husky, and a little harsh, yet in some way compelling and even charming, she dashed out of the studio at Dimbola [her mansion at Freshwater], attached heavy swan's wings to the children's shoulders, and bade them 'Stand there' and play the part of the Angels of the Nativity leaning over the ramparts of Heaven'" (Joseph 46).

Works Cited

Aleksiuk, Natasha. "'A Thousand Angles': Photographic Irony in the Works of Julia Margaret Cameron and Virginia Woolf." *Mosaic* 33.2 (June 2000): 125-42.

Chapman, Alison. "'A Poet Never Sees a Ghost': Photography and Trance in Tennyson's *Enoch Arden* and Julia Margaret Cameron's Photography." *Victorian Poetry* 41.1 (2003): 47-7

Davidov, Judith Fryer. *Women's Camera Work: Self / Body / Other in American Visual Culture*. Durham: Duke UP, 1998.

Farfan, Penny. "Freshwater Revisited: Virginia Woolf on Ellen Terry and the Act of Acting." *Woolf Studies Annual* 4 (1998): 3-17.

Flesher, Erika. "Picturing the Truth in Fiction: Re-visionary Biography and the Illustrative Portraits for Orlando." *Virginia Woolf and the Arts*. Ed. Diane Gillespie and Leslie Hankins. New York: Pace UP, 1997. 39-47.

For My Best Beloved Sister Mia: An Album of Photographs by Julia Margaret

Chapter 6 ■ Julia Margaret Cameron as a Feminist Precursor for Virginia Woolf   145

Cameron. Albuquerque, New Mexico: the U of New Mexico Art Museum, 1994.
Ford, Colin. *Julia Margaret Cameron: 19th Century Photographer of Genius.* London: National Portrait Gallery, 2003.
Gernsheim. Helmut. *A Concise History of Photography.* 1965. New York: Dover, 1986.
——. *Julia Margaret Cameron: Her Life and Photographic Work.* New York: Aperture, 1975.
Hill, Marylu. "'Shadowing Sense at War with Soul': Julia Margaret Cameron's Photographic Illustrations of Tennyson's *Idylls of the King.*" *Victorian Poetry* 40.4 (2002): 445-62.
Hopkinson, Amanda. *Julia Margaret Cameron.* London: Virago, 1986.
In Focus: Julia Margaret Cameron. Los Angeles: The J. Paul Getty Museum, 1996.
Joseph, Gerhard. "Poetic and Photographic Frames: Tennyson and Julia Margaret Cameron." *The Tennyson Research Bulletin* 5.2 (Nov. 1988): 43-48.
Lukitsh, Joanne. "Album Photographs on Museum Walls: The Mia Album." *For My Best Beloved Sister Mia* 27-31.
——. *Five Great Woman Photographers. Julia Margaret Cameron.* London: Phaidon, 2001.
Melville, Joy. *Julia Margaret Cameron: Pioneer Photographer.* Stroud, Gloucestershire: Sutton, 2003.
Millard, Charles W. "Julia Margaret Cameron and Tennyson's *Idylls of the King.*" *Harvard Library Bulletin* 21 (1973): 187-201.
Munich, Adrienne Auslander. *Andromeda's Chains: Gender and Interpretation in Victorian Literature and Art.* New York: Columbia UP, 1989.
Olsen, Victoria C. *From Life: Julia Margaret Cameron and Victorian Photography.* New York: Palgrave Macmillan, 2003.
Reid, Panthea. "Virginia Woolf, Leslie Stephen, Julia Margaret Cameron, and the Prince of Abyssinia: An Inquiry into Certain Colonialist Representations." *Bibliography: An Interdisciplinary Quaterly* 22.3 (Summer 1999): 323-55.
Rosenblum, Naomi. Introduction. Ed. Lothar Schirmer. *Women Seeing Women: A Pictorial History of Women's Photography from Julia Margaret Cameron to Annie Leibovitz.* New York: Norton, 2001. 11-17.
Ruotolo, Lucio P. Preface. Woolf. *Freshwater: A Comedy* v-ix.
Terry, Ellen. *The Story of My Life.* Woodbridge, Suffolk: Boydell, 1982.
Watson, April. "A History from the Heart." *For My Best Beloved Sister Mia* 14-26.
Weaver, Mike. "A Divine Art of Photograph." *Whisper of the Muse: The Overstone*

Album and Other Photographs by Julia Margaret Cameron. Malibu: The J. Paul Getty Museum, 1986. 15-60.

———. *Julia Margaret Cameron1815-1879.* London: Herbert, 1984.

Wolf, Sylvia. *Julia Margaret Cameron's Women.* New Haven: Yale UP, 1999.

Woolf, Virginia. "The Art of Biography." *The Crowded* 144-51.

———. *Between the Acts.* 1941. London: Penguin, 1992.

———. *The Crowded Dance of Modern Life.* London: Harmondsworth, 1993.

———. "Ellen Terry." *The Crowded* 173-78.

———. *Freshwater: A Comedy.* 1923. New York: Harcourt, 1976.

———. "Julia Margaret Cameron." *A Victorian Album: Julia Margaret Cameron and Her Circle.* Ed. Graham Ovenden. New York: Da Capo, 1975. 13-19.

———. "Professions for Women." *The Crowded* 101-06.

———. *A Room of One's Own.* 1928. London: Penguin, 1945.

———. *To the Lighthouse.* 1927. New York: Harvest, 1955.

Wussow, Helen. "Travesties of Excellence: Julia Margaret Cameron, Lytton Strachey, Virginia Woolf, and the Photographic Image." *Virginia Woolf and the Arts: Selected Papers from the Sixth Annual Conference on Virginia Woolf.* New York: Pace UP, 1997. 13-16.

Wynne-Davies, Marion. "The 'Anxious Dream': Julia Margaret Cameron's Gothic Perspective." *Victorian Gothic: Literary and Cultural Manifestations in the Nineteenth Century.* Ed. Ruth Robbins and Julian Wolfreys. New York: Palgrave, 129-257.

Chapter 7

Miyeko Kamiya's Encounter with Virginia Woolf: A Japanese Woman Psychiatrist's Waves of Her Own

To Dr. Noburo Kamiya (1913-1999)

I. Introduction

Miyeko Kamiya (1914-1979) is well known in Japan as a psychiatrist who devoted herself to working for the nation's largest leprosarium on an isolated island, Nagashima Aiseien, as a prolific essayist, and also as a Virginia Woolf scholar who eagerly took a psychoanalytic approach in examining Woolf's life, personality, and works.[1] In 1965 when Kamiya's paper "Virginia Woolf: An Outline of a Study on her Personality, Illness and Work" was published in English in *Confinia Psychiatrica*, there soon came praise from all over the world.[2] In *Virginia Woolf: A Biography* (1972), Bell remarks that the "Japanese psychiatrist Mme Miyeko Kamiya is, I believe, preparing a pathography of Virginia Woolf and this may enable us to know whether psychiatry could have helped her" (20). What Kamiya intended to compile was not, however, Woolf's "pathographie" or merely a medical record, but an "anthropographie" in

German which Kamiya defined as an interrelated study of Woolf's family background, personality formation, mental breakdown, and creative activities, and which could be an extended production, compared with Bell's *Biography* (*Virginia Woolf Studies* 138).[3]

While waiting for all the five volumes of Woolf's *Diaries* to be published, and while contemplating the first two volumes (1977 & 1978) as well as the first four volumes of Woolf's *Letters* (1975, 1976, 1977, & 1978) and *Moments of Being* (1976), however, Kamiya regretfully died in 1979, leaving the unfinished project of writing a book entitled *Virginia Woolfs Anthropographie*. In addition to publishing a number of professional articles on Woolf from 1965 till her death, Kamiya compiled the first part of Woolf's "Autobiography" with a multiple approach in 1974, and Kamiya's translation of *Virginia Woolf A Writer's Diary* (1953) was published in 1976. After Kamiya's death, *Virginia Woolf Studies* (1981), a collection of her writings on Woolf, was edited by her editor and her daughter-in-law, Nagako Kamiya, and was included in a complete collection of Kamiya's works which were published from 1980 through 1985 by Misuzu Shobo.

Kamiya's empathy with Woolf stems from Kamiya's discovery and recognition of the similarities between them in family background, personality, and psychological struggle. Reading Woolf through Kamiya adumbrates the intertwined and intertextualized representation of their internalized quandary, insurrection, vulnerability, and ambivalence which ultimately precipitated their quintessential talents. In her plunge into Woolf from the early 1960's till her death in 1979, Kamiya substantiated Woolf's core conflicts which ultimately led to Woolf suicide: her childhood sexual abuse, lesbianism, mental breakdown, and bombardment experience during the Second World War in London from which she and Leonard sheltered themselves at Monk's House, obsessed with an esoteric sense of fear of the Nazis. The more Kamiya learned about Woolf s life, the more she identified herself with Woolf because there are another set of similar core conflicts between them: the intellectual family background with the eminent fathers and elder brothers, the endless agony as a woman pursuing a career, the late marriage, the mental breakdown, and the wartime experiences.[4] Kamiya's obstinate pursuit targeted Woolfs de facto diaries as which Kamiya asserted embedded the intriguing interrelationship between Woolf's personality and work as she notes that Woolf's unpublished diaries might connote "Woolf's complicated and multi-layered aspects of personality" and "the origin of her creative activities" (*VWS* 139).[5] Rereading Kamiya's private diaries and letters as well as her essays and professional writings, moreover, empowers us with a profound understanding of Kamiya's studies on Woolf and eventually enables us to reconsider our contemporary Woolf criticism.

Kamiya's 1965 paper, "Virginia Woolf; An Outline," consists of several sections including "Life of Virginia Woolf in Outline."[6] In her 1970's Japanese version of that paper, however, Kamiya changed most of that section: the biggest four additions are regarding Woolf as a victim of the sexual abuse in her childhood days, her lesbian tendencies, mental breakdown, and the Woolfs' anxiety about the Nazis before her suicide. Between 1965 and 1970, Kamiya frequently corresponded with Dr. Eugen Kahn — one of the editors of *Confinia* —, Leonard Woolf, and Quentin Bell. In 1965, Kamiya realized her long-cherished dream when she was appointed as Chair of Psychopathology Department of Nagashima Aiseien, after her research there had begun in 1957, her appointment as a doctor had been made in 1959, and her monthly visit had started in 1960.[7] From 1965 through the 1970's, in spite of her heavy duty and bimonthly five-hour commute between her home in Ashiya, Hyogo and Nagashima Aiseien in Okayama, regretfully leaving her husband and two sons at home, Kamiya's writing activities flourished. During the most mature yet conflicting period in Kamiya's own life, Kamiya was deeply involved with Woolf so that it is significant to investigate Kamiya's studies on Woolf during such a crucial period. Kamiya's examination and interpretation of Woolf by way of recreating Woolfs persona and voice is intertwined with Kamiya's own autobiographical persona and voice in her letters, diaries, and essays.

II. Kamiya's Recreating Woolf's Voice as a Victim of Sexual Abuse

In Bell's letter of May 25, 1968, responding to Kamiya's request to inform her of the history of Woolf s mental breakdown, he writes that from the age of nine, "she [Virginia Woolf] and her sister were the object of improper advances from their half brother" (*VWS* 226).[8] It was at this point that Kamiya recognized Woolf as a victim of sexual abuse in her childhood days. This was twenty years before Louise DeSalvo's book, *Virginia Woolf: The Impact of Childhood Sexual Abuse on Her Life and Work* was published in 1989. In her 1970 article, consequently, Kamiya develops Bell's statement in his letter and notes that: the "experience that possibly damaged Woolf's sex life is, according to Bell, she had been a victim of constant sexual abuse by her step-brother who lived in the same house from her childhood days till she was over 20" (*VWS* 16). Kamiya's grasp of Bell's words and her deep understanding of what actually took place made her reconsider Woolf s once-inarticulate childhood days. Even though Bell has been attacked by such feminist critics as Jane Marcus, he had supplied Kamiya with the right reference before Woolf's *Moments of Being* was published in 1976. While translating Woolf's *Diary*, from 1973 through 1974, Kamiya was considering expanding upon her 1965 and 1970 papers of "Virginia Woolf: An Outline" into her *Virginia Woolf's Anthropographie*. Bell's 1968 letter provided Kamiya with an opportunity to reexamine, register, and vindicate Woolf s life as a suppressed self.

Kamiya's "Autobiography," which she began writing on Dec. 4, 1974, is the important piece of evidence which can be used to evaluate Kamiya's deep insight into Woolf's sexual abuse experience as the once concealed self-representation. She finished the first part exactly two weeks later, though she might have revised it after the publication of *Moments of Being*, which includes "A Sketch of the Past" and "22 Hyde Park Gate," two essays referring to Woolf's childhood sexual abuse experience.[9] In writing "Autobiography," Kamiya largely depended on Woolf's *Diary* and Bell's *Biography*. Kamiya's intention was, however, not to use those authorized and already-published materials but to recreate Woolf's voice by way of Kamiya's interpretation of those limited materials and to employ a multiple approach. This "Autobiography" opens at the time Woolf has just completed *Between the Acts* at age 59, traces back to her birth, and ends with her father's death at age 22 when Woolf suffered the mental breakdown. In this experimental "Autobiography," Kamiya resuscitates Woolf's voice of inwardly exclaiming her victimization of sexual abuse and the first serious mental breakdown.

Bell's *Biography* illustrates Woolfs sexual abuse fact at 13 in an indirect and gentle manner from an objective point of view as Woolf's official biographer.

> At what point this comfortably fraternal embrace developed into something which to George no doubt seemed even more comfortable although not nearly so fraternal, it would be hard to say. Vanessa

> came to believe that George himself was more than half unaware of the fact that what had started with pure sympathy ended by becoming a nasty erotic skirmish. There were fondlings and fumblings in public when Virginia was at her lessons and these were carried to greater lengths — indeed I know not to what lengths — when, with the easy assurance of a fond and privileged brother, George carried his affections from the schoolroom into the night nursery. (42-43)

On the other hand, Kamiya manipulates the technique of autobiography, "the narrative 'I'" which ultimately becomes "a fictive persona."[10] Kamiya retrieves Woolf's voice of the hidden anger of the recurrent sexual abuse after her mother's death.

> The most unpleasant memory around the age of six, which I even do not want to remember, is about my step-brother, George Duckworth. He is the eldest son of my mother's first marriage and was around 22 old then. In my early childhood days, he committed misconduct with me. He had me sit on the slab of the wall in a nursery room and invaded my private parts. I did not know what it meant in those days, but I tremble for shame whenever I remember that. His misconduct continued till I was 21 or 22, but I was so furious that I could not tell that even to my parents. Only my sister knows that, but neither of us could tell anybody because George was kind during the daytime. This experience made me hate throughout my life *the* mere sex. (*VWS* 41)[11]

Woolf's voice at age 6 is based on the female sex's intuitive perception and unavoidable unpleasant feelings; while Woolf's voice over 20 is grounded upon the more evident and direct feelings of aversion. Both voices of the past are revived in the moment where the narrator, "I," is situated and where Kamiya places herself.[12]

Focused on Woolf's introspection, Kamiya demonstrates the sequestered self which was contracted under the public face of the privileged "Victorian" brother as a challenge to Bell's description of George as abuser.

> Outsiders might have viewed my step-brother, George Duckworth, as blessed with his efforts to comfort us, as being a model brother. He was known as a good-looking, wealthy, well-mannered, and agreeable gentleman. He gave us gifts, held a party for us, and took us outside.
>
> But alas! This "model" step-brother had been fumbling my body and it became more often and more unbearable after our mother died. When I was studying, he came in and fumbled. Finally, he intruded into my bed at night. Both my sister and I were scared, but we were very shy, and moreover, it was considered that women should not tell such a thing, so that I could not tell either my father or Stella about that. This step-brother's incestuous behavior made me in a panic during the first part of my life. (*VWS* 52)

The gap between the model brother during the daytime and the abuser / sexual harasser at night is what the Victorian gentleman concealed and what the Victorian gentlewomen had to endure in its sexually suppressed society. DeSalvo infers that "Victorian ideology held girls responsible for the morality of their brothers" (108). Kamiya's aversion to the Victorian, male-centered, tyrannical household is so strong that her straightforward and powerful voice is inscribed within the frame of Woolf's persona.

A disparity between Bell's *Biography* and Kamiya's "Autobiography" is, thus, seen in several facets. Though Bell's description of George is compassionate, Kamiya's is hostile. Bell depicts Gerald's conduct as being initially based on his "pure sympathy" and "affections." On the contrary, Kamiya rejects this interpretation and instead she delves into the consequence of the sexual abuse both in Woolf's life-long psychological agony and her extreme rejection of physical sex. Bell's testimony deflected the readers from the depth of the sexual abuse issue; however, it was virtually modified by Kamiya. Compared to Bell's *Biography*, Kamiya's "Autobiography" describes the streams of intense emotions in a long-silenced voice in order to articulate the core of Woolf's trauma.

Bell also points out Woolf's breakdown at 22 in connection with George's sexual abuse: "When Virginia went mad in the summer of 1904, Vanessa told Savage of what had been happening and Savage, it seems, taxed George with his conduct" (95-96). Bell presents to us the fact that Woolf's mental breakdown largely originates from her sexual abuse experience in her childhood days, and he also infers that this secret was preserved between Vanessa and Virginia. In contrast to Bell's slight mention, Kamiya emphasizes that this secret could never be revealed to their parents, and even to their father and their step-sister after their mother's death, and that there was no shelter in their household.[13] Kamiya substantiates that Woolf was psychologically isolated and suppressed, and regards Woolf's silenced self as the core of her mental breakdown.

Kamiya's recreation of Woolf's voice in "Autobiography" can be evaluated when it is compared with Woolf's autobiographical memoirs, *Moments of Being*. In "A Sketch of the Past," which Woolf began to write in 1939, Woolf illustrates her sexual abuse experience, what Woolf calls "the looking-glass shame" (*MB* 78).[14]

> Another memory, also of the hall, may help to explain this. There was a slab outside the dining room door for standing dishes upon. Once when I was very small Gerald Duckworth lifted me onto this, and as I sat there he began to explore my body. I can remember the feel of

his hand going under my clothes; going firmly and steadily lower and lower. I remember how I hoped that he would stop; how I stiffened and wriggled as his hand approached my private parts. But it did not stop. His hand explored my private parts too. I remember resenting, disliking it — what is the word for so dumb and mixed a feeling? I must have been strong, since I still recall it. (79-80)

In her 1997 *Biography*, Lee defines "A Sketch of the Past" as an "uncompleted fragment of life-writing" where "the elusiveness of the self almost becomes the subject" and evaluates it as a "new kind of women's life-writing she has been recommending for so long" (18). Kamiya, in "Notes on Virginia Woolf's *Anthropographie*" (1978-79), regards "A Sketch of the Past" as one of the most important documents where the psychiatrists can know the depth of the patient's inner self by letting him or her tell the past memory freely (*VWS* 148). Kamiya points out three main characteristics of "A Sketch of the Past": first, the confession which can be traced close to the starting point of Woolf's personality formation; second, the dimensional structure consisting of the present self at Monk's House during the war and the past self; third, the division of daily life between "non-being" and "being" (*VWS* 148-50). In an attempt to create an innovative self / life-writing which aligns Woolf's personality formation, Kamiya's perspective is close to Woolfs in respect to reproducing the once-lost voice in which the discord ranging from refusal to survival are interlaced in the present self.

In "22 Hyde Park Gate," which was originally presented in 1921, Woolf declares a troubled incident with a cynical comment using the word, "lover," for an abuser, George.[15]

Sleep had almost come to me. The room was dark. The house silent. Then, creaking stealthily, the door opened; treading gingerly,

someone entered. "And don't turn on the light, oh beloved. Beloved
—" and he flung himself on my bed, and took me in his arms.

Yes, the old ladies of Kensington and Belgravia never knew that George Duckworth was not only father and mother, brother and sister to those poor Stephen girls; he was their lover also. (*MB* 180)

Woolfs adoption of narrowing and deepening the space from the house to the room and eventually to the bed is successful enough to embody the metaphorical invasion into Woolfs psyche as well as her body in a form of realistic and physical exploration. By quoting from the above part of "A Sketch of the Past," also by pointing out "22 Hyde Park Gate" and Woolfs letters to Vanessa in 1911 and to her friend in 1941, Kamiya defines Woolfs childhood sexual abuse as her "unforgettable 'trauma' which determined her sexual apathy after marriage and her life-long light lesbian tendencies" ("Notes on *VWA*," *VWS* 155). Liberated from Bell's discourse, Kamiya in "Autobiography" initiates into the inquiry about Woolf's private territory which has been intentionally half-hidden and half-revealed as it is a domestic violence in the sacred sphere of a Victorian home, and ultimately about Woolf's personality formation which determined the rest of her life.

III. Kamiya's Encoding Woolf's Lesbian Tendencies, Mental Breakdown, and Creativity

Kamiya's encoding of Woolfs lesbianism, mental breakdown, and creative talents in her papers and "Autobiography" is ferreted out by Kamiya's autobiographical writings. Woolf's lesbian tendencies conjure up Ms. X (Ms. Y in Kamiya's diaries), a person who desired Kamiya as an elder sister and lover, suffered a mental breakdown, showed an extraordinary creative talent, and committed suicide.[16] In her 1970 paper, Kamiya already added a significant factor about Woolfs lesbian tendencies.

> When she was 23, Woolf began to write seriously. But according to Bell, who has already proved it in his *Biography*, Woolf had started her writing activities at home at age nine. Woolf got married at age 30, yet until then she had quite often inclined to fall in love with women seriously. This lesbian tendency is considered as one of the most important elements to think about with respect to her life and writings. (*VWS* 17)

Kamiya's assumption is ascribed to Bell's assertion of Woolfs lesbian love to Madge Symonds. Bell's observation is founded upon his suave evasion from the dishonorable collision between Woolf and her kin. What Bell surrender is resumed by Kamiya in her "Autobiography." Kamiya recreates Bell's description of Woolfs "very pure and very intense passion" for Madge, which is a passion for the same sex resulting from the traumatic effect of the sexual assault: "Virginia at sixteen, for all George's kissings and fumblings, was by modem standards almost unbelievably ignorant" (60-61). In "Autobiography," Kamiya forms Woolf's voice: "I already had a strong hatred for men, so I can say Madge, a wonderful senior woman, was my first love" (*VWS* 57). Kamiya, using Bell's *Biography* (82-85), also evolves Woolfs voice of confessing her love to Violet: "Not only warmhearted, Violet also has a balance and masculine confidence, so that I entirely rely on her and behave like a child. While I was 22 to 25, this friendship continued, yet it is of course a very platonic one" (*VWS* 65). In these compositions, Kamiya presents to us the characteristics of Woolfs lesbian love — that is, a child-like pursuit for a mother / elder sister figure who gives

Woolf a sense of protection, psychological stability, and physical wholesomeness. Woolf's lesbianism is, moreover, interrelated with Kamiya's memoir of Ms. X, "Those Whom I Remember," which was first published in a Japanese journal, *Life and Science*, in 1971. Ms X's lesbian tendencies are very similar to Woolf's, as Kamiya employs the same expression as "a spoilt-child-like pursuing love to women."

Kamiya's redefinition of Woolf's lesbianism appears in "Notes on *VWA*," after "Those Whom I Remember" was first included in *Essays by Kamiya Miyeko II* in 1977.[17] At that time, Kamiya first intended to omit a part of Ms. X in that essay and crossed its part on the original sheet which was preserved by Noburo Kamiya (Personal Interview). Kamiya's sense of guilt to Ms. X, with which she was obsessed until her death, however, seems to motivate her to explore the depth of women's psychology when "Those Whom I Remember" is reprinted. In one of the late notes, Kamiya regards Woolf's lesbianism ranging from her passionate one to Vita as her "lesbian partner" to Woolf's friendship with Katherine Mansfield through correspondence and states that "Woolf has a very light lesbian tendency" and her "lesbianism represents her prematurity" (*VWS* 191-92). These two types of lesbianism can correspond to Ms. X who passionately needed Kamiya and for Masa Uraguchi to whom Kamiya wrote 624 letters during their 35-year friendship till Kamiya's death.[18] Kamiya recognizes that women have their natural emotions of love to women as Woolf describes, "Chole liked Olivia" (Woolf, *A Room of One's Own* 81):

> According to the first volume of Woolf's *Letters*, her childish love was in pursuit to some senior women in a baby-like manner. In her letters to those women, interestingly, Woolf compared her with different animals like their pets. After marriage, this childish love pursuit

mostly targeted her husband, but Woolf continued to seek for her love to Vita and Ethel whatever the age difference was, and especially to Vita throughout her life. Though Woolf had some male friends, she seldom showed the same childish love. Woolf's only lesbian partner among her female friends was Vita for three years in their long friendship. It was certain that Woolf preferred having a friendship with women. For example, Woolf's letter to Katherine Mansfield, a talented writer who passed away young can be considered as an evidence of their friendship. But, there is almost no evidence to define Woolf a lesbian. (*VWS* 191-92)

It is possible to assume the reason why Kamiya almost rejected her own hypothesis of Woolf's lesbianism centers around her own personal experience of being pursued by women, especially Ms. X and Masa. In the above statement, Kamiya excludes her first hypothesis which she borrows from Bell's *Biography* and constructs her own theory that lesbianism is not necessarily related with the childhood sexual abuse experience. Kamiya's autobiographical voice which retells her fated relationship with Ms. X and Masa results in Kamiya's altered attitude toward Woolf's lesbianism.

The interrelationship between the mental breakdown and creative talent is more acutely associated with Woolf and Ms. X through Kamiya's autobiographical voice. According to "Those Whom I Remember," Ms. X, who suffered from a sequence of mental breakdowns and committed suicide at age 29 in 1949 just after she was shocked by Kamiya's merciless rejection. From that time until her own death, Kamiya was obsessed with the sense of guilt and eventually exposed her blemish which, paradoxically, urged her to discover the interrelation between Woolf's mental breakdown and creative talent. In addition to Kamiya's involvement in Ms. X, Kamiya would "feel a personal attachment for the illness" which Ms. X suffered (*Diaries and Letters* 68). In her young days, Kamiya repeatedly describes her idea in her diaries that many of her family members possess "psychopathische Persönlichkeiten" (April 8, 1945, *DL* 62). Kamiya is convinced that she is herself "Genantinomie (double-personality)" (Jan. 4, 1946, *DL* 68) and she has "manic-depressive personality" (Dec. 4, 1946, *DL* 70) especially when she was so absorbed in her studies.[19] Kamiya believed that her manic-depressive personality might deprive her of a chance of marriage. Kamiya's discovery of a similarity in the interrelated bond between the mental breakdown and creative talent among Ms. X, Woolf, and herself is molded into the core of Kamiya's interdisciplinary studies on Woolf.

The connection between Ms. X and Woolf in their creative talents which is examined in "Those Whom I Remember" embodies the foundation of Kamiya's life-long studies on Woolf. Kamiya links one example of Ms. X's writings with Woolf's and states: "Such writers as Virginia Woolf and Neville describe strange figures and scenes, which are too vivid and even too extraordinary to be regarded as the products of mere imagination" (*The Significance of Beings* 43-44). As Nagako Kamiya states in the Epilogue of *Virginia Woolf Studies*, Kamiya had already written about Ms. X's creative talent just one month after Ms. X's suicide:

> Most of these images were awfully desultory, but vivid enough to grasp the entire structure clearly. For example, in depicting the beautiful evening sky, she said, "To the west, a man with a sword is sitting on the clouds and cries. He wears a hat with a blue feather." Also, she said, "I do not imagine that, but really can see that. I cannot help seeing that."
>
> What is hidden inside the brain of a woman with her hair bobbed short. I was sure that if she had possessed the unusual sensitivities

and would have improved them properly, she could have created a unique literature. (*VWS* 281-82)

Kamiya's encounter with psychopathology by way of Ms. X in 1943 strengthened Kamiya's pursuit for the interrelation between the mental breakdown and creativity at Ms. X's suicide in 1949, and eventually develops her intuitive analysis of Ms. X's uniqueness into her Woolf studies in the 1970's.[20]

Kamiya's conclusion that both Woolf's and Ms. X's cases are considered "the so-called 'atypical' psychoses" has been consistent till her late years. In her 1971 version of "Virginia Woolf: An Outline," Kamiya remarks that Woolf's "illness, showing both 'circular' and schizophrenic components, seems to belong to the so-called 'atypical psychoses' or 'schizo-affective psychoses'" (200).[21] This thesis is, interestingly, affiliated to Kamiya's observation and examination of Ms. X's case which Kamiya twenty years after Ms. X's death can define: "She showed a typical schizophrenic symptom, but it was circular. Her abnormality in her calm period was too subtle to recognize unless it was carefully observed (*SB* 47).[22] After struggling in defining Woolf's case where both schizothymia and manic-depressive psychosis are witnessed, Kamiya in her late note explains the process and the reason of reaching to the conclusion that Woolf's case can be classified into "schizo-affective psychoses" among "schizo-phrenic psychoses," yet rather close to the last stage of "affective psychoses," which is originated by the inherited symptom, yet caused by the defects of amino metabolism in the brain, and mentally and physically induced (*VWS* 245-46). All aspects of Woolf's several degrees of psychoses, its circular disposition, a series of conflicts in personality, and the driving force in her childhood days formulate Woolf's obsession with reaching the stage of perfection in her novels, and at the same time, cause the manic-depressive psychosis and the entire dismantlement of consciousness (*VWS* 247). Regarding the induction of Woolf's psychoses and all the symptoms, Kamiya makes a close examination by using the layered references of Woolf's published diaries, letters, and Leonard's autobiographical writings.

Kamiya's consistent examination of Woolf's psychoses is overlapped with Kamiya's exploration into herself by writing her autobiography during the last five years of her life. In writing this late note on Woolf's psychoses, Kamiya herself suffered heart attacks and had been in and out of the hospital since the first attack in 1971. During the last stage of her life, Kamiya was deeply devoted to reading and writing, especially Woolf's *Anthropographie* and Kamiya's own autobiography entitled *Pilgrimage*. According to Noburo Kamiya, this fragmented autobiography does not include all of Kamiya's personal experiences and Kamiya was worried if the last part of *Pilgrimage* which describes her hard time in her marriage and family life would be misread and even hurt her husband and sons (Epilogue, *P* 285). By reading this last part of *Pilgrimage* and rereading Kamiya's letters and diaries, however, it is possible to assume that Kamiya suffered a similar set of conflicts as Woolf's: the extraordinary energy and talents since her childhood days; being an outsider at the Japanese academic institutions both as a student and as a teacher; a conflict with her eminent father, Tamon Ueda, and her diligent elder brother, Yoichi Maeda; a struggle in pursuing her profession and establishing herself; her marriage to a well-established scientist to become an ideal wife; her joy and strife in bearing and bringing up two sons; and her struggle between a wife / mother role and a psychiatrist / writer in the middle of her career during her last 33 years till her death. Noburo Kamiya states both in the Epilogue and in the Personal Interview that Kamiya named her inner vital power "*oni*," or demon, and she was fighting with a number of demons under the mask of the ideal and obedient wife and mother (285). Kamiya's own examination of her psychoses in her autobiographical writings is engraved in her studies on Woolf's psychoses because of the identical backgrounds and conflicts.

Consistently responding to her own autobiographical discourse, Kamiya encodes the closely intertwined relationship among Woolf's lesbianism, mental breakdown, and creative talent by reexamining her past friendship with and reexamination on Ms. X and Kamiya's own personal perspectives as a motivation and energy to investigate into the deep side of human psychology.

IV. Kamiya's Reviving Woolf as a Bombardment Victim

In her "Notes on *VWA*," Kamiya concludes that inducement for Woolf's suicide was largely, "Entlastung," a state of stupor after her achievement of *Between the Acts*, rather than the war (*VWS* 248). Kamiya's autobiographical voice, however, seeks a crucial war-time crisis which influenced Woolf's psychoses. Kamiya once points out the reason of the low nervous breakdown and suicide rate among patients during the war: "people are too concentrated on putting forth their greatest strength for survival to ask themselves what they live for" and especially as for doctors and nurses in the clinics, "the sense of duty is the strongest force to prevent people from committing suicide" ("Suicide and the Meaning of Life — Suicide in the Clinics," *From the Memoirs* 111-12). Kamiya's above statement is tied with her autobiographical note: "Encouraged by their lively and bravely attitude, I remained myself all alone in Tokyo, temporarily inhabiting in an office of the Hospital's Psychiatrical Department, even after my house was bombed and all of my family left Tokyo" (*FM* 112). Kamiya is convinced that the war encouraged people to live, which connects with Woolf's case.

That Kamiya in her late years was perhaps unconsciously compassionate for Woolf is embedded in the fact that both Woolf and Kamiya had their houses burn down in air raids during the Second World War. Kamiya, moreover, witnessed the approaching danger of the war both in the States and in Europe from 1939 through 1940.[23] This shared ideological context must have motivated Kamiya to intend to unravel the elusiveness of Woolf's final mental breakdown and the reason of her suicide.

Kamiya's dramatic yet prominent life precipitates her argument concerning Woolf's tragic end. In her English version of "Virginia Woolf: An Outline," Kamiya describes the last stage before Woolf's suicide in 1941: "The war seems to have made her suffer not only in the form of material loss and shortage, but also and more in that of the 'loss of echo' to her work, of which she complains several times in her diary' (194). In her 1970 Japanese version, this last part is altered, since Kamiya might have been assured in her talk with Leonard of the real crisis with which they were confronted at Monk's House after she had read his *The Journey Not The Arrival Matters* (1969).

> There, another breakdown occurred to her and she struggled with it, but finally drowned herself in the Ouse, which she could reach from the garden. She was 59. Her husband is a Jew, so that the Woolfs planned to commit suicide together before the Nazi invaded into England. It was the worst wartime period in England. (*VWS* 18)

Kamiya recognizes the ideological context which influences both Woolf's suicidal longing along with her breakdown. Leonard states that Adrian Stephen offered Virginia and Leonard "a portion of this protective poison" to commit suicide "rather than fall into German hands" (*JNAM* 15). The crucial fact that Leonard is a Jew and both the Woolfs are obsessed with a strong sense of anxiety about the Nazi invasion into England is reexamined by Kamiya as the mortality of the society for which Woolf lived.[24]

"Autobiography" begins with the war-time evacuation life where Kamiya connects Woolf's unconscious plunge into her psychological col-lapse with Woolf's wartime experience just before her suicide. Kamiya first builds up the bombardment damages: "Our London apartment was bombed, and our Hogarth Press was completely burnt. During the past — years, I have kept writing and have purchased pretty furniture and paintings one by one, yet all were burnt down to ashes" (*VWS* 35). Kamiya's description of Woolf's last days of life is grounded on the gradual loss of life itself which is reminiscent of Kamiya's own wartime experience: first, the loss of materials such as houses; second, the loss of people; third, the loss of duty.[25]

> As I am now convinced that I will not be able to live long, I also have begun to feel like writing my memoirs since last November. Of course, I do not want to die yet. I would like to live another ten years. But, because of the terrible air raids, I sometimes imagine I will be killed by bombs. It is regretful that I — after observing everything — cannot describe my death bed scene. Is it painful to have eyes and head crushed? Yes. I'm scared. I am going to become faint, and then try to come to myself in a few breaths, but later. . . .
>
> Furthermore, we have our own specific reason. As Leonard is a Jew, both of us will be sent to a gas room if the Nazi invade into England. We have already decided to kill ourselves together before the invasion and prepared poison which Adriane had gotten for us. Leonard and I agreed that we would commit suicide together in a locked garage. (*VWS* 35-36)

The overall and most unbearable loss is, however, that of the sense of significance of self. In the worst wartime England, Woolf realized that the war would deprive her of the true meaning of life which transcends beyond the material loss and that of her calling. Kamiya writes as if Woolf and Leonard were enjoying the lone and simple country life; however, Kamiya is aware that they faced the invisible threatening. The possibly worst consequence of the Nazi invasion not only causes the loss of life but also the loss of significance of being. Kamiya enacts the idea that Woolf's condition before suicide is accounted for by Woolf's desire for dissolution after being in a state of stupor and as a result of despondency over surrendering the dignified self.

Induced by these elements, Woolf's suicide attempt is carried out during the early stage of mental breakdown where suicides are more often achieved (*VWS* 248). Along with the other suicide attempts after her father's death, after her marriage, and during the last breakdown, Kamiya remarks that the final attempt was easily carried out (*VWS* 148). In such an early stage, Woolf plunges into the abyss which cannot be avoided. In *What We Live For*, Kamiya analyzes two things that could prevent people from committing suicide: one of them is the grasp of "time," or the moment of being, which enables our physical existence to continue living and consequently sustains us in our unconscious situations (139); and the other is a more powerful force, that is, "the offensive spirit" which is assured in the grasp of "time" (141). Kamiya's autobiographical voice of Woolf in her last stage expresses the definite and logical theory which underlines the existence of the invisible force which will destroy the moment of being and the living inner force. In "Autobiography," Kamiya interfaces the absence of these objections to suicide with the direct route to Woolf's suicide attempt and its achievement.

V. Conclusion

Kamiya's waves of her own are her thorough examinations, analysis, and arguments on Woolf's personality formation and life. Her inner conflicts are classified into the traumatic effect of her childhood sexual abuse, the psychological constriction in her ingenuous lesbian tendencies, and the segregated self-existence and self-confidence. These three elements are concatenated with one another so that they accelerate Woolf's itinerary to suicide. As Kamiya was confronted with approaching death, she was eager to discover "what she lives for" in completing her Woolf studies in the form of a book as she states in *Miyeko Kamiya: Personality and Work* (140-41).

Notes

The abridged form of this paper was delivered at my panel, "Miyeko Kamiya's Encounter with Virginia Woolf," at the 7th International Virginia Woolf Conference, at Plymouth State College, on June 15, 1997. I would like to express my gratitude to Ms. Nagako Kamiya and Dr. Noburo Kamiya for their support and encouragement. This paper was originally published in *Doshisha Literature* 43 (March 2000): 1-16.

1 Kamiya's first encounter with Woolf was her reading of *To the Lighthouse* (1927) while she was majoring in English Literature at Japan's Tsuda College (Tsuda Juku Daigaku) in the mid-1930's. Kamiya reencountered Woolf around 1960 while she was advising a sociology student at Kobe College (Kobe Jogakuin Daigaku) on a B.A. thesis dealing with Woolf. This second encounter provided Kamiya with an opportunity to investigate Woolf from an interdisciplinary viewpoint. In her English papers, Kamiya used such words as "leprosarium" and "leper" without any sense of discrimination.

2 According to Kamiya's first letter of Leonard Woolf of Aug. 22, 1966, Kamiya received "more than fifty requests" for offprints from all parts of the world.

Kamiya corresponded with both Leonard Woolf (from 1966 to 1968) and Quentin Bell (from 1968 to 1975). In 1966, she visited Leonard Woolf in order to interview him.

3 Kamiya explains that Spoerri names "Anthropographie" or "Strukturanalyse" in "Virginia Woolf: Outline" (190). In the 1960's, Kamiya was deeply involved in "Anthropographie": she introduced "Anthropographie" in her 1962 paper entitled "On Two Major Trends in Modern Psychiatry —The Social and Existential Approaches in Europe, America and Japan —" which "Anthropographie," Kamiya again focused on the same subject (*Psychiatrical Studies 2* 125-38).

4 According to Noburo Kamiya, Kamiya was so absorbed in her studies on Woolf that she almost identified herself with Woolf (Personal Interview).

5 All English translations of Kamiya's works which were originally written in Japanese are mine. As for Woolf's diary and letters, Bentock states that "Woolf did not live to write her memoirs, and the bulk of the autobiographical Virginia Woolf exists in her diary and letters, forms whose generic boundaries she extended and reconstructed" (17).

6 This paper consists of Introduction, "The Sources," "Social and Literary Background," "Family Background," "Outward Appearance," "Life of Virginia Woolf in Outline," "Personality," "Mental Illness," "Virginia Woolf's Work," "Relationship among Illness, Personality and Work," "Discussion," and "Summary." Regarding some references on Woolf, Kamiya used mainly *A Writer's Diary*, Lernard Woolf's *Beginning Again*, Pipett's *The Moth and the Star: A Biography of Virginia Woolf*.

7 At age 19, Kamiya visited a leprosarium, Tamazenseien, with her uncle and Quaker priest, Tsuneo Kanazawa. Kamiya's first encounter with Hansen's disease determined her to be engaged in curing its patients even though she faced her parents' strong opposition (Ejiri 69-72).

8 Parenthesis is mine. The Japanese translation of Bell's letters are published in *Virginia Woolf Studies*. The original letters were privately preserved by Dr. Noburo Kamiya.

9 DeSalvo articulates her opinions about Woolfs repression as "'a common protective mechanism'" caused by her sexual abuse experience, considering the fact that Woolf had not confessed Gerald's abuse until late in her life (10).

10 It is because "the autobiographer can never capture the fullness of her subjectivity or understand the entire range of her experience" (Smith 46).

11 It is noted that Kamiya mistook George as Gerald because she used Bell's

Biography in which Bell himself mistakes George as Gerald, but later both brothers turned out to be abusers for Woolf.

12 According to Smith, the "autobiographer joins together facets of remembered experience — descriptive, impressionistic, dramatic, analytic — as she constructs a narrative that promises both to capture the specificities of personal experience and to cast her self-interpretation in timeless, idealized mold for posterity" (45).

13 DeSalvo argues that in her discussion of the environment of incestuous sexual abuse: "Feelings of profound betrayal and rage at other members of the household also existed; many times they remained unexpressed" (12).

14 Lee concludes that "there were many more long-term, problematic, and influential features in her childhood than" the incident of sexual abuse by Gerald (124).

15 King points out that Woolf "could be very loose in terminology: 'Lover' does not have to be taken to mean that George forced Virginia to have intercourse" (83).

16 Ms. X's elder brother, a friend of Kamiya's elder brother's, asked Kamiya to take care of his sister. Kamiya had just graduated from Tsuda College in 1935 and was staying at home because of the aftermath of consumption. Kamiya was about 21 or 22, and Ms. X was, at 15 or 16, an English major at Tokyo Women's University. Their friendship continued about fourteen years from 1935 to 1949. During those years, Kamiya studied in the States, both of them survived the Second World War, and Kamiya got married and had two children. According to Kamiya, Ms. X showed an extraordinary love to Kamiya, never forgave Kamiya for her marriage, and finally committed suicide just after Kamiya mercilessly told her that she would leave for the States with her husband and their children. Kamiya kept writing about Ms. X in her diaries in her young days and even about Ms. X's suicide one month after her death, yet never revealed it in public until she wrote "Those Whom I Remember" in 1971.

17 During her life, Kamiya's writings were compiled into four books by a smallpress in Kyoto, which was founded by Kamiya's former students.

18 Kamiya interprets Woolf's friendship with women which is proven in her letters by tracing back to Kamiya's own experience with Ms. X and Masa Uraguchi. In her diary of Sep. 15, 1942, Kamiya was very annoyed with both Ms. X and Masa for their serious pursuit of Kamiya as their idealized "ambassador of God" (*DL* 116). In a diary of Sep. 2, 1944, Kamiya again confesses that she hates herself because she "is passionately, dominantly, and absolutely loved by both men and women" who admire Kamiya as some "goddess" (*Diaries in Young Days* 207). Kamiya's brother, Yoichi Maeda, who later became a well-known scholar of

French literature, called Kamiya "androgynous" and insisted that because of this personality Kamiya would not be able to get along with any man (June 26, 1939, *DL* 18).

19 Parentheses is mine.

20 According to Caramagno, "Literary-psychoanalytic studies on her [Woolf's] life and art, however, have shied away from the biological implication of such a diagnosis" (6). Kamiya's 1965 paper consists of "Family Background," "Outward Appearance," "Personality," and "Mental Illness."

21 Caramagno points out that "DeSalvo's theory" that Woolf's madness is "the reactive depressions of incest victims . . . cannot account for full blown mania, for the cyclic and often seasonal form of bipolar breakdowns, or their severity" (7).

22 In 1943, Kamiya met Ms. X's doctor, Dr. Toshiki Shimazaki of Tokyo University, and determined to specialize in psychopathology. Though her parents were opposed to Kamiya's will to work for Hansen's disease patients, they ultimately agreed with Kamiya on studying medicine on condition that she would not work for Hansen's disease patients.

23 In 1939 while Kamiya was studying at Pendle Hill in Philadelphia, which is a Quaker Center for Study and Contemplation, and at Bryn Mawr College, she was confronted with the outbreak of the war. In her diary of April 2, Kamiya writes that "Hitler defied both England and France" (*DL* 10). On May 14, Kamiya told her friends at Pendle Hill that her father had finally allowed her to become a doctor, and they predicted that "Japan may call you back as more and more diseases will become prevalent in Japan as the aftermath to the war" (*DL* 12). In this critical period, Kamiya payed an unexpected visit to France and stayed there in July and August solely because she was asked to assist her sister-in law, who was having her third baby in Paris. On August 18, Kamiya finally left France for the States by ship which was "full of people who escape from the war" (*DL* 19). After this, she abandoned her graduate study in Greek literature and at 25 became an undergraduate in medicine at Columbia University. Because political relations between Japan and the States had become worse, Kamiya eventually retuned to Japan on July 8, 1940, and began her study at Tokyo Women's Medical School in 1941.

24 In spite of his discovery of the fact that the Woolfs "appear on a Gestapo arrest list prepared for the planned German attack," Zwerdling states that by 1941 the danger of invasion had passed and Woolf was fearless (289).

25 Bond announces that Woolfs suicide is caused by her reexperiences of "the multiple catastrophic stressors of her adolescence, as well as enduring the actual horrors of World War II along with the rest of her contemporaries" (169) and presents to us some specific "stressors" such as "the trauma of the war against Hitler," her marriage to a Jew, the deaths of people closest to her, especially Vanessa, Lytton Strachey, and Roger Fry, and the loss of the ability to write (169-70).

Works Cited

Bell, Quentin. *Virginia Woolf: A Biography*. 2 vols. New York: Harcourt, 1972.

Bentock, Shari. "Authorizing the Autobiographical." *The Private Self: Theory and Practice of Women's Autobiographical Writings*. Ed. Shari Bentock. Chapel Hill & London: U North Carolina P, 1988. 10-33.

Bond, Alma Halbert. *Who Killed Virginia Woolf?* New York: Human Sciences, 1989.

Caramagno, Thomas C. *The Flight of the Mind: Virginia Woolf's Art and Manic-Depressive Illness*. Berkeley: U of California P, 1992.

DeSalvo, Louise. *Virginia Woolf: The Impact of Childhood Sexual Abuse on Her Life and Work*. Boston: Beacon, 1989.

Ejiri, Mihoko. *Kamiya Miyeko*. Vol. 136 of *Life and Thoughts* [*Hito to Shiso*]. Tokyo: Century Books, 1995.

Kamiya, Miyeko. *Diaries and Letters* [*Nikki to Shokanshu*]. 1982. Vol. 10 of *A Collection of Kamiya Miyeko's Works* [*Kamiya Miyeko Chosaku-Shu*]. Tokyo: Misuzu, 1996.

——. *Diaries of My Young Days* [*Wakaki-hi no Nikki*]. 1984. Supplementary Vol. [*Hokan*] of *A Collection of Kamiya Miyeko's Works*. Tokyo, Misuzu, 1996.

——. *From the Memoirs* [*Tabino Techō Yori*]: *A Collection of Essays, 1945-1970*. 1981. Vol. 5 of *A Collection of Kamiya Miyeko's Works*. Tokyo: Misuzu, 1996.

——. *Kamiya Miyeko: Personality and Work* [*Kamiya Miyeko: Hito to Shigoto*]. 1983. Special Vol. [*Bekkann*] of *A Collection of Kamiya Miyeko's Works*. Tokyo: Misuzu, 1996.

——. *Pilgrimage* [*Henreki*]. 1980. Vol. 9 of *A Collection of Kamiya Miyeko's Works*. Tokyo: Misuzu, 1996.

——. *Psychiatrical Studies 2* [*Seishin Igaku Kenkya 2*]. 1981. Vol. 8 of *A Collection of Kamiya Miyeko's Works*. Tokyo: Misuzu, 1996.

———. *The Significance of Being* [*Sonzai no Omomi*]: *A Collection of Essays, 1971-1979*. 1981. Vol. 6 of *A Collection of Kamiya Miyeko's Works*. Tokyo: Misuzu, 1996.

———. "Virginia Woolf: An Outline of a Study on her Personality, Illness and Work." *Confinia Psychiatrica* 8 (1965): 189-205.

———. *Virginia Woolf Studies* [*Vajinia Urufu Kenkyu*]. 1981. Vol. 4 of *A Collection of Kamiya Miyeko's Works*. Tokyo: Misuzu, 1990.

———. *What We Live for* [*Ikigai ni tsuite*]. 1980. Vol. 1 of *A Collection of Kamiya Miyeko's Works*. Tokyo: Misuzu, 1991.

Kamiya, Nagako. Personal Interview. Masami Usui. 25 October 1996.

Kamiya, Noburo. Personal Interview. Masami Usui. 25 October 1996.

King, James. *Virginia Woolf*. New York & London: Norton, 1994.

Lee, Hermione. *Virginia Woolf*. New York: Knopf, 1997.

Smith, Sidonie. *A Poetics of Women's Autobiography: Marginality and the Fictions of Sept-Representation*. Bloomington & Indianapolis: Indiana UP, 1987.

Woolf, Leonard. *The Journey Not the Arrival Matters: An Autobiography of the Years 1939 to 1969*. 1969. New York: Harvest, 1975.

Woolf, Virginia. *Moments of Being: Unpublished Autohiographical Writings*. 1976. Ed. Jeanne Schulkind. London: Granada, 1978.

———. *A Room of One's Own*. 1929. London: Penguin, 1990.

Zwerdling, Alex. *Virginia Woolf and the Real World*. Berkeley: U of California P, 1986.

Chapter 8

The Trauma Caused by Mothers' Deaths in Virginia Woolf and Kyoko Mori

I. Introduction

Both Virginia Woolf and Kyoko Mori (1957-) experienced their mothers' deaths in their adolescence, and the mother's death trapped both writers as trauma throughout their lives. Woolf's mother, Julia Stephen (1846-1895), died at 49 from rheumatic fever and overwork when Woolf was 13; while Mori's mother, Takako Mori (1928-1969), committed suicide at 41 when Mori was 12. Whether their death was natural or voluntary, both mothers were victims of the patriarchy in different schemes: the British Victorian patriarchy whose values continued influencing the British society and the Japanese *ie* (household) patriarchy which long remained after the legal banning of *ie* after World War II. For daughters, mother's death is engraved as the first serious depressive experience which results in their everlasting opposition against their fathers, and ultimately against the male-dominant society and its culture which enforced the men's wills on their wives within the sacred sanctuary of the upper-middle-class and well-established families. The writer's trauma is transformed into an art form of healing the life conflict and establishing the strategy of empowering the once-silenced self.

This articulated art form cannot be categorized into the traditional genres but is integrated by novels, memoirs, and essays because it aims at resisting a consistent cultural icon. In Woolf's novels, memoirs, and essays, such as *To the Lighthouse*, *Moments of Being*, and *A Room of One's Own*, the mother's self-sacrifice enlarges and strengthens men, while her self-concealed or even lost privacy causes her physical or psychological mortality. In Mori's novels and memoirs such as *Shizuko's Daughter*, *One Bird*, *The Dream of Water*, and *Polite Lies*, the mother is totally victimized under the mask of the ideal image of woman, wife, and mother.[1] Woolf states that she wrote *To the Lighthouse* to do for herself "what psychoanalysts do for their patients" (*MOB* 94) because Julia, as Jane Marcus points out, "died just as her daughter reached puberty, linking sexuality and death forever in her mind" (85). In an interview, Mori says that her writing does not mean her looking back to herself, nor her setting herself free by reexperiencing the past (Editor's Note, *Megumi* 228). Like Woolf's works, however, Mori's works are "haunted by the mother's absence and by the question it raises" (Rosenberg 19).[2] As far as the life conflicts are internally recurring to the writers, their writings are, whether consciously or unconsciously, subordinated by their wills to recover from the conflicts. In concrete terms, both Woolf and Mori are haunted by mothers' ghosts. It is, therefore, true that both Woolf and Mori need to explore the old societies whose values and social customs largely influence and determine their mothers' lives. Their writings, however, do not represent the old societies, but are grounded upon their wills to discover the engraved proofs of the old societies whose fundamental value system is somehow unconsciously absorbed in their contemporary societies but is situated and recognized as the object to the contemporary societies. In both cases, the daughter attempts to formulate a cultural icon embedded within the mother and to recreate the cultural experiences that were shaped via the mother's death.

What Woolf and Mori examine in their works is, therefore, the mother's inarticulate self that is formed within a different sociocultural scheme, but that is shared as a cross-cultural embodiment. Both Woolf and Mori explore middle-class women in the patriarchal society who "have been sequestered from the world, isolated from one another, and their heritage submerged with each generation," so that "they are more dependent than men are on the cultural models on offer, and more likely to be imprinted by them" (Wolf 58). The myth of the middle-class women is the mirror through which the daughters perceive the hidden aspect of the seemingly well-protected situation and status. The middle-class mothers are dis-dained to convey their daughters the lack of the significance of women in the male-dominant societies.

Without the mothers, both Woolf and Mori experience homelessness in their adolescence and adulthood. In *Three Geuineas*, Woolf states that women have no country (109) as a political message. The country means the patriarchal society that controls and manipulates all the powers that are represented by the father. The woman's lack of the political, social, legal, and economical status and stability in men's land, therefore, signifies the woman's homelessness. Mori herself confesses that she possesses neither father nor country, nor a close family (*PL* 28) since her home country is controlled by the patriarchy from which she is culturally exiled. The trauma caught in the daughter's internal self is exposed and examined as the undercurrent of the writer's opposition to any form of patriarchy, especially in the image of woman, the paradox between the private and the public as for the roles and conduct of women, and the pursuit of women's language and art as forms of self-expression.

II. The Image of Woman: Breaking the Beauty Myth

First, the image of woman that is constructed within the social scheme of patriarchy is the first encounter for the daughter to perceive as the physical reality so that it leaves both the sense of pride and the sense of vulnerability. Both Julia and Takako left the beautiful image, or "vision," of women to their daughters. Woolf remarks that she "accepted her [Julia's] beauty as the natural quality" (*MOB* 95). Mori also remembers that her mother was praised for her beauty at the beauty salon: "My mother was beautiful. When someone praised her for beauty and she denied it with a smile, I could see that the exchange gave both of them a good, friendly feeling" (*PL* 104). The mother's beauty nourishes the daughter's pride as well as their keen sense of beauty as the same sex. As teenagers, both Woolf and Mori restore the matured image of their mothers as women in their forties. As for her mother's suicide, Mori explains that her mother "never completed her transition into the brown-and-dark-blue middle age" (*PL* 142). The mother's physical reality as the daughter's experience is so strong that the daughters cannot escape from the image of woman that was permanently engraved in their minds after the mothers' death. In this respect, the mother's physical beauty is a quality that is frozen in their daughters' memories so that it empowers them.

Woolf portrays her mother figure in Mrs. Ramsay whose beauty conquers the people around her and her consciousness about her beauty is also perceived.

And after all — after all (here insensibly she drew herself together, physically, the sense of her own beauty becoming, as it did so seldom, present to her) — after all, she had not generally any difficulty in making people like her; for instance, George Manning; Mr. Wallace; famous as they were, they would come to her of an evening, quietly, and talk alone over her fire. She bore about with her, she could not help knowing it, the torch of her beauty; she carried it erect into any room that she entered; and after all, veil it as she might, and shrink from the monotony of bearing that it imposed on her, her beauty was apparent. She had been admired. She had been loved. She had entered rooms where mourners sat. Tears had flown in her presence. Men, and women too, letting go the multiplicity of things, had allowed themselves with her the relief of simplicity. (*TTL* 47)

Mrs. Ramsay's monumental beauty that occupies the Ramsay's home space, the others' minds, and even her own self plays a role of echoing the psychological inclination toward her figure. As Naomi Wolf defines, the beauty myth is "composed of emotional distance, politics, finance, and sexual repression" and it is not about woman but about "men's institutions and institutional power" (13). Mrs. Ramsay's beauty at fifty represents maternity, motherhood, and domestic comfort that are desperately demanded by those who do not possess them, especially by men. Because Mrs. Ramsay's visual beauty exceeds any other woman's beauty and is considered as the core of her maternal love and compassion by her admirers, it connotes her isolated and forlorn self who always listens to others but is hardly listened to.

Though mother's beauty in Mori's novels, unlike Mrs. Ramsay's, does not represent the torch of the universal love among the people who gather in her home space, her beauty also reflects her loneliness and inarticulate self. Ms. Shimizu, Megumi's mother, in

One Bird and Shizuko Okuda, Yuki's mother, in *Shizuko's Daughter* are both described as beautiful and feminine mothers. The mother's beauty is ironically contrasted with her misfortune and loneliness in her marriage and home space: Ms. Shimizu leaves home and Shizuko commits suicide. For the daughters, mothers' absence and loss strengthen their visual image that corresponds with the mothers' love and obsession with the ornaments around them such as flowers, birds, clothes, accessories, and arts. Megumi's mother is a naturalist who loves wild birds, trees, and flowers; and Shizuko's gardening is presented as a token of her love of nature. Shizuko's white wedding dress in an old photo, her colorful clothes in her closet, her stylish scarf delineate her good taste as a modern woman in the postwar society. The mother's fashionable sense influences the sense of beauty to the daughter and reminds the daughter of the mother's beauty as shown in Mori's poem.

> At forty, my mother
> had a brown coat made, too old now
> for her peacock blue. She asked the tailor
> to line the coat with flannel, red and green
> tartan no one could see. The spring of her
> death, my aunt folded that coat for storage. "Your mother
> still liked such bright colors," she said, brushing
> the flannel with her fingers. I stored away
> that remark among what I wanted to remember
> most about her. ("To My Ancestral Spirits," *Fall Out* 9)

The woman's feminine and fashionable garment represents the woman's unavoidable form of expressing beauty and is remembered by the daughter as a token of the mother's engraved beauty. Mori's description of the mother's beauty in her works is mainly grounded upon the mother's tastes of nature, her own clothes and the daughter's clothes, embroideries, and paintings as the reflection of the beauty mask.

The mother's beauty, therefore, ironically coexists with the mother's isolation and vulnerability. The mother's beauty brings out an irony as Woolf indicates that "the pride was snobbish, not a pure and private feeling: it was mixed with pride in other people's admiration" (*MOB* 95). In Mori's case, the beauty in which the woman is created and which she creates in her house is "elegant but cold" because there is always a self-sacrifice behind its beauty (*PL* 94). The conflicting senses of the mother's beauty draw the first outline in the process of portraying the mother and the primary source for ultimately reading, examining, and interpreting her story deeply buried and hidden behind the image of woman which is absolutely disconnected with woman's body and soul.

The woman's body was scarcely examined, articulated, and expressed so openly in the Victorian and Japanese patriarchal societies as it is now. The body in the Victorian society was a taboo especially in the middle and upper-middle classes. In contrast to the fact that the spiritual aspect of the woman is emphasized, the physical aspect is minimized and ultimately vanished. The notion of home and family is strengthened as the wall protecting from the outside sexual evil and immorality. The idealized womanhood is also born as "the Angel in the House" whose purity, submission, obedience, and honesty women are encouraged. Even though Mrs. Ramsay bears eight children, her body is not discussed as the object of sex. Mrs. Ramsay's body is, however, sacrificed by having sex with her husband more than twenty years, giving birth eight times, taking care of each growing child, and doing housework and volunteering jobs as an upper-middle-class gentlewoman. Mrs. Ramsay's body suddenly vanishes in the middle of the novel as it is described, "[Mr. Ramsay stumbling along a passage stretched his arms out one dark morning, but, Mrs. Ramsay having died rather suddenly the night before, he stretched his arms out. They remained empty]" (*TTL* 140). The body that is confronted with the destructive force of the storm that implies the war both in human life and in human society is a victimized embodiment. Mrs. Ramsay's body is a representative of the minimized, destroyed, and lost meaning of existence of woman in the Victorian society.

The body in the Japanese society is a more intriguingly interwoven notion. As Mori insists, the English word, body, is contradicted with the Japanese word, *karada*, which can be literally translated as body in English. The difference in sounds, meanings, and contexts between body and *karada* are grounded upon the cultural differences of body-related issues, especially sex issues, and ultimately of the self-expression issues.

> Even the word *body* in English sounds heavy and portentous — the broad *o*, the solid *b* and *d*. It's one of the words we think of in pairs: body and soul, black and white, heaven and hell, good and evil. Words that come in pairs usually suggest a conflict or need for choice. The commonly used Japanese word for the body, *karada*, does not have the same associations. The word has connotations of health rather than those of sin or sex. *Karada ni yoi* means "good for one's health"; *Karada no choshi was [sic] yoi* means "My health has been good" even though, literally, the sentence says, "My body has a good pace." *Karada ni ki o tsukete*, people advise each other as a form of farewell: "Be careful with our body." It's a casual expression, just like "Take care of yourself." There is nothing personal or intimate — much less sexual — about these references to the body in Japanese. In English, I would not say to people who aren't close friends, "My body has been acting up," because any reference to the body seems too intimate. It is

more polite to say, "I haven't been feeling very well" or "My health has been poor." In Japanese, the word *karada* simply does not have the same feeling of taboo. (*PL* 110)

The lack of expressing the sex-related meaning in the Japanese *karada* influences the Japanese language expression patterns. The use of the word *karada* is, moreover, connected with the disuse of the notion of body in *karada*. Even though *karada* partially means body and there are expressions to connote the meaning of sex in *karada*, it is an indirect or polite expression. In Mori's novels, the woman's body is neither described nor discussed since it connotes the direct, bold, and even aggressive meaning of woman's body.

In addition to the woman's body, the woman's soul is another neglected or reversed notion in the patriarchal societies. The woman's soul is so idealized as to be marginalized and lost in the man's expectations and psychology. Though the soul is the innermost self and belief, it is protected and restricted under the image of woman and it should not be articulated. As Simons remarks, Woolf was "a woman who appeared to put all her energies into self-expression, yet who never told the truth about herself. Her most intimate thoughts and feelings seemed perhaps to her too fragile to survive the transfer direct onto the page, and were kept so deeply hidden that only those closest to her were aware of those dark recesses" (169). In Woolf's novels, the woman's soul is fragmentally conveyed in her monologue since it is profoundly buried in her true self and the true self should not be expressed openly. The mother's soul is, furthermore, always covered by her actual figure on duties within the home space. In *To the Lighthouse*, Mrs. Ramsay's soul is a ghostly shadow upon her body throughout the novel even during her lifetime and after her death.

In Mori's works, the mother's soul remains like a ghost and

restored not only within the daughter but also with the men around her, even the father who abandons the mother for another woman. Shizuko's soul is, like Mrs. Ramsay's, fragmentally remembered on the surface level, yet occupies the other people's minds throughout the novel. Even her husband, Hideki, who cannot retrieve his memory of Shizuko clearly and correctly is struck with one moment during the vacation when he had a quarrel with her, left her, and returned to her with "large clusters of hydrangea flowers that he had picked while wandering about the mountain paths all by himself, at first sullen and then sorry, very sorry" (*SD* 163).

> He had stuck the flowers almost into Shizuko's face, said something about their being blue rather than pink because it was or wasn't humid, and then sat on the chaise longue hoping that she would now go on as though nothing had happened. And she did. She took the flowers from him, put them in a large pitcher of water, and asked him whether they should go out to supper at a resort hotel nearby. She never referred to their quarrel. Smiling, she turned to Yuki, who looked frightened, and told her to look at the flowers, how the hydrangea changed colors depending on the level of moisture in the soil. That was how she was at her best — gentle, quiet, always considerate about saving his feelings. In all their time together, she had never raised her voice at him or walked away to slam doors and to sulk. (*SD* 163)

Hideki's betrayal almost throughout their married life is ironically supported and forgiven by Shizuko. The hydrangea whose colors change according to the weather or the level of moisture symbolizes the woman who can sacrifice herself and manipulate her emotions on behalf of the man. The dead woman's soul's returning to the living people in Mori's writing is an important procedure for constructing the mother / woman figure within a frame of portrait.

The visual image of woman in the mother is an illustration of the woman's disagreement of body and soul. The woman's beauty that coexists with her vulnerability sacrifices both woman's soul and body injured and hidden in the patriarchal societies. Both Woolf and Mori attempt to reveal this tendency and break the beauty myth as the initial step to their exploring the background of woman's paradoxical conditions between the private and the public and developing their self-expressions in their art.

III. The Paradox between the Private and the Public

The second aspect of the trauma caught in the daughter's internal self lies in the paradox between the private place as a woman's work place and the public place as a woman's free space. This paradox is observed in women's roles and conduct that are nourished in the patriarchy and registered in their daughters. The women of middle and upper-middle classes in the Victorian and Japanese patriarchal societies have to impose upon themselves their domestic duties within the private home space. The paradox is born when the mother / wife has to sacrifice her privacy for the husband's and children. The domestic space that gives its inhabitants comfort, rest, safety, and freedom from social strife is transformed into the invisible jail that imprisons the woman's self-esteem and self-expression. Therefore, the woman demands the purely private space, a psychological room of one's own, which liberates, embraces, appreciates, and discovers the woman's innermost self and her self-expression.

Mrs. Ramsay's home as an embodiment of her self-sacrifice outlines the lack of her own room. Woolf recreates Mrs. Ramsay as a woman on duty as a wife, mother, hostess, and volunteer. Within the private sphere of home, she is a caretaker for the poor people. Julia's motherhood is highly evaluated: "— she seemed typical, universal, yet our own in particular — had by virtue of being our mother. It was part of her calling" (*MOB* 95). Founded upon the Victorian ideal image of women, Julia's self-sacrifice is emphasized in contrast to Leslie Stephen's selfish, egoistic, and aggressive attitude toward the others around him, especially toward women. The Victorian ideology enlarges Julia as a part of the house as her work place and, moreover, intensifies her also as a part of the society as her public service place.

Mrs. Ramsay's public service places range from the dinner table, the drawing room, the nursery room, the garden, the kitchen, and even the walk passage to the drawing / bedroom of lower income family. Her private space is fragmentally obtained between and among those public service places.

> . . . it was a relief when they went to bed. For now she need not think about anybody. She could be herself, by herself. And that was what now she often felt the need of — to think; well not even to think. To be silent; to be alone. All the being and the doing, expansive, glittering, vocal, evaporated; and one shrunk, with a sense of solemnity, to being oneself, a wedge-shaped core of darkness, something invisible to others. (69)

Though Mrs. Ramsay's soul is admired, her self is always concealed and revealed only in her purely private space and time. The isolation occurs during a brief and temporal time that is extended and enlarged in the psychological space. The strength of this isolated yet purely private self is, however, reversed by the lack of privacy during her service, and its contradiction determines the position of woman's self.

The mother / wife figures in Mori's novels also face the contradiction between the public and the private within the home space in the postwar nuclear family in Japan. Just as Julia is a model image of the Victorian "Angel in the House," Takako is also grounded as a model *sengyoshufu* (housewife) in a nuclear family whose roles were ironically founded during the U.S. Occupation and were practiced by women who married in newly-democratic Japan after World War II. Different from Mrs. Ramsay, for example, Shizuko in *Shizuko's Daughter* once rejects a Japanese traditional arranged marriage expected to help her family in her home village, goes to a big city, Kobe, to become a secretary, and encounters Yuki's father at the company where she was working. Though once Shizuko possesses a room of her own, she returns to the traditional practice of being engaged in housework and childcare whose roles were emphasized after World War II. Even though there is a great difference between the large and extended Victorian family and the nuclear Japanese family, however, there is a similar consequence and subsequent conditions in women's psychology.

The phenomenon of the woman of Takako's generation is communicated to Mori by Shiro, Takako's brother, during Mori's travel to Japan: "People in your mother's generation were prone to depression when they got to be thirty-five or forty" because of the experiences of World War II (*DW* 190). Those women in their teens were deprived of freedom during the war; they had to sacrifice themselves to support their families after the war, and they again had to sacrifice themselves to their husbands and children after marriage. Takako's submissive life is here again enlarged in contrast to her husband's "impatience and insensitivity" that Mori remembers as her father's attitude toward his wife. Takako's motherhood is what she could enjoy in her unhappy marriage ("How One Daughter" 10). The Japanese paradigm of *sengyoshifu* imprisons Takako within a domestic sphere where the mother can find the only rescue and hope in the children.

Because the mother's self-expression is buried in a paradox between the private and the public, the daughters aim at looking for the mother's own language. As women, both Woolf and Mori stand against the male-dominant means of expressing the selves and attempt to create the unique voice. The mothers as women off duty are also discovered and articulated by the daughters. In such a free space, the women's pursuit for creative activities is a shared experience in the mothers whose roles and conduct imprison them within the home sphere. Inside themselves, therefore, Julia and Takako are in pursuit of the language of their own and their pursuit is accomplished by their daughters as professional writers.

The discovery of Julia's unpublished writings in 1979 provides us with an opportunity to examine the other yet more personal aspect of Julia's life. Woolf analyzes Julia's personality as being very "quick; very direct; practical; and amusing" and sometimes "sharp" and "severe" (*MOB* 96). Julia's insistent and sharp view is, however, supported by her silence in front of the others, yet it leads to her private writings. Gillespie remarks that Julia "is not among the previously neglected or undiscovered great women writers, but she is a far more interesting, complex, and talented person than most people realize" ("The Elusive" 25). The Victorian domestic life is recorded in Julia's works; with the sense of fancy, humor, and even satire in her stories for children (Steele 29-32) and with her "matriarchal view of the world," especially of religion and social concerns, in her essays (Gillespie, "Essays" 212). Julia's strength and uniqueness are observed in her creative activities that were accomplished during her heavy domestic duty in the large and extended Victorian household. Mrs. Ramsay's artistic sense of reading stories to children is often compared with Julia's one. Like Julia, Mrs. Ramsay is, moreover, devoted to investigating and recording the social problem.

... but more profoundly she ruminated the other problem, of rich and poor, and the things she saw with her own eyes, weekly, daily, here or in London, when she visited this widow, or that struggling wife in person with a bag on her arm, and a note-book and pencil with which she wrote down in columns carefully ruled for the purpose wages and spendings, employment and unemployment, in the hope that thus she would cease to be a private woman whose charity was half a sop to her own indignation, half a relief to her own curiosity, and become, what with her untrained mind she greatly admired, an investigator, elucidating the social problem. (*TTL* 13).

Mrs. Ramsay's concern and writings about the social issues symbolize her strong wish to be involved in her own self-expression regarding the dominantly male issues.

In Mori's case, the women's writings, craft and art are, directly or indirectly, associated with their wills to express themselves.[3] Takako's escape from the cold and barren house is achieved in her devotion to her journal writings. Mori encodes Takako's depression and her wish to commit suicide in her journals. Takako's initial wish to carry out *oyako-shinju* (parent-child suicide) is recorded in Takako's entry of October 1968 (*DW* 7). *Oyako-shinju* in postwar Japan is carried out mostly by mothers with children with a wish to unite in the next world. Mori analyzes that the "distinction between the private and the public also influences the Japanese attitude toward tragedy as an art form" (*PL* 184) and points to *shinju* (double suicide in order to show the inside of the heart) as its typical example. Having given up killing her own children, Takako's suicide still embodies the Japanese manner to leave her dignity instead of living with disgrace and dishonor, to say nothing of divorcing ("How One Daughter" 10). The mother's will to Yuki in *Shizuko's Daughter* is a final draft of mother's self-expression or her last letter to the daughter. The mother's last message that repeatedly occurs to Yuki is the voice that struggled to reveal yet was always to yield during her lifetime. Megumi's mother's letters to the daughter in *One Bird*, furthermore, plays a role to express what was not told within their house space. Megumi's discovery of several readings of her mother's letter means how complicated the woman's psychology is in her writing. The woman's writing that stores the women's voice is the dignified resource of women's self-expression.

Mori also remembers that Takako "had never been content just to live and be comfortable" yet "always wanted something more — some form of beauty" (*DW* 98), or art. Takako's desire for beauty is classified into two groups: one is her hand-made clothes and lines with her embroideries, and the other is her appreciation of paintings at art galleries. Takako's self-creation is deeply embedded in her creation of her own art in women's clothes as the art of the real world. Shizuko's hand-made clothes, similar to Takako's, embody her expressing love for her daughter. Megumi's mother's devotion to embroidery in *One Bird* is more professional than Shizuko's. Embroidery is, like Mrs. Ramsay's knitting, basically women's homemaking job: yet its sensitivity and creativity are more profoundly related with women's self-expression. Takako's desire to be involved in the objects outside reality, moreover, has the paradoxical meaning of her existence which is discovered in arts. Mori is reminded that her mother "was happier in rooms that weren't her own" as she loved to visit the art galleries and museums which are public places yet rooms of her private interests (*PL* 105). In *Shizuko's Daughter*, Shizuko's art book was discovered by her husband, Hideki, six years later. The drawing book that Hideki sent to Yuki at college in Nagasaki after Yuki's grandfather's death and funeral as a redemption is reexamined and reinterpreted this time by Yuki. Yuki as an art student succeeds her mother's will to draw the story of her own, and the stories of their own. Rosenberg states that art is "a tool of remembrance, a way back" and that it "also points a way forward, toward reconciliation with the world" (19). Both women's crafts such as sewing and embroidery and arts such as painting and drawing in Mori's works are important tools for mothers to withdraw the ignored and marginalized selves.

Both Woolf and Mori describe the truth that the mother's self cannot embrace both the public and the private in a well-balanced gravity with in herself. As women artists, Woolf and Mori are convinced that the daughter needs to articulate the mother's voice or self-expression in a form of their arts.

IV. The Pursuit of Women's Language and Art as Forms of Self-Expression

Both Woolf and Mori as daughters inherit their mothers' wills by devoting themselves to accomplishing their mothers' stories. Both writers launch into their writing career as a revolt against literature as men's privileged form of art throughout its history. Woolf is overwhelmed by the British literature that excluded women till Mary Carmichael can write "Chloe liked Olivia" in the early twentieth century (*AROO* 82). Especially against poetry as the most traditional form of British literature, Woolf emphasizes that Mary Carmichael needs "another hundred years" to write a better book as a poet (*AROO* 93). Mori rejects the Japanese classical literature as "a complicated system of symbols that few outsiders can understand" (*PL* 148). Mori believes that the traditional styles, symbols, poetic diction, and rules of the Japanese poetry such as *haiku* and *waka* cannot be adjusted to women and insists that the "women, who wanted to write about twentieth-century feelings of anxiety and frustration, were left to create a highly personalized and enigmatic system of symbols and dream visions instead of coming back" to Japanese traditional poetic diction (*PL* 151).

By rejecting the traditional literature, therefore, both Woolf and Mori explore their own voices. In *To the Lighthouse,* Woolf uncovers what is silenced, which expressions should be controlled, and which voice is revealed within the multilayered schemes of communications whose center is Mrs. Ramsay. Woolf attempts to unite "the mother's tongue, freeing language from bondage to the fathers and returning it to women and the working classes," as Marcus remarks, in order to seek "not only the overthrow of male culture but also a return to the oppressed of their rightful heritage and the historical conditions in which to enjoy it" (73-74). The tension between the matriarchal form of silence and the patriarchal form of language is what Woolf intends to express in *To the Lighthouse.*

Mrs. Ramsay's sharp insight into human nature and her criticism of the faults of others is not actually recited by Mrs. Ramsay, but conveyed to the readers as her inner voice by Woolfs writing. Though Sandra M. Gilbert and Susan Gubar expect to discover the woman's language or woman's sentence in Woolf's writing as such notable feminist linguists as Robin Lakoff and Dale Spender did, Woolf's employment of "a fantasy about a utopian linguistic structure" is a more intriguing subject to explore (*No Man's Land* 229-30). The conflicts among the people around Mrs. Ramsay are neutralized and moderated through Mrs. Ramsay's compassion for them. The discord, chaos, and reunion among her eight children are also modified in their mother's thoughts. Mrs. Ramsay's voice which expresses warmth, compassion, respect, and understanding of others is revealed with a series of interruptions of her works and small incidents. "The Window" is Woolf's recreation of the mother's communication style. Lily Briscoe's last brush to her portrait of Mrs. Ramsay in "The Lighthouse" is Woolf's accomplishment of describing the spirit of the mother who long haunts Woolf.

Mori, more radically, abandons her native language and chooses English as her own language. Mori's life has been a trial to revolt against patriarchal authority and power and to escape from her wrongly transplanted cultural sphere. Mori feels "uneasy in Japanese because we are supposed to say nothing about whatever threatens our safety" (*PL* 246).[4] For Mori, the Japanese language is not an appropriate means to express women's selves including herself because the Japanese language coexists with silence as the means of protection from intrusion and attention. The virtue of silence, however, does not help women but only deprives them of expressing their genuine, even negative or aggressive, emotions and thoughts. Mori's fears are caused by her mother's silence over her pain and sorrow that ultimately leads her to death. Takako is a woman of silence "who effaces — rather than expresses — herself" because she "is valued for her ability to pretend that her hard work is nothing, that she is scarcely there" (*PL* 94).[5] In *Shizuko's Daughter*, Mori describes Shizuko's unfinished will which is covered with a lie, saying that she would wish her husband's happiness after her death. The silenced truth is conveyed by Mori only to the readers.

Mori also imposes upon Yuki, Shizuko's daughter, the unavoidable tension between the voice without the body in the last telephone conversation between Shizuko and Yuki just before Shizuko's suicide and the body without the voice at the moment of Yuki's discovering Shizuko's dead body at home. Mori views the tension between these two as a destiny of the silenced self. Mori's intention to retrieve her mother's lost voice formulates Yuki's nightmare in which she cannot rescue Shizuko, whose voice is imprisoned within herself. The telephone wire is a metaphor of the invisible code of communication between the mother's spirit wandering in Japan and the daughter surviving in America. Connecting the mother and the daughter by a long distance call across the ocean means reestablishing the once-lost communication between them. Mori's pursuit for a language of her own is accomplished when she exiles herself from her native land and encounters another tool that frees her as she becomes an exile from all the bounds that imprison women and silence them.

By breaking the beauty myth, revolting against the traditional patriarchal values, and retrieving the once-silenced mother's voice, both Woolf and Mori struggled in establishing their own voice that can liberate them from physical and psychological restrictions imposed by visible and invisible men's forces.

V. Conclusion

What both Woolf and Mori share as common experiences in their teens provides them with the source of their creative energy and power. By recreating the truth behind what they witnessed and listened to while their mothers were alive, both Woolf and Mori overcome the past and strengthen the once-silenced and forgotten stories that have crucially haunted them. The traumas caused by mothers' deaths enabled both Woolf and Mori to nourish and establish the literature of their own.

Notes ■

The abridged form of this paper was presented on 10 June 2000 at the panel, "Life Matters / Historical Contexts," at the 10th Annual Conference on Virginia Woolf: "Virginia Woolf Out of Bounds" which was held at the University of

Maryland, Baltimore County, U. S. A. from June 7 through 11 in 2000. This paper was originally published in *Doshisha Literature* 45 (March 2002): 59-80.

1 Mori's most recent novel, *Stone Field, True Arrow* is different from her previously-published works in that the father is victimized and the mother is a free-spirited woman who leaves Japan and remarried in the States twice.
2 Mori herself frankly admits her strong emotions to and tie with her own mother: "I loved my own mother and value everything I learned from her" ("How One Daughter" C-10).
3 Brock-Servais remarks that Mori's mother "created a cultural home for her children, reading to Mori and her brother since they were small" (227).
4 In spite of her intention, her language is sometimes taken as something very Japanese or her book as a text through which American young readers can learn Japanese basic culture (Zitlow and Stover).
5 Mori does not receive good reviews of *Polite Lies* because she "writes an extended, vindictive essay on lies" so that "even the most sympathetic reader's patience begins to wane" (Barton 7-9).

Works Cited

Barton, Emily. "Polite Lies." Rev. of *Polite Lies,* by Kyoko Mori. *New York Times* 8 Mar. 1998: 7-19.

Brock-Servais, Rhonda. "Kyoko Mori." *Asian American Novelists: A Bio-Bibliographical Critical Sourcebook.* Ed. Emmanuel S. Nelson. Westport & London: Greenwood, 2000. 220-33.

"Editor's Note." Kyoko Mori. *Megumi [One Bird].* Trans. Kakiko Ikeda. Tokyo: Aoyama, 1996. 338-39.

Gilbert, Sandra M, and Susan Gubar. *No Man's Land: The Place of the Woman Writer in the Twentieth Century.* Vol. 1. New Haven: Yale UP, 1987.

Gillespie, Diane F. "The Elusive Julia Stephen." Gillespie and Steele 1-27.

——. "Essays for Adults." Gillespie and Steele 195-213.

Gillespie, Diane F., and Elizabeth Steele, eds. *Julia Duckworth Stephen: Stories for Children, Essays for Adults.* Syracuse: Syracuse UP, 1987.

"Kyoko Mori." *Contemporary Authors Online.* The Gale Group, 1999. 10 June 2000.

Kyoko Mori. *The Dream of Water: A Memoir.* New York: Fawcett, 1995

——. *Fall Out*. Chicago: Chucha, 1994.

——. "How One Daughter Honors Her Mother." *New York Times* 16 Apr. 1997 Sec. C: 10.

——. *One Bird*. New York: Fawcett, 1993.

——. *Polite Lies: On Being a Woman Caught between Cultures*. New York: Fawcett, 1988.

——. *Shizuko's Daughter*. New York: Fawcett, 1994.

——. *Stone Field, True Arrow*. New York: Henry Holt, 2000.

Marcus, Jane. *Art and Anger: Reading Like a Woman*. Columbus: Ohio State UP, 1998.

Rosenberg, Liz. "Children's Books." Rev. of Kyoko Mori's *Shizuko's Daughter*. *New York Times* 22 Aug. 1993 Sec. 7: 19.

Simons, Judy. *Diaries and Journals of Literary Women from Fanny Burney to Virginia Woolf*. Iowa City: U of Iowa P, 1990.

Steele, Elizabeth. "Stories for Children." Gillespie and Steele 29-35.

Wolf, Naomi. *The Beauty Myth: How Images of Beauty Are Used against Woman*. New York: William Morrow, 1991.

Woolf, Virginia. *Moments of Being: Unpublished Autobiographical Writings*. 1947. Frogmore: Panther, 1976.

——. *A Room of One's Own*. 1929. Harmondsworth: Penguin, 1990.

——. *Three Guineas*. 1938. San Diego: Harcourt, 1984.

——. *To the Lighthouse*. 1927. Harmondsworth: Penguin, 1992.

Zitlow, Connie S., and Lois Stover. "Japanese and Japanese American Youth in Literature." *The ALAN Review* 25.3 (Spring 1998) <http://scholar.lib.vt.eduiejournals/ALAN/spring98/zitlow.html>.

About the Author

Masami Usui, Professor of English, Doshisha Unviersity, Higashiiru-Kamigyo, Kyoto, Japan 602-8580

Short Biography

Masami Usui received her BA and MA from Kobe College, Japan, and her second MA and Ph.D. from Michigan State University in 1989. After teaching at Hiroshima University, she is currently Professor of English and at Doshisha University, Kyoto, Japan. She has been doing her research and writings on Virginia Woolf and women writers, Asian American literature and culture, and popular culture. She published papers in Japan, England, Korea, USA, Germany, etc., and contributed to *Virginia Woolf and War* (1991), *Asian American Playwrights* (2002), *Literature in English: New Ethnical, Cultural, and Transnational Perspective* (2013), *Virginia Woolf and December 1910* (2014), etc. Along with MLA, International Virginia Woolf Conference, International Popular Culture Conference, American Studies Association Conference, she has presented her papers in English at Academia Senica in Taiwan, ASAK and KAFSEL in Korea, MESEA in Hungary, CISLE in Canada, International Conference on Asian American Expressive Culture in Beijing, China, International Conference: The Cultural Translation and East Asia, Bangor, U.K., The 20th Annual Conference of EALA in Taiwan, and International Popular Culture / American Culture Association Conference in Poland, and the 2014 International Symposium on Cross-Cultural Studies, Taiwan, International Conference: English Studies as Archive and as Prospecting the 80th Anniversary Conference, University of Zagreb, Zagreb, Croatia, The 3rd International Conference on Linguistics, Literature and Culture 2014, Penang, Malaysia, Expanding the Parameters of Asian American Literature: An International Conference, Xiamen University, Xiamen, Fujian, China, The CISLE 2015, Gottingen University, Germany, the MLA International Symposium in Dusseldorf, Germany, Oxford Symposium on Religious Studies, and Oxford Woman's Leadership Symposium, Oxford, U.K., etc.

Her hobbies are Kado or Japanese Ikebana (Ikenobo), Chado or Japanese Way of Tea (Urasenke), and Shodo or Japanese Calligraphy.

A Passage to Self in Virginia Woolf's Works and Life

2017 年 10 月 31 日　第 1 刷発行

著　者　臼井 雅美　© Masami Usui, 2017
発行者　池上 淳
発行所　株式会社 現代図書
　　　　〒 252-0333　神奈川県相模原市南区東大沼 2-21-4
　　　　TEL　042-765-6462（代）　　　FAX　042-701-8612
　　　　振替口座　00200-4-5262　　　ISBN 978-4-434-23935-9
　　　　URL　http://www.gendaitosho.co.jp　E-mail　info@gendaitosho.co.jp

発売元　株式会社 星 雲 社
　　　　〒 112-0005　東京都文京区水道 1-3-30
　　　　TEL　03-3868-3275　　　FAX　03-3868-6588

印刷・製本　モリモト印刷株式会社

Printed in Japan

落丁・乱丁本はお取り替えいたします。
本書の内容の一部あるいは全部を無断で複写複製（コピー）することは
法律で認められた場合を除き、著作者および出版社の権利の侵害となります。